Transfusion

I0674030

Victoria Buck

Transfusion
COPYRIGHT 2017 by Victoria Buck

Contact Information: titleadmin@pelicanbookgroup.com

Cover Art by *Nicola Martinez*

Harbourlight Books, a division of Pelican Ventures, LLC
www.pelicanbookgroup.com PO Box 1738 *Aztec, NM * 87410

Harbourlight Books sail and mast logo is a trademark of Pelican Ventures, LLC

Publishing History
First Harbourlight Edition, 2017
Paperback Edition ISBN 978-1-61116-959-1
Electronic Edition ISBN 978-1-61116-960-7
Published in the United States of America

Dedication

For those who do not grow weary.
Revelation 2:3

Other Books in the Series

Wake the Dead
Killswitch

Part I

1

Chase considered his audience. Thirty men in ragged coats snarled like wolves judging bait in a trap. The alpha wolf—a guy they called Ep—paced at the far end of the narrow room. Long, bony legs. Impatient puffs of frigid air raging from his flared nostrils. A polished wooden nightstick dangling off his belt.

Alpha Wolf had decided it would be beneficial for Chase to tell the pack what he could do for them. Outlaws seeking revolution couldn't be trusted with too much information, even if revolt was the solution. But Chase had to gain the wolf's trust. Or at least secure the respect of the pack.

He smiled—he always smiled for the crowd. Millions of fans once adored him. But his last audience was a hundred believers stowed deep in the Underground Church. The fans had likely forgotten him. The believers...

The smile left him.

Now this—renegade dissenters holed up in an old campground two hundred miles from Chase's destination. He'd been here three weeks, captured on his way from Quebec to Detroit. Nothing good remained in Quebec since the destruction of the underground's base. He wasn't sure what he'd find in the rundown city of Detroit, but God told him to go there.

"What do you know about God?" Switchblade grumbled behind him.

Chase angled his vision to the left. "Did I say that out loud?"

"All those superpowers and you don't even know when your stupid thinking is coming out your mouth. These people don't care what you think God told you."

Murmurs filled the room as Chase swung around. "You know as well as I do God is sending us to Detroit."

Switchblade folded his thick black arms. A vein bulged up the middle of his forehead. "Then how'd we end up in this Godforsaken place? Huh? Why ain't we in Detroit?"

"Why don't you just rub it in? I thought I could get us there and I failed. You think I don't want more than anything to wake up to my wife's beautiful face instead of *your* ugly mug? You think I don't wonder how we're going to find her if we even make it to Detroit? All I can do is to follow what little instruction I get from God."

The muscles in Chase's throat tightened and his tone rose an octave. "I can't depend on intel from the underground, because it shut down. Remember? But God will get me there. *That* is what I know about God."

Switchblade's furrowed brows relaxed. "Now you're ready." He placed his big hands on Chase's shoulders and forced him around to the stunned audience.

Alpha Wolf snarled.

Switchblade smacked Chase across the back. "Go on and tell them what you know about God."

"I don't think that's what the boss man wants."

"You scared of that old dog? We got stuck here for a reason, robot."

Laughter rose among the men's agitated whispers. Alpha Wolf slapped the nightstick against his leg.

Tell them what he knew about God? These men weren't waiting for a Sunday school lesson. During his time here, Chase had read the irises of most of the outlaws. Files kept by the Western Republic listed them as thieves. Murderers. Swindlers. Hackers. People like that served a purpose in the Dissenters of the Republic. The leader had no felon's record, but he was an outlaw just for going rogue. Anybody bowing out on the government's agenda was a criminal. Including Chase, who'd long since found his own name among the WR's Most Wanted.

But he wasn't a felon—not like this bunch of none-too-smart, freezing, half-starved men. Most of their weapons were stored away by the wolf in charge. Chase could outthink them. Overpower them. So why was he still here?

Patience.

The message didn't come from the exoself. Chase had learned to tell the difference between the constant stream of information flowing through his processors and the whisper in his soul. God would get him and Switchblade out of here. In time. Right now, they were just a couple more freezing, half-starved men in need of shelter during the worst winter in recorded history. Soon the snow would melt. The men's hearts would soften. Chase had to be patient.

He allowed the signature smile to return. With an out-of-control beard and hair nearly to his jawline, he barely resembled the man he used to be. But he still had the smile. And the voice.

"Gentlemen, your leader"—Chase eyed Alpha Wolf—"has asked me to explain how I came to have, as he puts it, a supercomputer inside my head. It's actually not confined to my head. Sensors and processors run throughout my body. They not only give me access to government intel, they also regulate my lab-grown organs. They work with my muscles to increase upper-body strength. My hearing is enhanced. I can see in the dark. But most of you already know all that. I guess what I'm supposed to tell you is how my ability to worm into WR programs might prove useful."

Switchblade cleared his throat.

Chase's shoulders tightened. He sucked in a breath. "But I'd like to tell you my story. My real name is Charles Redding. I became Chase Sterling when the WR made me a game show host. A star. Then they turned me into a transhuman. I want to tell you how it happened. How I became a believer. Where I was headed when your leader detained me."

"Never mind," Alpha Wolf bellowed. He leaned against the plywood wall and crossed his arms. "I don't want to hear about your life as a pretty-boy celebrity or as an outlaw convert. Just tell us what you can do for us. You can plant information in WR systems, so you could have turned us in. Of course, a raid would mean your capture. You'd never get out of here before the Feds showed up. But come springtime, you might make it work. So now, while I've got you trapped, work that transhuman magic and make us all upstanding citizens."

Chase lowered his eyes to the floor. "It's true—I've entered false data in government programs before. To protect my people." He lifted his gaze. "When I got rebuilt, a change took place in me. I'm not talking about the technical transformation. I didn't like what they did to me, so I ran. But I wasn't running away from something as much as toward something else. And I found what I was looking for. The Underground Church. My mother and my closest friend were there." He motioned to Switchblade. "And this guy—he got assigned to guard me. And there were others I came to love. I used my abilities to keep them safe."

He ran his hand through his hair. "I thought I could save them, but the friend I'd searched for told me what I needed to hear—that I couldn't save anybody. She told me I needed the One who calms the seas and shuts the mouths of lions." He glanced at the leader, who waited with unexpected silence. "And wolves."

Chase pulled his arms tight around his chest and raised his eyes to the decaying ceiling. "So I found what I was running to. And I married the girl who'd told me the truth." His gaze met the stillness of the meager crowd.

"And then the transhuman failed. I lost them. My friends. My family. My wife. All I've got left is this ill-tempered bodyguard and the whisper of God telling me where I need to go. What He is *not* telling me to do is plant some bogus story in WR intel about *you*. I'm sorry. When I'm ready to go, I'm going. I won't turn you in. But I can't help you."

Alpha Wolf laughed. "You *will* help us. And you're not leaving—not in one piece." He skulked to the door and pulled it open. A cold gust carried flurries into the room before the leader marched out and slammed the door. The pack didn't move, except to tug on their coats.

Switchblade launched forward and planted himself between the men and Chase.

"That's rough," a voice called out. "You ain't got no idea what happened to 'em?"

"I think…" Chase drew his brows tight. "I pray my wife and some of my people are in Detroit."

"God told you?" another voice asked.

"I'm sure of it. And Mel—my wife—sent me a clue. But others are dead. Killed by the WR. The ones who escaped need me." Chase blew out a breath. "I need *them*. Soon I'm getting out of here. But I could use some help." He stepped off the platform. "Who's with me?"

2

Sunlight reflected off the snow. Chase squinted as he eased down the wooden steps of the bunkhouse and into the crunch of day-old, foot-deep snow. After three weeks in confinement, freedom to walk the compound offered some hope. Alpha Wolf had moved his captives to the main bunkhouse when he figured warming another building was using up too much firewood. The unrelenting winter made escape impossible anyway. So Chase and Switchblade settled in among the outcasts. None had been eager to make conversation. Especially after Chase's plea for help yesterday. They'd asked a few questions. Some had even shown a bit of sympathy. But that was all.

"They're not helping me."

For the first time in a month, the frozen assault had ceased on what was, according to the exoself, the southwest corner of a former national forest near Saginaw Bay. Now the land was abandoned to the wild, no longer listed among the WR's protected properties. They still owned it—just didn't maintain it. Which made it the perfect place for people like the dissenters.

If Chase could make it to the bay, he'd find a way to get around it. Or across it.

What he needed was a sympathizer—somebody assisting the underground. If this area held dissenters, there must be believers too. Christians still existing in the world up top were faithful to offer a hand to the ones who'd gone under. Ten weeks ago, it would have been easy to find that kind of help. But Mel had cut him off from the underground. She'd done it to protect him. *He* was supposed to protect *them*. But he lost them.

He lost *her*. His wife of one day.

"It wasn't even a whole day," he said to the sky. Frigid air slapped his face. White breath escaped his mouth. Tears puddled and he quickly swiped the moisture away with his gloved hands. "God, I can't do this. I got Your people connected and then You took it all away. Now they're worse off than before. I don't understand."

The rhythm of a steady drip drew his sight to the overhang on the bunkhouse. Melting snow. Just a bit. But tomorrow, if the sun held, more sweet percussion would accompany this beat.

He trudged through the snow to the building where lunch waited. Other men marched alongside him. But not Switchblade. Maybe he had kitchen duty. As though they'd agreed to join the renegades, Chase and Switchblade had been ordered to perform chores like permanent residents.

Two men reached the steps alongside Chase. Both turned away. No surprise. The unreasonable request of helping a transhuman get to Detroit was too much for these poor guys.

At least they didn't run to their leader. Alpha Wolf would've forced Chase and Switchblade back into confinement by now if the men had squealed. Cold wind delivered a few flurries. Chase ran a check of weather reports and groaned at the news of more snow. No need to confine anyone. Nobody was leaving.

The exoself streamed data of snowbound towns. Impassable roads. The Feds wouldn't find Chase here—not anytime soon. And in the middle of the frozen wilderness, at least he couldn't hurt anybody by trying to help them.

Maybe the world was better off without a transhuman.

He pulled on the door of the mess hall and entered a room warmed by the wood-burning apparatus used for cooking. Chase slid his hands out of the brown gloves and dropped them to the floor as he sat at the nearest table. He pushed back the hood of his jacket.

Rations were limited to a few crates of apples, some dried beef, and several sacks of potatoes. The makeshift stove supported a huge aluminum pot where today's potatoes were boiling. Would the food hold out until spring? Alpha Wolf had a computer. He had connections. But he'd secured himself and his men too far off the grid. The mega blizzard made it impossible to get supplies in.

Or get Chase out.

Where was Switchblade? Chase counted the men. Twenty-six. Alpha Wolf sat at a table on the other side of the bunker. Four men had skipped lunch. Five, counting Switchblade.

Chase rubbed his face and then slapped his hands against the rough wooden table. "What's he up to?"

A young man with blond hair past his shoulders yanked a chair away from the table and slid a plate in front of Chase. "Who? Your bodyguard?" The man lowered another plate and sat in the chair. He was nearly as big as Switchblade.

Chase eyed the plate in front of him. A strip of jerky. Half an apple. Four chunks of potato. "For me? You shouldn't have." He picked up the meat and bit it.

"You're welcome," the man said. "Switchblade's in a meeting. He sent me to get you, but he said I should feed you first. Said you can't let a transhuman go too long without food. Is that true?"

"He's in a *meeting*? What the—"

The man elbowed Chase.

Alpha Wolf crept toward them. He stopped behind Chase and poked the nightstick between his shoulders. "My cabin. Four-thirty. Don't keep me waiting." He exited the mess hall.

Chase picked up a steaming potato, dropped it, and rubbed his fingers together. "One hundred forty-seven degrees. Don't you people have forks?"

"You know the temp just by touching it?"

"What sort of meeting? What's going on?"

The man smiled. "You want out of here. Right? Some of us are ready to help."

"You weren't too eager yesterday."

"We had to talk it over. You know how it is."

"No. I don't. What are you all doing here with that drooling dictator wannabe?"

"Waiting for the revolution." The man pulled out a pocketknife. "And we got no place else to go." He stabbed a potato, blew on it, and eased it into his mouth.

Chase bit his apple. "None of you have family? You've got to know somebody besides Henry Theodore Epsin."

The man's brows went up.

"Your leader."

"Oh. Right. Ep's the only name he ever told us."

The man smiled again. "I guess you know my name too."

"Jeffrey Allen Turner. From Ohio. Arrested for relieving the WR of an armored transit. Two years in prison. Released to the custody of your grandparents." Chase eased his finger onto a potato. "So you do have a family."

"True to the Western Republic. Kicked me out when I refused to report for my job assignment. I took up with some dissenters and ended up getting recruited by Ep. None of us has any strong attachments. Couple of guys were married, but their wives booted 'em when they went rogue."

Chase popped the rest of the potatoes into his mouth. Followed by the jerky. He left the browning apple on his plate. "Enough getting to know each other. Tell me where I can find Switchblade." He reached for his gloves.

Jeff grabbed the apple off Chase's plate and held it with his teeth. He pulled his tattered jacket closed and motioned Chase to the door.

They crossed the frozen ground toward four small cabins. One was Alpha Wolf's personal living space. Another housed the latrine. The third was Chase's former prison cell he'd shared with Switch for three weeks. The fourth, he'd never been in.

Jeff headed toward it.

Chase shuddered. The building resembled the one behind the WR detention center in Quebec, where the Feds housed the device called Bloodless. The execution machine. He followed Jeff through the door. A dim bulb hung on a wire from the ceiling. Switchblade looked up from a map. Four others sat with him around a small table.

Chase examined the map, the men, and the room. Some sort of storage building. Shelves filled with notebooks lined a wall. The men showed little expression except for a hint of fear. They shivered—this building had no heat.

Across the top of the old map—*Michigan*. Across the bottom—*United States of America*. Maps like this had disappeared a decade ago.

"What are you doing?" Chase asked.

"Planning our exit," Switchblade said. "Nothing transhuman about it. Just old-fashioned hightailing it out of here. You ready to go, Charlie?"

3

"More snow coming." Chase slid a chair across the bare wood floor and sat next to Switchblade. Jeff stationed himself at the one small window and peered out.

"I don't need a robot to tell me that," Switch said. "We've got a radio. Supporters are broadcasting a signal nearby. Well, not too—"

"Supporters? You mean...believers?"

Switchblade eased into a grin. "That's right. Somewhere between here and the bay."

Chase slumped back in the cold metal chair. He'd lost the ability to pinpoint transfers between believers, but Switchblade and these good-for-nothing dissenters had done it. Somewhere between gratitude and relief, something ugly wriggled inside. Envy? Pride?

"Great." Chase leaned forward, his elbows on the table. "But we don't have a two-way, so how are we supposed to find them?"

"You're the one with a computer in your head," Switch told him. "Figure it out."

A scrawny man with a tattoo of a lion on his neck pulled a small radio from his jacket. The type of signal the antique picked up—the kind sent out by supporters—was illegal. But their signals still roamed the airwaves.

The man rubbed his hand over his greasy black hair. "If we could get to Ep's outgoing signal, we could—"

"Hack into their transmission," Chase said. "But my programming is limited to WR applications and satellite signals. I haven't accessed a rogue band since I lost Mel's programs."

"So give it a try," Switchblade said. "Just because you got cut off from one access doesn't mean there ain't another. Maybe Sparky has some new tricks. Look at what happened back at Blue Sky Field—you did stuff you didn't know you could do."

"Who's Sparky?" Jeff asked. "And where's...You were in a field?"

Chase crossed his arms and lowered his head. Searching the recesses of his programs for a connection to rogue radio signals, he closed his eyes.

Switchblade offered Jeff an explanation. "Nah, the name of our base was Blue Sky Field. See, we had this painting...It's a long story. And Sparky's just a stupid name we gave the exoself."

Chase looked up and shook his head.

Switchblade changed the subject. "Look at this road." He pointed to the map. "If we can get some kind of transport that can handle the snow...like a fuel-cell sled-glider, we can make it. We're only twenty miles from the bay."

"Which is frozen," Chase said. "I already looked into the possibility of ferrying across. Not happening until the ice melts. Even then, four WR boats cross those waters."

"Could be somebody off the grid has the right equipment," the guy with the lion tattoo said. "And you can confuse the Feds. That's what Switchblade says."

Chase sprang out of the chair. "Look..." He ran a

sweep of the man's record. "Trevor, I can't hack a rogue signal. I can't get out of here until the snow melts. And even then, getting on a ferry and crossing the bay would be risky. I'd have to hide in plain sight." Chase shuffled to the bookcases and picked up a dusty notebook.

He pulled back the cover. More maps. Smaller than the one on the table, but just as old. "What are you all thinking? You can't help me. I was a fool for asking. Don't get yourselves in trouble on my account." He faced the men. "I'll stay here. At least until the snow melts."

Switchblade folded the map and slid it onto the floor. "What's wrong with you?" He pushed out of his chair and folded his arms. "We've been stuck in this place for weeks. You finally showed some nerve the other day. Now you're backing off. You scared, Charlie? I thought you'd move heaven and earth to get to Melody. We're trying to come up with a plan. And you're stalling."

"I'm not stalling." Chase slipped the notebook back onto the shelf and returned to the table. "I just…"

Jeff tugged on his jacket and rubbed his hands together. "He's got a meeting with the boss this afternoon."

"What about?" Trevor asked.

"No idea," Chase said. "Why are you people afraid of that man? What's he going to do if you all walk out?"

"You gonna tell him we're helping you?" The question came from the oldest of the men. Seventy-nine—so said the exoself.

"You're not helping me," Chase said. "This is a waste of time."

Switchblade huffed before marching out the door. Trevor rose from his chair. The lion on his neck seemed to flex. Like it would pounce if the man swallowed too hard.

"Look, I don't know how the stuff inside you works," he said. "But if you can hack a satellite, what's so hard about locating the source of a radio signal? The WR does it all the time, and you're connected to their programs. So use their programs."

"Yeah. I'll work on it."

"You don't deserve to be stuck here." Trevor held out his hand. Chase returned the gesture. That's all it took for the exoself to reveal the man's terminal condition. There'd be only one more spring for the man with the lion tattoo.

Chase followed him out the door. No point in telling him he wouldn't live long. Something flickered inside Chase. The dying man could live forever if…

Trevor headed for the latrine. Chase watched him for a moment, then spotted Switchblade on the steps of the bunkhouse, staring at the roof. Chase joined him.

"What are you looking at?" Chase asked.

"That drip. Snow's melting."

"More's coming."

"So you're not going anywhere. I get it. Your wife is out there wondering if you're dead or alive and you're not ready to go. Never thought a blizzard would be what came between you two."

The muscles in Chase's arms tensed. "Are you going to try to make me mad every time I don't behave the way you expect me to? Because I've had enough of people controlling me. I don't need it from you."

Switchblade looked him in the face. "Then talk to me, brother. I know you're scared. Tell me why."

4

Chase examined his boots. The right sole had worn thin. He rubbed his beard before dropping to the step at Switchblade's feet.

The big man sat beside him. "Charlie...Chase—"

"You know, you were a lot tougher looking when your head was shaved."

"Well, look at you. Melody ain't gonna like that three-month growth." Switchblade picked up a handful of snow, formed a ball, and threw it across the compound. "We need to get out of here, man. I can feel it."

"Wishful thinking. I don't see any way out. And the boss man is not letting us go—he has his own agenda."

"Why do you care? What's wrong? Talk to me."

Chase lowered his head.

Switchblade eased his arm around Chase's shoulders. "Come on now. You can't give up."

"How did we end up in this mess? I thought if we avoided the cities, we'd make it. Then the worst blizzard ever known to mankind hit. And that wolf brought us here at gunpoint. And now my feet are frozen in solid ice." He groaned and wiped his face. "If we'd just stayed close to the highway, we'd be in Detroit. I messed up. I'm so...messed up."

"I thought we did right too." Switchblade pulled

back his arm and shoved his hands into his pockets. "We probably would have died out there if we hadn't gotten caught. But we've been here long enough. Ep ain't gonna get in our way. He's ridiculous—walking around with that nightstick. And you're not messed up. I don't even know what you mean by that."

"Of course you do. How long was I at Blue Sky Field before it was destroyed? A week? I went there with all these grandiose ideas and I ended up getting people killed. I married a girl who deserves better, and then I lost contact with her. I left the underground with nothing. I got trapped in the woods with a bunch of dissenters. And I brought *you* along. You must hate me. All you Christians must hate me. Mel must—"

"Melody loves you," Switchblade snapped. "*She's* the one who shut down the underground's communication—not you. And *I'm* the one who wouldn't leave you behind. And that lousy dissenter, Kirel, was the reason behind it all. None of it was your fault. Things just went wrong."

"Things always go wrong when I'm around. Since the day they blew a hole through me and turned me into a freak. I can't let Mel spend her life with a freak. And I don't want to go to Detroit. The world will be better off if Ep and I stay right here."

Switchblade launched off the steps and put twenty feet between him and Chase. "Man, you *are* messed up." He formed another snowball and threw at Chase's face.

Chase sucked in a breath and wiped the snow from his eyes. He brushed the cold mess from his beard.

Again, Switchblade gathered a handful of crunchy snow and hurled it at Chase.

Chase stood and shook the snow off. "You're just trying to make me mad."

"Trying to get you to act like a man."

"Yeah?" Chase yelled. "*You're* acting like a stupid kid."

Another snowball hit Chase between the eyes.

"Cut it out!"

"Make me!"

Chase flew off the steps, sprinted toward Switchblade, and shoved him with both arms. Switchblade flew fifteen feet before landing on his back. He sank into the snow. And he didn't move.

Chase stumbled to the imprint in the snow and fell to his hands and knees. "Dear God, what have I done now?"

"There's the transhuman we all know and love." Switchblade grunted as he sat straight in the man-size hole. "Last time you knocked me down, my feet didn't come two feet off the ground. I think you're getting stronger." He brushed the snow off the top of his head and smiled.

"Did I hurt you?" Chase stood, grabbed hold of Switchblade's arms, and pulled him up.

"Nah. Good thing I hit snow and not asphalt. Am I right about you getting stronger?"

"Seems like it."

"So, at your meeting with the boss man, take that stick of his and crack his skull with it. These poor fools will follow anybody. Get 'em on your side and let's get out of here. Tonight."

Chase wiped off his jacket and headed back to the bunkhouse. "I'm not cracking anybody's skull."

"Are you at least over all that 'poor little transhuman' talk? If Melody heard that, she'd be knocking *you* down."

Chase pictured her soft black curls. The fire in her brown eyes. Switchblade was right. He couldn't let her down by giving up. "I'm an idiot," he said. "A self-centered idiot. Always have been. Some things just don't change."

"Everything changes. The old man is gone. The new—"

"I know. I've got a Bible in my head. Remember?" Chase entered the bunkhouse. A few other men rested on their cots. Chase slid down a wall and sat on the floor near the heater.

Switchblade joined him. "Melody put that Bible in your head to let you know she was out there. But really, God did it. If all the Bibles in the world disappear, we got one left in the head of a transhuman. You're a blessed man. And I'm blessed to know you. Even if I do have to straighten you out once in a while."

"I'm sorry I pushed you so hard." Chase snickered. "Well, I barely touched you. I'll be more careful."

"Tell me something, Charlie. If you're getting stronger, what other changes are going on in there?"

Chase rubbed the sides of his head. He powered the hearing enhancer. Nothing out of the ordinary—if ordinary was hearing every sound within a six-hundred-yard radius. "I don't know. But something's happening."

5

At quarter past four, Chase stood from his bunk and pulled on his jacket. Most of the men were in the bunkhouse—too cold to be anywhere else. Switchblade stood by the door. He'd insisted on attending the meeting with Alpha Wolf. The dissenters eyed Chase. They must be as curious as *he* was about the summons to the boss's office. Jeff gave him a nod. Trevor eased off a rotting wooden bench near the door and crossed his arms.

Chase and Switchblade headed out into a light snow. As soon as the door shut, voices filled Chase's ears with speculation.

"Ep's gonna let him go," one man said.

"No way," another said. "Ep's gonna kill him."

"Why would he invite him to his cabin to kill him?" someone else asked. "Ep's gonna torture him into giving up his secrets—make him do something for us."

Chase waited for Switchblade to catch up. "They're wondering what's going on."

"So am I. This guy gives us any trouble, one of us is taking him down."

"Nobody needs to get hurt."

"What if Sparky feels a threat? You might not have a choice."

"The exoself does not have feelings. I can control

it. Besides, Ep knows we could've left. He's not the one keeping us here—you can thank the weather for that. I think he just wants to do a little bargaining."

"For what?"

"For some misinformation. Like he said. He wants a fresh set of facts in WR intel."

"You ready to do that?"

They reached the steps of the cabin. "I might give a little," Chase said. "If I get something in return." He knocked on the door.

"Enter," a voice called.

Switchblade stepped in front of Chase and pushed open the door. Ever the loyal protector. As if Chase needed protection.

"I didn't say anything about bringing *him* with you," Ep said to Chase.

Chase took three steps into the small room and dropped into a chair. Switchblade stood beside him and crossed his arms.

"Fine." Ep pulled a laser gun from a drawer and laid it on the desk. He looked from Switchblade to Chase. "I know some of my men have been swayed by you. And I know which ones. There are no secrets here. I can't have you gaining allegiance."

He picked up his weapon and turned it over and over. "You and I both know these poor saps are only here because they have no place else to go. But you, on the other hand, have important business in Detroit. So I've decided to do one of two things."

"You've decided to let me go if I cooperate with you. Or kill me if I don't. The first solution, you get what you want and get me out of here with the respect of your men intact. The second, you offer a display of power to keep the troops in line, and you still get rid of me."

"That brain of yours has great aptitude for reason and probabilities."

Chase leaned forward. "That's right—*my* brain. I don't have to use any superpowers to figure you out."

"But you're ready to use those powers now. Right?"

"I can set up shipments of food and supplies, but only after I get to Detroit and reinstall my connection to the underground."

Alpha Wolf laughed. "You think you can make empty promises for things I can already access, and I'll let you walk out of here?"

"You can't stop me."

Ep's steely gray eyes met Switchblade. "I've decided to alter my plan." He pointed the gun at Switchblade's head. "You'll give me what I want—full pardon from the government for me and my men—all except the ones who met with you earlier today. Or I'll kill *him*."

Chase was off the chair and across the desk before Ep could react. His shoulder drove under Ep's arm. The man let out a yell as his arm twisted upward. The weapon fired and blew a hole in the ceiling. Ep's arm continued to twist up and over until it dangled at an odd angle. He fell behind his desk and wailed. The laser gun spun in circles on the floor.

Switchblade picked it up. "So much for nobody getting hurt."

"I didn't mean..." Chase bent to help Ep off the floor. One touch told Chase the man's arm was completely pulled loose from the joint, the bone from shoulder to elbow shattered.

Ep screamed as Chase eased him onto the nearby

cot. "You'll pay for this." He shivered.

Chase spread a blanket over him.

Switchblade shoved the gun under his belt. "I'm firing up his old radio. Might catch onto that transmission from the supporters. You can hack in and we'll get somebody—"

"I need another day here."

Switchblade huffed and put his hands on his hips. "I'm getting you out now."

"I'll try to hack the signal. But I need another day. I can't leave this man all busted up, and I've got to have a talk with at least one of the men here."

Switchblade grumbled as he sat at the desk and turned on the radio.

Ep let out another scream, followed by curses. "You plan to put me back together? Just get away."

The man shook and his teeth chattered. Chase found another blanket as he searched data on the men in the bunkhouse. He found a medic who'd served in the military in the 1990s.

"Switch, you know which guy is named Gunner Foster?"

"They don't use real names much around this place."

"Go find him. He's had medical training."

Ep cried out again and then seemed to drift into delirium.

"You really gonna try to save this jerk?"

Chase lifted his brow.

Switchblade shook his head. "Thanks for not lettin' him shoot me. I'll go find…"

"Gunner Foster."

"Right. What about the radio?"

"I'll see what I can do."

Cold air swirled in through the hole in the roof, and more came in the door as Switchblade went out. Chase stoked the fire in the cast-iron heater and tucked the blankets tighter around Ep.

"I didn't even see you coming." Ep groaned. "You moved so fast. You busted my arm without even trying. How come you didn't work that stuff three weeks ago?"

Chase sat at the desk and turned the knob on the old radio. "I can't melt snow. I couldn't keep us alive in these conditions."

"So I saved your life. Now you're returning the favor? You just tore my arm loose."

"If the exoself had sensed an imminent threat against *me*, you'd probably be dead." Chase picked up a transmission. "But I didn't mean to get so rough."

"Is that an apology? Doesn't help me now."

A barely audible voice came over a rogue frequency.

"The word from Detroit—" Static muffled the woman's voice.

Then a man spoke. "Doubt he'll ever show. Probably in some detention center getting the wires pulled out of him. She seems to believe—" More static. "But it's been too long."

Chase's mind raced. Were they talking about him? Who else would get his wires pulled out? He sparked every processor in his systems, hunting a way to use WR applications to hack into the transmission without getting these people caught. Within seconds, he was inside a tracking system at a Federal station in Grand Rapids.

He pulled the system out of WR reach and made it appear inactive. Didn't seem it'd been used in months, so no one would notice. Then he reinstalled it in his own processors. It would have been easier with Mel's programs intact, but the exoself made it work. Chase adjusted the signal inside him, relayed it to the radio, and pressed the button on the transmitter.

"Hello. I'm...a believer in need of assistance. Can you hear me?"

Static.

"I need safe transport. I'm north-northwest of Saginaw Bay. I've picked up enough of your transmissions to know you're not too far. I'm requesting help."

Silence.

"I know this is a rogue channel with limited access. I found my way in and there is no danger of Federal tracking."

The woman replied. "How do you know whether or not the Feds could track us? Who are you?"

"Name's Charlie. Can you access a sled-glider?"

Laughter seemed to meld with the static. Even Ep offered a pained snicker.

"No can do, Charlie. State your location."

"Don't do it," Ep said, his voice weak.

"Seven point six miles due north of National City. Is there an underground base there?"

"Nothing there. Dead town."

Chase grinned. "Then it's the perfect place for a base, isn't it?"

No reply.

"Look, I only need to get out of this blasted snow and get to Detroit. I'm not interested in messing with your operation. Please."

The man responded. "What's your reason for going to Detroit?"

Chase didn't trust these people any more than they trusted *him*. Their earlier conversation indicated they'd been told to watch for him. But he'd hold out on identifying himself.

"Family business."

More laughter.

The woman filled Chase in. "The city's got no business except the shady kind. What are you into?"

Switchblade flung open the door and pushed in an old man wearing a torn, soiled coat and wire-framed glasses taped together in the center. Chase had seen him of course, but they'd never spoken. The man stumbled into the cabin and looked from Chase to Ep.

"He didn't want to come," Switchblade said. "Took some persuasion."

"More like force," the man said. "Been many years since I worked as a medic."

The door remained open and more frigid air rushed into the cabin and overtook the small heater. Several men waited on the steps outside the door. Peering in, one of them addressed his leader.

"You want us to take care of these two, boss?" he asked.

"Don't even try it," Ep whined.

Chase let his finger off the transmission button. "This was just an accident. A couple of you find something to repair the roof. The rest of you go back to the bunkhouse. We're going to take care of—"

Switchblade shut the door. "You got anything?" He motioned to the radio as he pushed the old man toward Ep.

"Communication between a man and a woman. I hacked the transmission and asked for assistance. But they're not real hospitable."

"Then you gotta do some convincing." Switchblade reached for a cabinet door and swung it open. He pulled out a metal box. "Charlie, break the lock off this thing."

Chase smiled. "Looking for your blade?"

"Dog locked it up when he brought us here. Now I'm taking it back."

Chase snapped off the padlock. Switch retrieved the knife and stuffed it into his pocket.

"Reunited. They don't call me Switchblade for nothin'."

Chase pushed down on the button. "It's Charlie again. You still there?"

Static.

"Are you in touch with anyone in Detroit? I hear there's a new base there."

Before Chase could let off the button, Ep screamed, his pulverized arm in the grasp of the medic.

"Who's that yelling?" the woman asked. "You got a problem there?"

"Injury. We could use a poly-cast for a broken arm."

"We've got some supplies," she said. "But no sled-glider. Got the old-fashioned kind. I think the snow's packed tight enough for us to make the trip."

"Nobody's going anywhere." The man broke into the conversation. "Not until you tell us more about yourself."

"Can you communicate with the base in Detroit? Have you talked to their leader? Her name is Melody Reese. Or Redding. Or she might be going by Sterling."

Silence.

"She's my wife. I'm Chase Sterling."

6

Static returned as footsteps on the roof shook an abundance of snow into the room. A tarp covered the hole and the pounding of nails drowned out whatever sounds might have been coming over the radio. But the men finished their task quickly and stepped to the side of the roof.

"Are you still there?" Chase clicked the speaker button repeatedly.

At last, the woman responded. "We haven't spoken with Melody, but we know who she is. Her group set up operations somewhere in the city. They've got radios, and a man called Leo sent word to watch for..." She paused. "How do we know it's really you?"

Chase looked at Switchblade.

"Leo?" Switchblade's eyes widened. "It's our people."

Chase pushed the speaker button. "Check me out. Tell Leo I'm traveling with Switchblade. I gave my wife a wedding ring that belonged to my mother. I had a dream about a painting called *Blue Sky Field*. Tell him those things and he'll know it's me."

A crash accompanied the sound of a man sliding off the snow-capped roof. The old radio let out a pop. Then nothing.

Chase fiddled with the controls as Switchblade ran

from the cabin. He returned in a hurry, his arms crossed, his black eyes glaring.

"Goon kicked the antenna down." Switchblade shook his head. "Used to be one piece—now it's four. Maybe we can fix it."

"Is everybody all right out there?" Chase asked.

"One of 'em's limping. He took the fall better than the antenna did."

Chase pushed the transmitter aside. Did he get enough information to the supporters? It was the only contact he'd made since he left Quebec.

"Mel." He closed his eyes as an ache welled up inside him. "Hold on, sweetheart."

The old man wrapping Ep's arm in a sheet looked up. "Feds probably heard everything. You think you can hide? They'll get us all now."

"The Feds are not as capable as you think. Can't track us as well as they'd have us believe."

"You think they didn't pick up on that transmission? I say they're on the way."

Chase looked away from the man. Maybe they were. Or maybe the supporters were checking his story and sending a rescue team.

Or maybe nobody was coming at all.

Switchblade walked in with the broken antenna sticking out from under his arm. He dropped it on the desk. Chase met his friend's eyes. The threat of Switchblade getting shot had been enough for the exoself to take charge. And the speed of the reaction was something new. Was Chase losing control?

"Can you fix it?" Switchblade asked.

Chase examined the broken antenna and mentally pulled a repair manual from his programs. The thing was not designed for rehabilitation. Only replacement.

He took a breath and internalized a prayer. "Can't be done. But they're coming." He glanced at the medic. "The supporters will check us out and they'll be here. Tomorrow."

"Just like you planned. One more day." Switchblade gathered the faux-metal pieces and tossed them into a trashcan. "Or a week. Or a month. We don't know if they even got what you were telling them."

Ep let out a cry as Gunner bound the crushed arm against his torso.

"Tomorrow," Chase said. He pulled his jacket tight and headed out of Ep's cabin. "Tonight we tell a dying man how to live forever."

Switchblade followed. "What are you talking about? Who's dying?"

"The guy with the lion tattoo." Chase slowed his pace. A light shone from the mess hall. Supper was cooking—boiled potatoes.

"You know from the touch?" Switchblade put his big hand on Chase's shoulder. "I almost forgot Sparky could do that."

"Me too. But it still works."

"Anything ever goes wrong inside me, I don't need no diagnosing. Ain't none of us long for this world anyway."

"Nothing's ever going wrong inside you—you're too tough."

"Wouldn't have made any difference if Ep pulled the trigger. I think he was bluffing, but you—or Sparky—took him serious. Never saw you move like that."

Chase followed his nose—even the smell of more potatoes stirred his hunger. "Let's go to the mess hall.

Maybe Trevor is already there."

"You telling the guy he's dying?"

"I don't know. Like you said—none of us are long for this world."

"Except you, robot."

"Not even me." Chase pulled open the door and stepped inside the warm building. Trevor sat alone at the table nearest the stove. He stared at the food on his plate.

Most of the men sat in groups, shoving hot potatoes into their mouths. The guy who'd fallen and taken the antenna down sat alone, rubbing his ankle.

Chase dropped into a chair beside him.

"Sorry if you was trying to get somebody on the radio," the man said. "Guess I ruined it for you."

"You didn't do it on purpose. Did you?"

"You think I'd fall off a roof just to keep you from calling for help? I don't care whether you stay or go." He sniffed and glanced around the room. "How's Ep?"

"I was trying to get him some help on the radio. Hopefully—"

"And get yourself some help?"

Chase nodded as he rose. "Can I have your attention?"

The men looked up from their plates.

"Ep has a broken arm. Badly broken. Yes, I did that to him. He threatened Switchblade and I…reacted. I spoke with believers in the area, and they'll be coming for me. Like I said, I won't turn you in. I'll do what I can to make sure Ep gets the medical attention he needs. Then Switchblade and I are leaving."

The men showed little reaction, though some kept their eyes on Chase. Others simply went back to their jerky and potatoes. Chase took the seat beside Trevor.

"You and I need to talk," he said.

Trevor looked up from his plate.

Switchblade pulled out the chair on the other side of Chase, swung his long leg over it, and eased down. Other men moved closer, including the limping roofer. Chase studied the lion on Trevor's neck.

Half the dissenters joined Chase at the table and waited with Trevor and the lion. The rest continued eating and talking, seemingly uninterested in the exchange about to take place.

A group meeting was not what Chase planned. He smiled. It wasn't up to him. Before he could open his mouth, Switchblade spoke.

"You all gathering around to hear something? This man's got something to tell you."

7

Next morning, long before sunrise, Chase eased off the top bunk and lowered his feet to the floor. Switchblade slept in the bottom bunk, his breathing deep and steady. The snores of others reverberated through the bunkhouse.

Boots in hand and jacket over his shoulder, he slipped out the door. Once on the steps, he hurried to tug on the outerwear. Frigid air shook him. But the temperature was already up to thirty-four degrees. Today would be warmer than yesterday.

He peered from one side of the camp to the other. The supporters were coming. Of course, it was too early. He marched through the deep snow to Ep's cabin and swung open the door. One of the men from the bunkhouse dozed in the desk chair. Ep slept peacefully. Thank God for that.

The man—Chase had identified him as an identity exchanger—opened his eyes. "Gunner took a break. Told him I'd sit with the boss for a while." The man pushed himself up in the chair. "Guess I nodded off."

"How's he doing?" From the foot of the cot Chase studied his captor. His enemy.

"Woke up about an hour ago. Told me to kill you."

Chase turned his gaze to the man.

A grin crawled up one side of the man's face. "He was delirious. Can I ask you something?"

Chase stepped toward the man. "Ask away."

"All that stuff you said last night—"

"You didn't join us. Were you listening?"

"You taking your new converts with you to Detroit?"

Chase lowered his head as the question sank deep. "It's a small group. I suppose…" He looked up. "I don't know. I'll have to—"

"Pray about it?" The man blinked.

"You planning to join us?"

"Nah. There's no saving somebody like me. Just wondering who we got left in this sorry band. We're not doing ourselves or anybody else any good. I'm thinking about moving on. Thought I might head out with you, then break off before you get to Detroit."

"You've had some practice doing what your leader asked *me* to do—turning a person into somebody else," Chase said. "Does he know that?"

"I'm useless as a changer without the right programs. And no, Ep doesn't know. You're the only one who can give him what he wants. You could make him a new man." He snickered. "And I don't mean like you did for the saps in the mess hall last night. Ep wouldn't fall for that any more than I would."

"I didn't change anybody."

"Right. It was the good Lord." The man rolled his eyes.

"I used to think dissenters were fighting for their rights as Christians," Chase said. "You know, God bless America and all that. Then I met a dissenter who claimed to be a Christian. He even went underground. Turned out he just wanted to rid the world of the transhuman element."

"Where is he now? I'm guessing you didn't kill

him, since you're too soft for that."

Chase shuddered as the exoself seemed to surge with defiance. It could make him a killing machine. But the Spirit remained constant. Peace flooded in. "The guy's in a detention center. He's the reason I'm here. The reason my wife had to disappear. The reason our base was destroyed. I…"

"You wish you'd killed him."

Chase looked the man in the eyes. "I forgive him."

The man laughed loud enough to stir Ep. "Well, forgive me too, for leaving you here alone with the boss. He's no threat since you busted him up. Must be some weird stuff going on inside your head. You hang out with Ep and sing a hymn or something. I'm getting some shuteye."

The man left. Chase took the seat. Deep sleep returned for Ep. An hour passed. Then two. Sunlight filtered through the grimy windows. Chase pressed the button on the transmitter. Nothing. But they were coming—the supporters. Believers living in the real world and not in a hole in the ground.

Chase pushed out of the chair and stepped outside. Thirty-nine degrees. A veritable heat wave. He surveyed the narrow paths between the trees. No sign of visitors. It was still too early.

Switchblade stumbled out of the bunkhouse and took long strides toward Chase. His brows angled inward as he shook his head. Chase met him ten feet in front of the mess hall.

"Woke up and thought you left without me," Switch said.

"Without my bodyguard?"

Switchblade snickered. "We both know who's guarding who."

"I could get us back to the road, but I wouldn't know where to find the supporters. We'll wait here for them."

"I'm gonna believe with you. Been praying since before sunrise. Didn't notice you was gone till I got up." Switchblade turned toward the south. "They'll be coming from that direction. Doubt they'll ever find this camp if somebody don't go out to meet them."

"Don't even think about it." Chase stepped in front of Switchblade. "If they've been in the area long enough, they'll probably know there's an old campground at the coordinates I gave them. They might even have a detection-free coordinate tracker."

"They don't got nothin' so high-tech if they're using old ham radios."

"We wait here." Chase stepped up to the mess hall. The weather-beaten door caught a stream of melting snow in a deep crevice, and Chase watched the water run its course to the steps. "Switch?"

"Yeah, what is it?"

"They're bringing some medical supplies."

"So?" Switchblade stepped up beside Chase.

"You think they'll have an IV? And some—"

Switchblade swung him around and gripped his shoulders. "No. You're crazy. Just as crazy as that loony old doctor of yours, and *he* said you can't do that no more. You are no longer a blood donor."

"But it could make him heal much, much faster. I hate that I broke him up so bad."

Switchblade shook him. "The doctor told you no more."

"What he said was I couldn't do it more than once or twice."

"Look, you did it for Amos, and I pray it worked.

But truth is, we don't know how Amos is doing."

"He's cured. I know it."

"You hope it. That's all. And you ain't giving no more of that transhuman blood of yours. Not as long as I'm here to guard you."

Chase smiled. "Like you could stop me."

Switchblade raised his hands, palms open. "I can break every needle I see coming your way. And break anybody who tries to poke one into you." He dropped his hands. "Now quit this foolishness."

Chase tugged at his jacket and sucked in a breath. "I wish Robert was here. He could just whip up a new arm for Ep."

"And make him strong like you? Old man would probably do it. But you better hope that don't happen. We don't need no transhuman dissenters."

"I wonder…"

Switchblade opened the door. "What?"

"Robert said they were making another transhuman. Like me. I wonder how it's going."

8

That evening, Chase ate a quartered potato and a strip of jerky. Then he braved a cold wind to wait at the camp's southern perimeter and listen for voices, for footsteps. But there was nothing.

Switchblade had the six new believers in a huddle in front of the mess hall. Trevor was there. Chase closed his eyes and thanked God for saving the man. And Jeff, the big guy. He'd be an asset to the underground. Four more men Chase barely knew. Now they were brothers.

What were they planning? Would the men leave with Chase and Switchblade? Could they be trusted? They were still dissenters. Taking them into the underground would be risky. And trying to get to Detroit with six more people in tow was too much to consider.

Some of the other men—hard-core dissenters from what Chase could tell—had retrieved weapons from Ep's gun safe. But they hadn't made any threats. Seemed the pack was ready to abandon their injured leader.

A graying sky softened the bright white of the snow-covered forest as the sun sank behind trees. Chase headed for the small group of converts. He'd take them as far as the nearest underground base— assuming the supporters approved. Assuming they even showed.

"They're coming. Don't start doubting now." Chase headed toward the mess hall. A sound in the distance turned him around.

Drone.

Chase hadn't heard or seen a drone the entire time he'd been here. Too much bad weather for surveillance on an area WR programs classified as uninhabitable. No report had been filed regarding local covert activity for over three years. The area was clean—so said the records.

So why the drone?

But it didn't come near. Soon the faint rhythm faded to nothing. It headed south. Detroit?

Chase joined the men as Switchblade spoke in a soothing voice. The big brute could be as soft as his real name—Leslie Honeywell. Chase laughed. He didn't dare say that out loud.

Switchblade looked up and raised his brows. "Did I say something funny?"

"Sorry. I was just..." Chase lowered his head and walked toward the latrine as Switchblade continued his pep talk to the newly faithful.

"God already did something astounding for us," Switch said. "Even if we die tomorrow, or we end up in a center, He's got us. Ain't nothin' gonna change that."

A shiver crawled up the processors in Chase's spine. So many uncertainties. He should go back and join Switchblade in encouraging these men. They'd face greater resistance as believers than they'd ever met as dissenters. Chase pulled on the rusty door handle, but he stopped before he went in.

Footsteps. Three people—one lighter than the

other two. Sounded like they had some dogs with them. And a sled.

He let the door slam. "Switch," he yelled.

"Yeah?"

"People coming in from the south."

"You stay here. I'll check it out." Switchblade headed for the woods at the south end of the camp. Jeff hurried after him. Despite the blond hair and fair skin, the guy was as tough looking as Switchblade. A couple of big guys forming a welcome party was a good idea. But they weren't going without the transhuman.

Chase caught up with them before they got too far past the tree line.

Switchblade whipped around. "I told you to stay put, robot."

"Listen," Chase said. "One of them is on a radio."

"I don't hear anything," Jeff said.

"You wouldn't," Switchblade told him. "Got to have robot ears to hear like Charlie."

"They're a thousand feet out." Chase stepped forward. "Hey," he yelled. "This way."

Switchblade stomped in the snow and drove his fist into Chase's arm. "You crazy? You don't even know who's out there."

"I can hear what they're saying. They're looking for us." Chase ran between the trees, stumbling, calling out to the believers. Switchblade and Jeff were at his back.

In only a minute the party of two men, a woman, and four huskies came into view. The dogs pulled a long sled packed with canvas sacks.

The rescue team stopped. And stared.

"Are you in touch with our people in Detroit?" Chase eyed the radio held by one of the men. "Did you tell them I'm nearby?"

"I'm guessing you're Chase Sterling," the man said. "Would've never known it was you if I wasn't out here looking for you."

"My people. My...my wife. Have you talked to them?"

"We had to drop communication. There's drone activity in the area."

Switchblade crossed his arms and looked up. "For the love of...Charlie, did you know about this?"

"I picked up on one a little while ago. It headed south." He stepped toward the sled. "I checked intel. They don't know anything. The drones are headed for Detroit."

"You checked intel?" the woman asked. "You can do that?"

Chase met her eyes. "I'm doing it right now. Your base—wherever it is—is safe. The drones were sent out because the dissenters are rallying in Detroit. It's got nothing to do with the Underground Church. But..."

"But what?" Switchblade kept his arms crossed as he stepped between the three newcomers and Chase.

"They plan to check the whole area for activity tonight."

"Then we need to do what we came to do and get out," the woman said. "It won't help though. Will it? They'll spot us if they come back this way."

"I'd like to say I could turn them," Chase said. "But the best I can do is blow them up if they get too close."

"Well, praise the Lord for that," Switchblade said. "But it don't mean they won't send back data. You sure you can't send 'em somewhere else?"

"Wait," the woman said. "What do you mean you

can blow them up?" She looked up to the sky.

"It's in my programming. I can make them self-destruct."

"Unbelievable." She smiled. "I guess the rumors were true."

The rumors likely carried stories of death and destruction. "I'd be of far greater help if I could get to Detroit."

The woman dropped the smile. "Then let's get you to Detroit."

The tightly fastened hood of her gray parka circled her face, and the cold had turned her fair skin pink. Hazel eyes seemed to search Chase.

"Camp's this way," Switchblade said. "Let's get moving—it'll be dark soon." He led the way, and the supporters who'd braved the weather and the unexpected visitation of drones followed.

"I'm Hillary," the woman said. She motioned to the men on either side of her. "Gavin and Bloodhound."

Chase nodded. "Nice alias," he said to the one called Bloodhound. "Good at tracking?"

"You got it," the short Hispanic man answered.

"Thank you for coming after us. My navigation is good, but I lost my way in this blizzard."

The other man—Gavin—gave a whistle, and the dogs followed. "We've got a few medical supplies and other provisions. Not feeling great about giving this stuff to dissenters."

"If it makes you feel any better, as of last night at least six of them are believers," Chase said. "Could be more. You know how people are about admitting it."

Hillary easily kept up with the men. "How'd that happen?"

Victoria Buck

Chase shrugged. "How does it ever happen? The Spirit moved."

Switchblade grabbed the satchel slung over Hillary's shoulder, and she didn't protest. "Man's being modest. He had church last night. And some of the men answered the call." Switchblade pointed to Jeff. "Including this guy."

Jeff dipped his chin. "Any room at your base for a new guy?"

Gavin was quick to answer. "No room for dissenters. Not after what happened to the headquarters in Quebec."

Chase stopped and faced the man. "What did you hear?"

"Dissenters told the Feds where to find it, and they wiped the place out. We were hooking up computers to get into the new system. But it never worked. We heard the Feds shut your wife's programs down, but then we found out she did it herself. Lots of rumors flying, Mr. Sterling. One of 'em says the poor girl doesn't want you anywhere near Detroit."

A surge ran through Chase. "It's not true. Mel sent me a clue she was headed for Detroit. And now that our group has made contact with you, I know she made it. She's waiting for me."

Hillary rested her hand on Chase's arm. "When you find her, will the two of you be able to reconstruct the programs and connect the underground? We heard some crazy story about the whole program being hidden in verses from the Psalms. Is that true?"

Chase nodded. "Melody put the code inside my programs, but I could only get it operational by finding the right combination of chapter and verse. The numbers unlocked the code."

44

She shook her head. "Bizarre. So...you think you can do it again? Get the whole thing working?"

"Yes." Chase marched through the snow. Switchblade and Jeff were up ahead. The men with the sled came behind. Hillary trudged along beside Chase.

"But I need Melody's help." Even as he spoke, he searched the exoself for any hint of Mel's programs. Just like he'd done every day for the last ten weeks. Nothing remained except 32-7. The code that allowed him to manipulate WR programs and blow up drones. Among other things. But the rest of the code, so valuable to the underground, was useless. And he needed Mel to get it working again.

9

The supporters drugged Ep with something in a hypodermic. They slid the crushed arm into a poly-cast. The guy named Gavin seemed to know what he was doing. Soon Ep was sleeping.

Chase sat on the edge of the desk. "What'd you give him?"

"Morphine," Gavin said. "And some bio-antibodies."

"Where'd you get the drugs?"

Gavin faced him. "We have resources. Been taking care of outcasts in this area for years. Long before the underground felt the need to go transhuman." He pulled a blanket over Ep.

Chase smirked. "It wasn't my idea. Just another unbelievable plan I got dragged into."

"So how does it…did it work? We heard you were about to get the whole underground connected. That you could set up transportation for a believer in Timbuktu, if that's what needed to be done."

"Do you know the four Ss?"

"Sympathizers, supplies, secret houses, safe travel," Gavin answered.

"Information about such things traveled by word of mouth," Chase said. "And the underground stayed clear of computers. But Mel hid a code inside me to connect believers via an untraceable system. Each S was represented by a chapter and verse from the Psalms. Up-top believers still communicate via electronic methods. I was able to latch onto that information and compile it in a system connecting the underground."

"So this Melody we've been hearing about—the woman who replaced Amos as the leader. She's a programmer? Why didn't she just hook all that up without going through...you?"

Chase smiled. "It's complicated."

"I guess it didn't work, huh? We're right back where we started. We work up top, so we're using computers. But we're careful. The underground—what there is of it in this area—depends on us. So what happened to the plan to get them hooked up?"

"The headquarters in Quebec was infiltrated by a mole—that dissenter you heard about. The WR got him, and he talked. Before the base was destroyed, Melody turned me off, so to speak. She shut everything down. It was the only way she could—"

"Keep you safe?" Gavin sat on the end of the cot.

"Keep the Feds from destroying every base around the world. And yes, keep them from finding me."

"When did you get married?"

"The day before we lost contact."

The man lowered his head. "They caught my wife. You got any idea what's going on in the detention centers? They used to hold first-time offenders for a while and then let them go. But not anymore."

Chase shivered. "I don't know."

Gavin stared at Chase. "You've still got access to WR records. Otherwise you wouldn't have known what the drones were up to."

"I could get into their systems before Mel's programs. And after."

"Then you must know something."

Chase bent forward and rubbed his face. "Do you know where they took her?"

"Grand Rapids."

He ran a check of the largest detention center in the city. The machine was in place. And functional. "How long?"

"Six months."

Should he tell the man? "I'm sorry. Detainees' records are deeply imbedded. I can't get in. I'm...so sorry."

"If you get the underground connected again, then you can find out?"

"It doesn't work that way."

The man rubbed his hands together and stood. "But keeping us all connected will help us not get caught. Right?"

"Yes. It will."

"Look, there's nothing else we can do for this man. We need to leave. How many are going with us?"

Chase rose from the desk and looked at Ep. The man remained deep in sleep. And that's where they'd leave him. And as many of his men as wanted to stay. Chase would do what he could to alter the view of the compound. He picked a satellite photo out of the WR files and reset it to real time. Maybe that would keep the drones away.

"I'll find out how many of the new believers want to leave with us." Chase eased out the door.

Gavin followed him. "I'll get the dogs ready."

Darkness covered the compound. The supporters had insisted they let the heaters and lamps go out. Not that it would do much good if a surveillance drone flew over. It'd pick up body heat.

Switch had already gotten the men together. He waited near the bunkhouse with Jeff and three of the other new converts, along with Hillary and Bloodhound. Food and clothing had been moved off the sled and stored in the cabin with the maps. A gift from the Christians for their enemies.

"Where are the other two?" Chase asked as he came up beside Switchblade.

"Not coming. Four in. Two out."

Bloodhound stepped close. "I tried to talk these four out of it. We'll be lucky to make it back alive. We would've never made this trip if we'd known about the rally in Detroit. Too much activity."

"Is that it?" Chase asked. "No other reason you discouraged the men from joining us?"

"They were all listening—new believers and otherwise. We can't show up back in our little town with a parade of dissenters." The man heaved a satchel onto the sled. "We don't like attention."

Chase nodded. "I understand. But the others—"

"I talked to them," Switchblade said. "They want to stay here. To shine a light. You know?"

Chase nodded. Trevor might not even survive the trip in his condition. Chase hadn't told him he was dying. But maybe he knew. "Then I guess they should stay."

"All right, if that's settled, let's get out of here," Bloodhound said. "There's nine of us. We'll head out three at a time, and we'll walk thirty feet apart. Everybody got it?"

"No lights," Gavin said. "We'll just have to feel our way home."

"Let me go first," Chase told him. "I can see in the dark."

Gavin's brows went up. "Take the two big guys and head out. We'll come behind you with the dogs." He eyed the other three who were ready for a new life. "You can bring up the rear."

The men from the camp drew close. "You're all in my prayers," Chase said. "God be with you."

"And with you," Trevor said.

Facing the dark woods, Chase began the march to the small town of National City, where he and Switch would leave these supporters, and probably the new believers. They'd find a way around the bay and continue this painfully slow trek to Detroit.

An hour passed.

"Switchblade?"

"You doing all right, Charlie?"

"Drones are coming near. Not just the surveillance kind. S-drones. Intel says no one is permitted outside tonight within a three-hundred-mile radius of Detroit. They'll shoot to kill."

10

"You gonna take 'em down, robot?" Switchblade came up beside Chase. "What are you waiting for?"

"For the exoself to feel the threat. They're too far out." Chase took long strides. He pulled the code—32-7. "I have to wait until they're closing in on us. But…"

Switchblade grabbed Chase's arm and stopped him. "But what?"

Jeff was right behind them. "Why are we stopping?"

"They'll pass over us in less than a minute," Chase said. "I'm going to try something."

Jeff looked up. "You can crash them. Right?"

"Too many of them. Ten downed drones would be reason enough to send out twenty more. I'd rather just let them go by. But we need to hide."

The others had caught up now. They gathered close.

"Why did we stop?" Hillary asked.

"Be very still," Chase said.

A small red light shone from the first drone passing overhead. Then another. They operated in silent mode, unseen except for the light. The rest passed by quickly.

"I think it worked," Chase said. "I read their outgoing data. No report."

"What worked?" Gavin asked. "Those little beasts

pick up everything. And we were standing right under them. How'd you do that?"

Switchblade rubbed his hand over his mouth. "Couldn't be that real-time trick—they'd pick up on our heat imprint with or without it. You can't use Melody's security code. So what was it?"

"Some kind of shield," Chase said. "A barrier between us and them."

"Something new. Right?" Switch grinned and looked up again. "Praise the Lord."

"You made us undetectable?" Jeff asked. "Can you keep it that way?"

Chase nodded. "I think so. Everyone stay close."

"The evolution of the transhuman," Switchblade said as they headed forward. "Glory be."

Gavin came up beside Chase. "Do you mean to tell me changes occur in your processors without anybody reprogramming you? It's spontaneous?"

"I'm afraid so."

"Afraid? Why?"

"I don't know what I'll become."

"Isn't it obvious God's got His hand in this?" Hillary asked. "Don't be afraid."

He'd almost forgotten. "Thank you."

"For what?" She walked on past him.

"For reminding me I don't have to be afraid." Chase smiled. "I have been. I will be again, I'm sure. But I needed to hear it."

She nodded. "We all need to hear it."

They went on toward the village north of Saginaw Bay. Daylight would beat them. They'd spend the day—maybe more than a day—formulating a new plan to get to Detroit. As long as they were in transit and the drones were sweeping the area, they'd have to stay off the radio. But in a few hours Chase would be in a safe house where he could try to contact Mel. He quickened his pace.

Sunlight spilled into the woods when they were an hour out. Chase ran a check on the drones. Still two in the area. The rest had returned to Grand Rapids. The rally had ended before it began. No casualties. What kind of place had Detroit become? Mel once called it a ghost town. Things had changed. Seemed outcasts there represented every rogue group. And if WR surveillance and infiltration reports were to be believed, the place was filled with crime.

Switch once said he'd gotten into trouble there. Years ago. Nothing new about the crime. Just the number of criminals.

With most of the drones gone, the exoself's new shield had come down. Chase was aware of this, but he'd done nothing to deactivate it. He glanced over his shoulder. The group had spread out. Switch was a few yards behind him. The rest lagged farther back. Except for the three converts from the camp. Chase listened. Then he stopped and swung around.

"What's wrong?" Switchblade caught up with him.

"Three missing—the men from the camp."

The supporters, along with Jeff, drew near.

Chase started toward them. "Jeff, where are your buddies?"

Jeff kept moving. "Must be close. Maybe they had to take a break."

"They're not within hearing distance. And I can hear a long way. When was the last time you saw them?"

"It was still dark," Jeff said. "I don't know. Hour

maybe."

Switchblade dropped his pack. "Well, if that don't ruin a perfectly terrifying morning. As if we don't have enough to worry about."

"Jeff and I will go back and look for them," Chase said. "The rest of you keep going."

Switchblade rubbed his head and then crossed his arms. "You got yourself a new sidekick? If you're going back, I'm going back."

Chase fished a water bottle out of a satchel and gulped from it. "Relax. One of us needs to get to the base and try to contact Mel. I'm better equipped to track down the stragglers. You go ahead and see if you can get through to Detroit."

Bloodhound stepped near. "I'll go with you and Jeff. Three of us looking is better than two."

Chase nodded. "The rest of you keep going. We'll catch up. The guys probably just got too far behind and lost their way."

"I don't like this." Switchblade grabbed his pack and marched forward.

Hillary and Gavin followed. Chase headed in the opposite direction with Jeff and Bloodhound.

"How far back you plan to go?" Bloodhound asked. "Could be they changed their minds and went back where they came from."

"Unlikely," Chase said. "They've got to be close." He listened. But the only thing he heard was a drone.

"We've got company," he said. "Drone just to the north. I've got us covered, but I can't do anything about the lost guys. Or the rest of our group heading south."

In only a minute the drone was overhead. Bigger than an S-drone, it hovered. Chase scanned its readout.

The cover the exoself put up seemed to confuse the thing. It wobbled, then eased away.

Chase groaned as he plodded through the snow. In the wrong direction. He gritted his teeth. "I can't believe this. I'm backtracking because some dissenters couldn't keep up."

Jeff and Bloodhound spread out to search the brush. Soon they disappeared. Bloodhound to the left and Jeff to the right. Chase moved straight forward and listened. Wood cracked nearby. He pivoted and surveyed the trees. The branches of one pine a hundred feet due north seemed to have been blown away. A ten-foot limb dangled. Another crack, and the limb fell.

Chase moved closer. "I think a laser took out a tree," he said loud enough for the other men to hear. He broke through the brush. From thirty feet, he saw the men. Two with the fallen limb over them. The other on his stomach in a stretch of red snow.

He ran and fell between the men—his new brothers—and touched their arms. All three dead.

Chase lowered his head and shut his eyes tight. "God help us." He rose and hurried back to the path. "Jeff. Bloodhound," he called. "You can stop looking. Come on—we've got to go."

The men plodded out of the bush.

Bloodhound stepped close. "What did you find?"

"They're dead. Drone got them. Let's go." Chase headed south.

"Just like that?" Jeff asked. "We're just going to leave them out here?"

Chase stopped and huffed out a breath. He faced the men. "We need to catch up with the others."

No more was said about the men. But Chase remembered Switch's words: *If we die tomorrow...*

The men followed him. Three more miles and they'd be in town. Chase kept the exoself's shield in place.

Two more miles. He caught the sound of an S-drone up ahead. He picked up its frequency just as it readied to fire. Two blasts. Chase stepped up his pace. "They're shooting again." Switchblade and the others were up ahead. Unprotected.

Chase broke into a run.

11

The crunch of snow beneath his boots lessened as Chase stumbled down what seemed to be a widening path. Perhaps even a road. The temperature rose. Within only moments the snow turned to slush. It didn't slow Chase down. Bloodhound and Jeff were somewhere behind him. Switchblade was ahead. Along with Gavin and Hillary.

The path stretched out at length now and the snow seemed not only to be melting but to have also been plowed. Would Switch and the others have taken the road? Or would they have kept to the tree line?

No sound nearby. No travelers. Town was a half mile away. "Switchblade?" Chase slowed to a jog. "Hillary?"

Nothing. Jeff and Bloodhound came up behind, both out of breath.

Jeff grabbed Chase's arm. "You think the drone—"

"I think we'd better keep looking. Don't jump to conclusions."

Another fifty yards. "Switchblade!" Chase calculated the direction of the blast he'd heard when the drone fired. He yanked a couple of small pines right out of the ground to clear the way. "They must have taken to the woods to stay under cover." He made his own rough trail through dense brush until he came to another path. Not a road—just a line cleared for hikers.

Then he saw them. Hillary sat upright, her hands pressing down on Gavin's stomach. And Switchblade. Heaped over a fallen tree. Face to the ground. Blood streaming into the snow.

Chase dropped next to him, wrapped both hands around the man's big shoulders, and pulled him off the log and onto his back. "Switch. Can you hear me?"

Vitals were stable. Chase found the entry point where the laser had hit. He pulled off his jacket and stuffed it against Switchblade's side.

He glanced at Hillary. Bloodhound and Jeff were on their knees next to her. "How's Gavin?" Chase asked.

"Not breathing. Can you help him?"

"Jeff, come over here and press this against the wound," Chase said. "He's bleeding heavily."

Jeff rose and then dropped next to Switchblade. "Got it."

Chase moved over and laid a hand on Gavin's chest. He closed his eyes and exhaled. "I'm sorry."

Hillary let her hands slide off Gavin. "Go in peace, brother. We'll all be with you soon." She rose off the cold ground, stumbled, and let out a soft groan.

Chase sprang up and supported her. "You're not badly injured. Just some bruising. How'd you manage that?"

"Switchblade jumped in front of me. Then he fell on top of me. Fooled the drone, I guess. Must've thought it got us both." She reached the fallen tree and sat on it. "He tried to crawl back to the road, but...Let's get him to town. We've got a doctor."

"Why'd you all move off the road?" Bloodhound asked. "You know that's not going to keep a drone off you." He turned to Chase. "And you—you got some kind of transhuman med lab inside you? How do you know she's not hurt bad?"

"Part of my programming—I can make an accurate diagnosis."

Hillary pulled her jacket tighter. "Then how bad is Switchblade?"

Surveying the area, Chase said, "I guess the dogs took off with the sled."

"Probably back in Gavin's barn by now," Hillary said.

Chase lifted Switchblade off the ground and hoisted him over one shoulder. The difference in their sizes made it awkward, but Chase would have no trouble carrying his friend half a mile.

"It's bad," he said. "Lacerated liver. His spleen is done for. He's bleeding out."

"Then we have to hurry." Hillary ran toward the road.

Chase stumbled through the brush. Jeff and Bloodhound kept a few paces behind him.

Seemed like another hour to get to town, but the exoself only counted ten minutes. A few small houses lined the road. No one greeted the rogue element entering the little village. Surely Hillary or Bloodhound would try their radio soon and let somebody know an injured man needed care.

"Where's the doctor?" Chase shifted the weight on his shoulder. "Why don't you get the radio out? The drones are gone."

"We're here," Hillary said. Her eyes darted all around, as if she expected someone to be watching them. Then she eased down an alley between two rotting buildings.

Chase followed with Bloodhound and Jeff close behind. Switchblade let out a sigh. The first sound he'd made.

"Hang on, Switch," Chase said.

The door of a shed behind the building to the left was where Hillary stopped. She knocked, and the door swung open. No words were exchanged with the woman who stepped aside to let Hillary in. Chase turned sideways to get in with Switchblade slung over his back. Once free of the doorframe, he searched the dimly lit room. He quickly moved to the nearest of three cots and maneuvered Switch onto it. Then he looked up at the woman standing beside him. He didn't have to think about scanning her iris. He just did it.

June Hakimata. Fifty-seven. A general surgeon assigned by the WR to provide services to the legitimate population of every small town within a hundred miles to the northwest of Bay City, where she ran a nice facility. She had connections. And a fully equipped medical transport.

A chip in her left arm reported her every move to the WR.

"You're a supporter?" Chase asked. "How do you manage that? You're high-profile WR." Even as he spoke, the exoself pulled a line of code to protect him from this woman, though she didn't give any indication of being a danger. Her slight build and kind eyes told Chase he had no reason to panic. But what was she doing here in this old shed?

She leaned over Switchblade and pulled his jacket open. Then she used a small blade to cut his shirt free. Blood still trickled from the wound.

Chase reached up with his right hand and touched

the back of his shirt. Wet with blood. Both his hands were bloody as well.

"I assume you read my iris," the doctor said.

"I'm afraid it's just habit now. Unless it's someone I know." Chase knelt at the side of the cot. "If any chance exists that you could turn me in, I'll put an end to it. I can confuse the Feds faster than that chip in your arm can report your location."

She looked into his eyes and smiled. "The chip says I'm in Bay City."

Chase smiled. "Only person I know—other than me—who could pull a stunt like that is my wife."

She tilted her head and lowered the red-rimmed glasses resting on her upturned nose. "You have a wife? Too bad." She smiled again.

Switchblade coughed and blood dripped from his lips. He stirred a bit but his eyes remained shut.

"Tell me you can help him," Chase said.

"I've got enough equipment here to repair the damage. If we can stop the bleeding in time, he should be fine. Of course, he's lost a great deal of blood already. We need to act quickly."

Jeff and Bloodhound waited near the door. Hillary had disappeared. The little doctor—this mystery WR citizen/supporter of the underground—moved like a graceful bird as she prepared a table of supplies beside the cot. No sterile environment, but she seemed to take great care in giving Switchblade the best chance at recovery in this shed of a hospital. An IV went into his arm and a drip of clear liquid filled the tube.

Hillary returned with two men. Chase read them both. Local farmers. No records. Law-abiding citizens. Like Dr. Hakimata. Only not so important. No monitoring. Not that it mattered around here—the doctor could fool the Feds.

"I've got him sedated," she said. She swabbed a bit of blood from his torso and dabbed it onto a slide. "Harold, type it for me. Then see what we've got."

"B Positive," Chase said.

The doctor's narrow eyes opened wide. "Never mind, Harold. I'm sure we don't have that one." She looked up at Chase. "A rare one, is he? Well, today he's O Positive. Plenty of that in stock. But we'll pray the bleeding stops." She looked up at Chase. "You are a praying man, aren't you, Mr. Sterling?"

"Call me Chase. I'm praying right now. If you need blood, the type doesn't matter for me. It's…"

"It's what?"

"I'm kind of a universal donor."

She drew her brows together. "O Positive. Like I said, we have some in reserve. No need for you to roll up your sleeve."

12

The doctor widened the hole under Switchblade's ribcage cut by a drone's laser. The wound wasn't much bigger than if it had been caused by a standard laser weapon. Why hadn't the thing blasted him to bits? Must not have been a direct hit. The woman's small hand reached right through the muscle and tissue. After that, Chase excused himself from the makeshift operating room. Hillary followed him outside.

The afternoon sun brought a steady drip from icicles jutting from the eaves of the shed. Chase reached for one and broke it loose. He tossed it to the ground. "If this surgery is going to take a while, I think I'd better go ahead and try to contact my group in Detroit. Where's your base of operations?"

"Already tried. Every post within a three-hundred-mile radius of Detroit seems to have shut down their communications. Or somebody did it *for* them."

"Are you saying there is no way to send word that I'm nearby?" Chase yanked another icicle loose and crushed it in the palm of his hand. "I don't believe this. How long will it last?"

"Could be a while. It happens when WR activity spikes. Last time, it lasted four days."

Chase left her standing between the buildings and walked to the middle of the narrow road. A couple of people shoveled slush off their driveways. They both eyed him for a moment, then went back to their chore. Chase didn't care who saw him, but Hillary hurried to the street, grabbed his arm, and pulled him back into the shadow of the buildings.

"Not everybody is town is a sympathizer," she said. "And *their* communication is working just fine."

"Nobody's going to recognize me. Not without a DNA scanner."

"You're going to have to be patient."

Chase closed his eyes. She was right. He breathed in and out. In the flow he offered a silent prayer. For Switch. For Mel. For peace. He opened his eyes. "This doctor—what's her story? It's one thing for somebody still in the system to help the underground, but she *is* the system. She's one of them. What's she doing here in this old building in the middle of nowhere?"

"She's a believer. We had a hard time learning to trust her. But she *can* be trusted. Before we headed out to find you—before communication shut down—we sent word that we might need her. Thought we might be bringing in the guy with the crushed arm. Turned out we needed her for something more urgent. God put her here. Wouldn't you say?"

"I've been running data on her. It says she's in Bay City. She's found a way to fool the system. Like I do. Well, she uses a computer. I'm guessing it's her AI training that makes it happen. She attended the same school as my wife."

"You know all that just by using…" Hillary loosened the collar on her jacket.

"It's called the exoself. Systems outside me linked to systems built inside me."

"And the WR can't use those systems to get to you?"

Chase shook his head. "Same as the doctor. Only I don't need a computer. I *am* one."

"Amazing." She tilted her head. "But you're still a man. You miss your wife."

The statement brought a lump to Chase's throat. "How do I get across the bay? I'll walk if I have to."

"A transhuman can walk on water?" She smiled.

"Only if it's frozen." Chase returned the smile.

The door pushed open and Jeff stepped out, his face a little green.

"You through observing the procedure too?" Chase asked.

"You know, I didn't mind the cutting and the blood. It was the stitching that got me. Doc said she had to do it the old-fashioned way. No lasers. Just a needle and thread."

"She's done already? It must not have been too bad."

"Says she won't know for a few hours."

For the moment, Chase forgot his need to move on. He had to see his friend. He stepped inside and closed the door behind him. Then he rested his hand on Switchblade's chest. No monitors needed. Heart rate was good. Temperature normal. Blood pressure a bit low.

And dropping.

Panic rose in Chase. He turned to the doctor, who was washing her implements in a little sink on the other side of the room.

"He's still bleeding inside."

The metal instrument hit the sink with a clank. Dr. Hakimata rushed over and lowered a stethoscope directly over the incision. "You can tell by touching him? I should have kept you here while I had him open." She positioned the scope. "I can't hear it. With better equipment, I would have known. There was so much damage around his liver—must be where he's bleeding. I'll have to go back in."

"I'll stay with you. It never occurred to me I could act as a monitor. I guess my diagnostic ability isn't as useless as I thought."

The doctor carefully removed the stitches and probed into Switchblade's gut a second time. She found nothing. But the slow blood loss continued.

After nearly an hour, the small woman gave Chase a look of desperation. And hopelessness.

"If we were back at my surgical center, this would not be an issue. Even in my mobile lab I could find the bleed and repair it." The doctor sighed and pulled the bloody gloves from her hands. "But here, there isn't anything else I can do."

Chase bit his bottom lip. He nodded. "We can give him a transfusion."

"I've been giving him blood for the last two hours. We've used up our supply and giving him more would only prolong the inevitable."

"He needs *my* blood." Chase slid out of the jacket he'd borrowed and rolled up his shirtsleeve. "I should have done this to begin with. Take some out of me— you won't need much."

"What's so special about your blood?" She shook her head. "What did they do to you?"

"Do you know anything about nano—"

"Nanobytes? Is that what's in your blood?"

"My doctor—the one who built me—said it's more like nano*bots*. Dr. Hakimata, it heals. It'll save his life."

She dropped her hands to her sides and drew her brow tight. "Call me June. If you're sure you want to do this, I'll get what we need to take your blood."

Chase nodded. "I'm sure."

Jeff and Hillary came back in from the alley while Chase lay on the cot next to Switchblade's. The blood seeped from his arm and into a bag. From there it dripped down another tube and into Switchblade.

"How is he?" Jeff asked. "Did you run out of blood? I'm O Positive. I can donate too."

Chase could hardly hold his eyes open. "Won't be necessary. Once he's got my blood in him, he won't need any more." He nearly laughed. "But listen—all of you. Don't tell him about this. He wouldn't approve."

"Why not?" June asked. "What's the downside?"

Chase's lungs seemed to close up. But that wasn't possible. He sucked in a breath. He'd get through this. He just needed to relax. "I might need to sleep for a while when we're done. That's all."

Jeff knelt beside him. "I got the impression back at the camp that you hardly sleep at all. You don't need it. Giving up a little blood changes that?"

"Yes." Chase looked at the doctor. "Try to keep him out until I get my strength back. If he sees me like this, he'll know what I did."

"He won't wake up today," the doctor said. "By morning, I'd say."

Chase closed his eyes. "Good. Take care of him."

"I'll take care of both of you. Anything else I need to know? Anything I should do?"

Chase pried open his eyes. "No. I just need to power down." He met Hillary's gaze. "Please...keep trying to get through to Detroit." His eyes fell shut. "But don't tell my wife I did this. Just tell her I'm coming. Tell her I..."

The old, familiar blackness carried Chase away.

13

"Charles Redding, what do you see?"

The voice. The darkness. Chase reached beside him, but there was no metal bowl filled with water like in dreams past. He opened his eyes. No movie screen. And no peaceful green hillside like the last dream he'd had—the one in Quebec. This time, it was different. This time...he knew the One speaking.

"I see my life. My future. I want to follow You home."

"In time. Look again."

Chase pushed himself off the cot. No—the cold, crumbling asphalt of a desolate street. He opened his eyes wide and looked up. "Where am I?"

"The place where you will speak."

"What will I say?"

Chase grabbed the edge of the cot as a rough punch to his bicep knocked him sideways. He rolled flat on his back and opened his eyes.

Switchblade knelt next to him. His jaw clenched tight, his nostrils flared. His eyes glared with something between hatred and gratitude. He shook his head and punched Chase again. "Oh, I'm sorry, robot. Did I wake you? It's only been about sixty hours. Maybe I should've let you sleep"—Switch's volume rose as he spoke—"forever."

Chase smiled. "You're OK. I'm—"

"You're stupid." Switchblade slugged him again.

"Will you stop hitting me?"

"I need to get out of here." Switch rose and headed for the door. He turned back, but only for an instant. "I'm glad you're awake." Then he left the room and slammed the door.

Chase propped up on his elbows and breathed deeply. He found June sitting in a chair, staring at him.

"I couldn't keep him sedated for two and a half days. In fact, he was awake, out of bed, and hovering over you after only a few hours. And he knew what you'd done. There was no hiding it."

"I can't believe I was out that long. It seemed like just a few minutes."

"How do you feel?"

Chase lowered his eyes and let his head fall to the pillow. "Rested. Peaceful. When I'm out, I dream. Well, I think they're dreams. I wanted…"

"You wanted what?"

"To go. I wanted to go home. But…"

The doctor came closer. "A near-death experience? Your heart rate and blood pressure never varied. You were just sleeping. But Switchblade told us your doctor said you shouldn't do this again. He said it might shut you down permanently. You should've let me know that before I stuck a needle in your arm."

"I had to do it. He's like a brother to me."

She nodded. "Well, your brother is not too happy with you now that he's got—as he put it—robot blood."

Chase smiled. "He'll get over it."

"He says the nanobots don't replicate. What will happen to you?"

"I don't know. Probably took a couple of years off

my life. Maybe now I'll only live to be a hundred seventy-three."

"I wish I knew more about how you function. I trained in AI, but this is beyond me. Your wife must be one smart woman."

Chase sat straight. "Is communication open again? Have they contacted Detroit?"

"Bloodhound came by earlier, but he didn't say anything about getting through on the radio."

"Have you been here the whole time? Seems too long for you to be missing from your clinic."

"I'm making rounds in the area. I returned for my mobile unit, came back, and checked on the local communities. That's my job." She brushed her hand over Chase's hair. "Nobody has to know I spent a good deal of my time looking after a transhuman in National City."

"Thank you. I'd have lost my best friend if it wasn't for you."

"I'll take a walk to Hillary's—that's where the radio is. Maybe they've gotten through. I have a feeling it's important for you to get to Detroit as soon as possible."

"You know something I don't?"

She shook her head. "I'm quite sure none of us knows anything you don't already know. Just a feeling. I'm praying, Chase. I don't think this will be easy."

"Getting there?"

"No. *Being* there."

Chase lay back as the doctor walked to the door.

"I'll send Switchblade to stay with you while I'm gone. I'm sure he didn't go too far. He's been so worried." She looked back and chuckled. "Well, he was worried between bouts of anger."

She slipped out the door. After a few minutes, Switchblade came in.

"You doing all right, Charlie?" He sat in the chair and rested his elbows on his knees.

"Now that I know you're OK, I'm doing great."

"Yeah. Look at this." Switch pulled up his shirt. The hole left by the laser and the incision made by the doctor were nearly healed.

"I'm glad you're—"

"Well, I'm having a little trouble with it."

"You're alive. That's all that matters."

"I've got your blood—transhuman blood—inside me now. I'm changed. I don't know what to expect."

"I wish I could tell you."

"Listen, robot, you ain't doin' this again. Understood? If it's meant to be that somebody dies, then somebody dies. We got the blood of Christ to take us home. You're just gonna have to let us go."

Chase had wanted that for himself—to go home. "It wasn't your time."

"It wasn't your call."

The steady drip of melting snow thumped on a windowsill. For a minute, it was the only sound.

"Charlie?"

"Yeah?"

"Thanks."

"You forgive me?" Chase asked.

"Nothing to forgive, brother. I would've done the same thing. I mean, if I was a transhuman and you was the one dying."

"I know." Chase looked his friend in the eye. "You won't tell, will you? Melody can't know about this. If she finds out, you *will* have to save my life. You'll have to save me from *her*."

Switchblade snickered. "Not making any promises. Not sure I can hide it when I cut myself shaving and it heals in twenty minutes. But I won't say nothing."

"Speaking of shaving. You think we could clean up before we head out?" Chase pushed up on his elbows.

"They got clothes and supplies here. You feel like you can get out of that bed?"

"Yeah. I'm ready. Let's get this horrible long walk from Quebec over with."

"About that—we ain't walking."

Chase grunted as he pushed off the bed and rose to his feet. "What are you talking about?"

"June's taking us in the med transport. At least she'll get us within five miles. I told her you can screw with the onboard spybots. But she says five miles is close enough. Any closer and she might get robbed."

"Detroit sounds like a charming place. I'm going to get my wife and we're leaving."

Switchblade shook his head and laughed. "I don't think so. I think Detroit is going to be home for a while."

Chase smiled. "Yeah, I know. We could be there tomorrow."

"No way, man. We'll be there tonight."

14

The doctor returned from her mission to check on radio contact. Nothing to report. Communication in the underground was near nonexistent.

What was going on? Chase reached as far as the exoself could take him. Even WR communication was slow. Nothing appeared to be going on in Detroit. Not since the rally that never took place.

"Are you sure you want to take this risk?" Chase asked June as she stocked the little medical shed with new supplies from her transport.

"More than sure. It's time I did something daring for the Lord. Soon..."

Chase straightened the collar on the clean white shirt he'd been given. "What is it?"

"I don't know how long I can remain up top."

"You thinking about joining us?"

"Not yet. These people need me to keep going as long as I can."

"It's pretty amazing that you're able to use your resources—WR resources—to support the cause of believers."

"God makes it work."

Chase let the words sink into his spirit. "Yes, He does."

"I'll get the transport ready. Switchblade said you'll fool the onboard cameras into thinking the bay is empty. How do you do that?"

"I take a mental picture, then tell the system to run it in real time. So what's actually going on is not what the monitor sees."

She nodded. "And you're sure everything is in working order after your recent blood loss?"

"I've run a check of my systems. Nothing to worry about."

She opened the door to leave just as Jeff arrived. He walked in and leaned against the wall.

"I'm staying here. At least for now," he said. "They could use my help since they lost Gavin."

Chase nodded. "Gavin was clear to stay up top. Considering your record—"

"Not much difference between up top and underground here."

Chase nodded. "Right. It's like that in a lot of places. I'm sure you'll do fine." He put his hand on Jeff's shoulder. "I'm glad you're a brother now. Tell me, do you still consider yourself a dissenter?"

"You worried I'm going to cause trouble here? Or turn you in?" Jeff lowered his brow.

"Are you?"

"I'm here to help the believers. I'm one of them now. Like you."

Chase patted him on the back. "I'm sorry. Past experience makes me ask. God be with you."

"And with you." Jeff left the little building.

Chase stepped to the small mirror he'd used when he trimmed his beard. It'd been months since his last haircut. He almost didn't recognize himself. How had he come to this? Running from the government. A renegade. A believer. Married to the head of the Underground Church. It was all much stranger, more difficult to fathom than the fact he was the world's first transhuman. He lowered his gaze. "God help me. I belong to You now. Hold me together, because I don't know how much longer I can…" Words failed. But his spirit's commune with God kept on.

The opening door drew his glance. Switchblade entered the room. He'd cleaned up too. The close-shaved head gave him back his intimidating appearance. He said nothing. Did he know Chase was praying? His deep breathing was the only sound. Was he praying too? At last, he spoke.

"It's time," he said. "Let's go find our people."

A tear slid down Chase's cheek. His people. His sweet Melody. Soon he'd hold her. "I'm ready."

The goodbyes were solemn. Bloodhound and Hillary, along with a few believers Chase hadn't met during his brief stay in National City, gathered near the med transport. They were praying too—Chase knew. He instructed June to busy herself in the bay of the transport, and he recorded her. The exoself made it replay for the Feds. It'd last a few minutes, then the bay would appear empty. Then it would play again. It was doubtful anyone would even be watching this doctor, who, at least for the time, was considered an asset to the government. And not a threat.

After a couple of replays, Chase would change the view. Just in case. It'd take less than an hour to get to the drop-off point. All this time. All the distance. And now he'd be close to Detroit in less than an hour.

But of course, there was the five-mile walk through more snow. And apparently Detroit's skirting held a danger all its own. Dr. June talked about the people living there as though they were pirates. And she wasn't sailing her ship into their waters.

As he stood at the rear of the transport, Chase saw

no need to mention the dead. In circumstances past, guilt overwhelmed him when people were lost for the cause. But he couldn't hold up under that self-reproach. Their lives—all of them—were in God's hands. And four more believers had gone home.

He faced Hillary and Bloodhound. "Thank you for all you've done. God will remember your faithfulness."

Hillary hugged him. "Thank you for all you're *going* to do."

Chase pulled back and looked her in the eyes. "What am I going to do?"

She shook her head. "God knows."

He reached for Bloodhound's outstretched hand.

"Our prayers follow you," Bloodhound said.

Chase climbed into the transport. Switchblade was already seated on a detachable gurney. The doctor sat at the small workstation. Data streamed across a holographic display. Chase caught every bit of information without even looking at the readout.

Bloodhound pushed the door and it latched with a sound like a puff of air. June touched a green bar on the side of the workstation and the transport lurched forward. Within seconds they were moving at sixty-five miles per hour. When they reached the snowplowed highway, this thing would increase its speed.

Four gurneys lined the walls of the transport. Chase stretched out on the one across from Switchblade.

"You doing all right, robot?" Switchblade asked. "No side effects from your recent hibernation?"

"Is that what I was doing? Hibernating?"

"Seemed like it. How long could you live that way?"

"Ask the doctor."

Switchblade turned his head.

"With a feeding tube, I guess you'd live a long time," Dr. June said. "As if you were in a coma. Your vitals never altered."

"They never do." Chase closed his eyes. The slight vibration and quiet rumble relaxed him. But days of insomnia would follow his sixty-hour nap. Even on a normal day Chase had to force himself to sleep. Now sleep would run from him. "Normal day? When was the last time I had one of those?"

"Man, what are you saying? Quit talking," Switchblade said. "Let your poor injured bodyguard get some sleep."

"Sorry, buddy."

The restful period didn't last more than half an hour.

The doctor spoke. "WR is calling me back to—"

"Back to Bay City." Chase sat straight. "I'm trying to omit the request from the system, but somebody's on live. Who would be calling you back?"

"My partner. He doesn't message through the system. He's calling my VPad. I'll have to tell him something."

"I take it he's not a believer."

Dr. June shook her head.

"Tell him you're on your way." Chase reached over and jostled Switchblade. "Wake up. Looks like our walk will be a bit longer than five miles."

"I can't leave you on the side of the road," June said.

"We can take care of ourselves," Chase told her.

Switchblade stretched and dropped his feet to the floor of the transport, which still zoomed along at ninety miles per hour. "Absolutely." He yawned. "We got trouble?"

"June's being reined in." Chase pulled every bit of intel coming out of Bay City. "Reports of a fire. Apartment building."

"Then the doctor needs to go." Switchblade faced her. "We can't be too far from where you planned to leave us. What are we—ten miles out?"

"A little more. I shouldn't even be out this far. They'll wonder what took me so long to get back to the med center."

Chase came off the gurney. "Then let us out. The last thing we want is to cause a problem for you."

June touched the green bar and the transport slowed to a stop.

"I take it you messed with the tracker without my help," Chase said.

"I've been doing that for years," she answered. "But I wish you'd tell me how to fool the cameras like you did today."

"I can't explain it. I just do it." Chase touched her shoulder as the door at the rear of the transport slid open. "Thank you, June. God willing, you'll never see us again."

"Not this side of heaven," Switchblade said. "God be with you." He squeezed her outstretched hand before climbing out.

"And with you," June said.

Chase lowered his feet to the cold ground next to a desolate highway that went someplace nobody wanted to go. Except for the ousted. Some of whom were brothers and sisters. Some were dangerous criminals.

Ten miles. They were bound to run into the dangerous kind.

15

Switchblade pulled his jacket closed and headed off the road and into the woods. Chase followed him, but was there any reason to leave the highway? It couldn't be unusual to find people walking where vehicles didn't often travel. Surely most of the renegades entering Detroit did so on foot. Self-drives were too easy to track. Even the older trucks and buses used by supporters might draw attention.

He glanced over his shoulder and watched the med transport speed away. No one else in sight. Nothing but bare trees and the whistle of a distant train. Maybe it'd be best to make the ten-mile hike through the woods and not out in the open. He caught up with Switchblade and they headed south.

A mile, then two. No problems. And little conversation.

"Switch, you OK?" Chase marched with long strides to keep up.

"Yep. How much further?"

"A little less than seven miles."

"Don't know if we can make it by dark."

"My calculations put us in the city limits at half past eight. So no, we won't make it before the sun goes down. But it might be for the best. We won't know where we're going anyway. We'll just find a place to hide out until morning."

"You serious? You're not gonna look for Melody tonight?"

"I don't know where to look. I can't run through the streets, calling her name. It might take a while to find the underground."

"Won't take no time at all, robot. You just got to ask the right questions of the right people. You ain't got no street learning." Switchblade huffed and increased his stride. "I'll find our people."

"You've been throwing out that word—*robot*—for days now. I thought we had an agreement. You don't call me robot and I don't call you—"

Switchblade spun around and pushed Chase backward. "Shut up. Just shut up. Don't let me hear you use that name. Not around here."

"What's the matter with you?"

"Nothing. I'm just in a hurry to get underground. OK?"

"And you think I'm not?"

"I wonder sometimes. Maybe you don't want to face our people after what happened in Quebec. Maybe you think Melody don't trust you no more."

"I don't think any such thing, and that's not what's bothering you." Chase put his hands on his hips. "You told me you had some trouble in Detroit. Does the name Leslie Honeywell mean something here? Is that what has you worried?"

Switchblade continued down the overgrown path.

Chase ran after him. "You'd better tell me now, before we get there. Are people going to recognize you?"

"Just don't mutter that name again."

"Fine. But quit calling me robot."

"Fine. Now come on. Let's get on with this."

Two miles out. Lights shone in the distance. Above them all, a tower of light. "The Cosimo building," Chase said. "Why is that failed attempt at revitalizing this city lit up like a candle?"

"Don't know what good they thought a high-tech skyscraper would do." Switchblade pushed his way through some underbrush. "Only took two years for that waste of money to end up as empty as every other building."

"It is a sight though. I guess they left the solar panels operational." Chase followed close behind Switchblade. "I bet there's some organization using it under the radar."

"Yeah. An organization of crooks. And pimps. And drug dealers. This ain't Chicago, Charlie. And that building ain't nothing but the WR's own Tower of Babel."

"That's what Amos said about transhumanism." Chase stopped. "Listen."

Switchblade tripped on a root as he turned around. "What is it?"

"Music. Laughter. Two hundred yards ahead. Maybe we should find another trail."

"By music and laughter, you mean—"

"I mean they're stinking drunk."

"Then maybe they won't notice us. If they do, just play along. Might be something worse waiting if we change course now."

"Yeah. I guess so. Seems like you know more about this atmosphere than I do. I'll let you lead."

"Don't say nothing if they spot us. We're just cuttin' through. Got some business in town." Switchblade walked on. "Don't need no assistance. No directions. Don't want no refreshments. We're just trying to get to an appointment. That's all. You got all that, rob—Charlie?"

"Got it, L.H. Lead on."

Switchblade growled. "Just let me do the talking."

Lights shone through the woods. A campfire. Some laser lights. Didn't appear to be any structures. Chase and Switchblade moved closer. Soon they could see the group. Ten men, seven women. Not much sense of modesty and seemingly no call for privacy.

They passed within twenty feet of the little party. Maybe Switch was right. Maybe this group wouldn't even notice two travelers.

"Hey! Look what we got here!" A man's slurred outburst brought others off a pile of blankets, and they stumbled after Chase and Switchblade.

Switchblade jumped between the men and Chase. "Just passing through," he said. "You all don't need to stop what you're doing on our account. Got some business on Eight Mile Road. We'll just be on our way."

One of the men lurched forward and grabbed Switchblade's arm. "Oh, now, you don't need to go all the way to Eight Mile Road. We got what you're looking for right here." The man grinned. Two front teeth were missing. And the hand on Switch's arm was cut up and caked with dried blood.

"We ain't looking for nothing," Switchblade said as he yanked his arm free. "Just got to get to a meeting."

"Them's bad ones working off Eight Mile Road. What you got going on? You got any goods on you?" The man pulled the front of Switchblade's jacket open.

"Nobody ever told you to keep your hands to yourself?" Switchblade shoved the man off and fastened the jacket. "We ain't got nothing for you."

Chase came from behind Switchblade's shadow. "I have no silver or gold, but what I have I give you."

Switchblade slipped his hand around the back of Chase's neck and whispered, "Now is not the time." He attempted to direct Chase from the crowd.

"Silver and gold?" one of the men asked. "What're you talking about?"

Now the rest of the men, and the women too, had gathered around.

"Some new drug," a woman said. "Right? But you don't have any. So, what is it that you do have?" She moved closer. "I'd love for you to share it with me." She smiled and ran her fingers through Chase's hair.

He grasped her hand and eased it away. "I come in the name of Christ. He offers life."

Laughter rose in unison from the ragged crew. The woman seemed to suffer an immediate loss of interest. She went back to the fire and pulled on a blanket.

"You some kind of preacher?" one of the men asked. "Don't know what kind of meeting you got, but you go to Eight Mile after dark, you gonna end up dead. Where you want to be is over by the old cemetery. Mount Olivet." The man folded his arms and twitched his nose. "But better wait for daylight. We won't bother you or nothing."

The rest of the group shrugged and grumbled. They all returned to the fire and the blankets. But the party ended. Half the group pulled covers over themselves and seemed to pass out. But the rest sat by the light of the fire and lifted their collective gaze to Chase, who remained twenty feet away with Switchblade at his side.

Switchblade shifted on his feet. "Morning *would* be

safer. And I guess you got something to say to these people."

"Yeah. We'll leave before dawn."

"All right, we're staying," Switchblade said to the crowd. "But don't try nothing or you'll find out real quick this ain't no regular preacher man. Now listen up. He's got something to tell you."

16

The eastern sky began its swift revolution from black to pink. Chase had not slept, though the outcasts who'd listened for hours were now restfully tucked into their soiled blankets. Switchblade slept too. But it was time to wake him. To get to the city and begin the search.

For days...weeks...Chase had wavered between wanting to rush in and find Mel as quickly as transhumanly possible and trusting God's timing that sometimes seemed to hold him back. And Switchblade—at times pushing Chase forward and other times letting his apprehension show. Something about Detroit scared the big guy.

None of five new believers had volunteered to accompany Chase and Switch into town. They all seemed sincere but unwilling to join the underground. Maybe in the future. But not now. They'd stay put.

The converts, and even the ones who didn't feel the call, gave Chase good advice. Told him what to look out for. He shouldn't make it too obvious he was hunting believers. He should stay clear of the buildings around the old people-mover stations. Nothing too high tech in town except the Cosimo building, but DNA scanners at the stations could pick out a wanted man in a hurry.

Chase let out a quiet laugh. He'd take care of that.

He didn't tell these people who he was. He was just Charlie. A believer looking for some old friends who'd settled in Detroit. The group didn't seemed surprised that Christians would congregate in a city filled with derelicts and crime bosses. All kinds came here. Anybody who wanted to be where the WR didn't waste too much time reeling in the unlawful element.

Unless somebody provoked the general public. Or got too verbal. Or planned an event. As long as they kept quiet, the Feds left them alone. Some of the local authorities—and there weren't many—even took payoffs. Chase got a few names from the outcasts, and the exoself ran a check. This former ghost town had become a bustling city. A neutral safe zone. But why? How did all these people end up in Detroit? The exoself seemed to struggle to latch onto...something.

The sun would soon peek over the treetops. Chase reached beside him and jostled Switchblade.

He rolled over and blinked his dark eyes. "I'm coming. We got anybody joining us?"

"Not today. They'll stay with their group. Hopefully..."

"Hopefully, they'll shine a light and not get killed."

Chase lowered his head and prayed silently. He opened his eyes and found Switchblade pulling on his boots.

"Are you familiar with the cemetery?" Chase asked.

"I can get us there. But you got a map in your head."

"I mean the neighborhood. You know of any gathering places?"

"Besides the one for dead people? Not really. We'll

just go take a look around. You gonna wake up these bandits and say goodbye?"

Chase stood and pulled his jacket shut. "No. Hey, Switch, do you think a person can truly understand what happened if he comes to Christ while he's inebriated?"

"God knows, Charlie. Only God knows."

"Yeah. Let's get going."

Low clouds hung over the city and distorted the sunrise. "I can't even see that monstrous skyscraper this morning," Chase said.

"It's there. Stupid building named after a stupid president." Switchblade continued with his fast-paced stride.

"We're getting close now. I put out a new report that I've been spotted in the southeast territory. And I made a dead man's DNA mine."

"What? How'd you do that? Won't they know he's dead?"

"No. He died a week ago," Chase said. "Here in the outskirts. There's no report."

"OK, start talking. What'd those people tell you after I went to sleep last night?"

"The guy used to repair cyber-guards. He came with a load of food and clothes, and they killed him. There's no report of his death. Not even any data that he's missing."

Switchblade shook his head. "And now you got the scanners picking up his DNA when it's really you they're scanning."

"Exactly. They're sorry now that they killed the guy. There was a lot of confessing last night. Like I'm a priest or something."

"I'm sorry I missed all that."

Chase watched the clearing sky. A patch of blue appeared, but the city remained under thick, moist cover. "I didn't worry about your DNA, because there is no record of you. When are you going to tell me about that? Why don't you exist?"

"I guess it's time you knew." Switchblade slowed his steps. "Witness protection. WR took me out of the system after I turned in some of my buddies. So far out that even *they* couldn't track me. That way, they'd have no report to file when I ended up dead. They call it being a—"

"A free prisoner," Chase said.

"That's right. Freedom is the reward for talking. But the WR don't plan on a free prisoner surviving."

"And then you got saved?"

"Happened before then. I got caught by a rival gang. They was ready to kill me. But there was a believer called Turk. He witnessed to the gangs. And he negotiated my release and told me the truth. Then he took me straight to the Feds. Said it was God's will. And he was right. I squealed and got wiped out of the system."

"Switch, tell me the truth. Did all that go down in Detroit?"

"Afraid so."

Chase stopped.

"Come on now. We made it this far. I won't mess nothing up for you. Been a while and I'm thinking nobody here will remember me."

"What about Turk?" Chase caught up with his friend—his brother.

"Dead. Rival gang got him after I talked."

"And then you joined the underground."

"That's right. WR had me dropped off in NYC. I

went north. A year or so later, Molly found me in Herouxville, and I offered to help set up the base."

Blue Sky Field. Chase wiped a single tear from his cheek. Molly and the others who died there would not be forgotten.

"Now don't start worrying. God got us this far." Switchblade led the way past the edge of the woods and right onto a street on the north side of Detroit.

Not a soul in sight. Old, broken houses and a ton of litter lined the unrepaired road.

"I guess nobody enforces the use-less-paper law here," Chase said.

"Too busy rounding up the axe-murderers."

"That's comforting."

The sky cleared, and the buildings of downtown marked the way to the huge old cemetery. A left turn up ahead. A few homeless men stretched out in an overgrown park. The smell of liquor rose like the morning mist.

Chase rounded a corner. "Must be good income in supplying booze to Detroit."

"Yep. The WR has its outlets. And so do the crooks."

"You worked as a guard at SynVue before you ended up in Detroit. Must have been a glitch that left one job assignment listed."

"I was there two years. Left about the time you arrived. Got replaced by a cyber-guard. Didn't like my new assignment, so I took up with some dealers and headed for Detroit."

"What was your assignment?"

Switchblade drew a breath.

"What?"

"Crowd control for a new show. Biggest show

ever."

Chase stopped. "You would have been working at the *Change Your Life* studio? Why didn't you tell me?"

"Tell you I hated the whole idea for your stupid show? I don't know. Thought it might cause some bad blood between us."

"I've got no good feelings left about my old life. It's nothing. Forget it. But I'm sorry I didn't know you then. Maybe I could have kept you out of trouble."

"Changed my life? I doubt it. I was already into some bad stuff in Chicago. But things worked out. We both got our lives changed."

As the sun rose higher, children wrapped in jackets and scarves gathered on street corners. This town of ill repute still had families. WR schools still sent transports to pick up the kids for a day of learning. Or brainwashing. A mother stood in front of her shanty and waved goodbye to her daughter. Neither of them smiled.

Two old cyber-guards held position at the next corner. The robots were painted up like women from a brothel. They'd obviously not left their post in a long time.

Chase poked one of them in the chest and it toppled backward and broke in two.

"I see why the poor guy who used to maintain the guards went out of business."

"People here don't tolerate cyber-guards." Switchblade snickered. "I took out a few myself. The police don't do nothing about it. They know the same thing might happen to them."

"Only four Federal agents left here. I can't get a number on the population. Not even a count on legitimate citizens."

"That's because even the ones who managed to stay on the WR payroll are not what you'd call legitimate. I'm telling you, this ain't like no place you've been. But I can't believe all these people live here. Didn't used to be like this."

Self-drives were outnumbered by hydro-buses and old-fashioned electric transports. A gas-powered truck passed by. A rarity. Gasoline was a black-market product sometimes used by the—

"Did you hear the engine roaring in that old truck?" Chase changed course and followed the truck.

"You thinking it might be in service for the underground?" Switchblade asked as he came up behind Chase.

"I got the ID. It's fake. It's a rogue vehicle."

"Man, don't get your wires in a wad. Lots of rogue transports in Detroit. And the cemetery is the other way." Switchblade grabbed Chase's arm and pulled him back. "Don't go chasing every clue. We need to keep moving in the right direction. Maybe that truck is headed *out* from where we want to be."

Chase swiveled around. "You're right. Lead the way."

Ten more blocks, and the three-hundred-acre cemetery spread out before them. The old iron fencing remained intact. Gravestones dating as far back as the 1880s seemed well kept. Even the winter's fierce assault had done little to disturb the tranquility.

Switchblade dropped to a wooden bench along the eastern edge. "Believers tend the grounds. Nobody tells them to. And nobody tries to stop them. This is the one place in the city where people show a little respect."

"I can tell." Chase sat beside him. "I can feel it.

We'll find somebody around here. Or they'll find us."

"Only one problem."

"You're starving?"

Switchblade laughed and nodded.

"Me too. Any idea where we can get breakfast?"

"Used to be a shelter on Division Street. Ain't too far."

A booming voice came from behind. "The shelter's for locals. And you two aren't locals. Are you?"

Chase eased around to find a hefty black man in uniform. A nightstick like the one Alpha Wolf carried dangled at his side.

17

"New in town?" The man smiled. His DPD uniform and jacket were probably twenty years old. No gun—laser or otherwise. Matted hair poked out from under a regulation hat with two holes in the front.

"Been gone for a while," Switchblade said. "My partner and I got some business to take care of. You know—import and export." He wheezed out a laugh. "We'll be collecting on a transaction later today, and then we'll head out...sir. But right now, we could use a bite to eat. So, is the shelter still open?"

The man narrowed his eyes. "Do I know you?"

"Oh, no, sir. Don't believe we've met. How long you been a cop here?"

"Forty years. Of course, my unit shut down a decade ago. But some of us still walk our beat."

Chase nearly laughed. "We wouldn't want to cause any trouble on your...beat. We'll just go on over to the shelter and see if they can spare a meal for two travelers. OK?"

The officer sniffed and nodded. "See that you're out of the city by nightfall. I watch out for folks. Don't want any trouble here."

Chase nodded once. "No trouble from us."

They headed away from the old police officer, who no longer held any real power. Chase followed

Switchblade a block south and two blocks west. The shelter was open and active. Sad-looking people in ragged clothes passed in and out of the double doors of the old storefront.

Warm sausage and scrambled eggs went down too quickly—the best meal Chase had eaten in months. Even though no one looked him in the eyes, the fearful atmosphere of the outside streets succumbed to sweet peace inside the shelter. The same peace Chase found at the cemetery. Believers must run this place.

He listened to the conversation beyond the dining area. No clues. Unfamiliar voices. No mention of anything but supply lists and a shortage of beds.

Switchblade gulped the last of his coffee. "You think we should start asking questions?"

"Definitely." Chase took his plate to the pile at the end of the long table. Then he went back to the serving line.

A tall man with a long beard eyed him. "You got yours already. Sorry, pal. Only one helping."

"I'm looking for some information," Chase said.

"That is something we don't hand out here, mister. You'd better go. And don't come back unless you ready to follow the rules. The only reason you open your mouth is to put food in it. You don't ask. And we don't tell."

"Look, I need to find some people. Believers. New in town."

The guy came around the table. "Out. Right now. If you're a Fed, you might as well go back where you came from. People in the neighborhood will sniff you out and take you down."

"I'm not a Fed."

Switchblade grabbed Chase by the arm and

dragged him to the door. "Can't rush this. These folks got good reason not to trust us."

They hurried out of the building and crossed the street.

"I can't believe that," Chase said.

"I told you they got reason to be wary of strangers."

Chase huffed and dropped to the curb. "At least we got some food." He looked up and smiled. "Best breakfast I've had since I went rogue. This place isn't all bad."

"Hah. Don't speak too soon."

Chase held the smile as he scanned the neighborhood. Dozens of people passed by. Some rushing down the middle of the street. Didn't seem to be any vehicles in this area.

He rose off the curb and they headed back toward the cemetery. A girl came toward them, carrying a large box that almost covered her face. But her stride seemed familiar. And her gentle eyes that peeked over the top of the box.

"It's Finley." Chase ran ahead.

Switchblade followed him. "*Our* Finley? Where? You sure?"

Chase caught her by the arm. She gasped as she dropped the box. He picked her up and swung her in circles. "I can't believe it." He squeezed her—probably harder than he should have—and she laughed and cried at the same time.

"Put me down. Chase, you're hurting me!" She laughed again.

He dropped her to the ground, but Switchblade picked her up and swung her around.

"Enough," she said as her laughter continued.

Switchblade set her down easy and kissed the top of her head. "Little girl, you're a sight to behold."

"Oh, you don't know how glad I am to see you two." She wiped the tears from her cheeks.

Chase grabbed the sides of her face and ran his fingers into her long brown hair. "Finley, sweetheart. Mel—where is she? Take me to her."

18

Either from fear or excitement, Finley cried again. Poor girl was only eighteen. She'd lost her parents— thanks to Kirel. Chase eased his grip and let his hands fall to her shoulders. "I'm sorry. I just—"

"No, I understand. You came all this way to find her. But she isn't here."

"That's not...What do you mean she isn't here?" He stepped back. "What are you talking about?" he asked too harshly. "Where else would she be?"

Switchblade eased his arm around Finley. "It's all right. Just tell us what you know."

"She got a lead on some computers. She said we had to have equipment ready when you got here. So she could reconnect the underground and all that stuff." Finley shook her head. "But she's been gone too long. We expected her back in a few hours, but then there was this rally. Well, it never actually happened, but communication shut down. And now it's been days and we don't know what happened to Melody. Or her two brothers—they went with her."

Chase crossed his arms and marched to the curb. He dropped down, rested his elbows on his knees, and covered his face with his hands. How could this be happening? After getting caught by dissenters. The blizzard. The loss of life. How could she not be here?

After a moment Finley's small hand grasped his

shoulder. "Now that you're here, I know Melody will be all right. Don't be mad."

Chase breathed in, stood, and drew his arms around her. "I'm not mad, sweetheart. I'm so glad to see you. Tell me everything. Exactly where did she go?"

"Ann Arbor. She found a guy who deals in merchandise retired from WR service. It's supposed to be clean and untraceable."

"And expensive. Where'd she get the money?"

"Lots of bartering going on. Like always. I'm not sure how she worked it out."

"At least she didn't go far," Switchblade said. "Finley, how many of our people are here?"

"Well, we got here with forty-four from our old base. We picked up a few more on the way. And there are about...I'd say six hundred in the underground. Plus lots of supporters living on their own in town." She shrugged. "Doesn't really matter. We all come and go as we please."

Chase glanced at Switchblade. "Six hundred all in one underground base? How on earth do you manage?"

She rolled her eyes. "It hasn't been easy. Some of them don't think Melody should be the head of the underground, even though that's what Amos wanted. And we—the believers from Blue Sky Field—have tried and tried to get the guy who was in charge before we got here to go look for her. But he acts like if it's God's will for her to be the leader, then He'll bring her back."

"And if it's not?" Chase asked.

"Then *he'll* be in charge." Finley wiped her face again. "Chase, most of the people here decided you weren't going to show. They gave up on you weeks ago. So they thought it was crazy for Melody to go after the computers. They're happy with the radios."

"Well, I'm here now. And I'm going after Mel. And we're going to get things back in order. OK?"

She smiled and nodded. "I believe you. I never stopped believing you'd find us."

Switchblade reached for her hand. "All right, young lady. Take us to this underground base packed tight with believers. You got every basement in town connected by tunnels?"

"Oh, no, Switchblade." Her wide-eyed gaze met the horizon as she pointed upward. "There's our base. Straight ahead."

Chase followed the direction of her finger. He laughed. Then drew his brows tight. "The Cosimo building?"

Switchblade rested his hands on his hips. "Great."

"Yep. That's our base," Finley said. "From the tenth floor to the twenty-third."

"How in the world did you end up *there*?" Chase crossed his arms and stared at the monster. A cloud still circled its top. "You're hiding in fourteen floors of the tallest skyscraper in the WR? What goes on in the rest of it?"

She giggled softly. "You'll have to see it to believe it."

19

Chase shook his head. "To tell you the truth, Finley, the only thing I want to see right now is the road to Ann Arbor. But I guess I'd better get as much information as I can before I head out."

"Before *we* head out," Switchblade said.

Chase eased forward. "Right. Of course."

Finley spun around and faced the street behind her. "My box—I have to get it to the shelter."

Switchblade stepped around her. "I'll take the box and catch up with you."

Chase didn't move his eyes off the building. "Hurry."

Switchblade grabbed the box and ran toward the shelter. Chase pulled on Finley's arm. "So Mel found her family."

Finley nodded. "Her brothers and her mom. They were already living in the Cos—that's what we call it." Her eyes widened. "Do you remember Erin? I share a room with her."

"Of course. And Leo? He's with you. Right?"

She nodded.

"I didn't get to know too many of the believers at Blue Sky Field. There just wasn't enough time."

"What happened to the rest of our people?" As they passed the cemetery, she shifted her sight to the graves. "We never saw the older ones again after we got split up. I ended up on a truck with everybody sixteen to forty who didn't have families. All the little kids went with their parents on two buses." She slowed her pace and a tear slid down her cheek. "Chase, what do you think happened to them?"

"The elderly believers are in a good place." Chase tried to smile.

"You mean heaven?"

He touched her cheek. "You ended up on the truck I sent using Mel's code. It was the last thing I did before she shut down communications. It could've been any of the groups that ended up in the truck. If I'd had more time, maybe I'd have sent another transport."

"Melody said she had to cut you off. And then she cried. For like a week. But without you getting us out the way you did, we wouldn't have made it. You know what happened to the people on the buses. Don't you?"

Chase shook his head. "They were headed for the center north of the base. But that...is all I know."

"Things are much better in Detroit. No detention centers. No Feds. We can live our lives here. Once we've got communication again, we can just tell everybody to join us." She seemed to study Chase. "Right?"

"I don't know. Something doesn't seem right about the way they just let you exist."

"Well, I think it's a blessing from God," Finley said. "He gave us this place to wait for Him."

"For the Lord Himself will descend from heaven."

"Exactly."

"Right down on Detroit." Chase laughed.

Switchblade caught up. "What's so funny?"

"The Lord has chosen Detroit for His re-entry," Chase said.

Finley struggled to keep up as Chase and Switchblade hurried toward the Cosimo. "You're making fun of me. I didn't say He was coming *here*."

"Eschatology can wait." Chase was jogging now. "I want to be in Ann Arbor before nightfall."

"Yeah, no time for whatever *ology* you two are talking about." Switchblade grabbed Finley by the hand.

The closer they got to the skyscraper, the more ominous it appeared. Two city blocks wide at the base. One hundred twenty-four stories into the sky. Thirty more below. The underground support structure housed safe rooms. Tunnels. And the believers had settled in the upper floors. Did they even know about the underside of the Cosimo?

The bronze skin of the building gleamed. Thousands of windows reflected sunlight. They stopped in front of the structure. Massive glass doors trimmed in brass welcomed them. Electric beams ran through the glass in shades of blue and green. The pattern varied, and at times came together to form letters.

THE COSIMO. A BRIGHT NEW BEGINNING. THE GIFT OF THE FUTURE FOR THE GOOD PEOPLE OF DETROIT.

And yet the place, according to WR data, was abandoned to deterioration. How could they not know it was being used for purposes contrary to the government's agenda? What else waited beyond the miraculous doors?

Finley swung the door open and walked through. Chase and Switchblade followed. The lobby—bigger than the whole underground base in Quebec—sparkled with more digital displays. Why didn't somebody just flip the switch and shut off all this propaganda? Clusters of sofas and chairs, desks and workstations dotted the expanse. But there was not the expected blend of computers and kiosks. According to the exoself, the criminal element cleaned out the technology years ago. That's when the WR virtually moved out and cut off funding for most of Detroit's programs. Mel might have gone to bring back computers stolen from right here.

People came and went. Chase scanned the lobby for cameras and spybots. They'd all been disabled. The funny old police officer he'd met earlier leaned against a wall and picked his nose. Seemed the Cosimo was on his beat.

"Finley, I need to talk to the man you told us about—the one who thinks he's in charge." Chase hurried to the nearest lift in a long row.

Finley waved her hand in front of a hyper lift and the door disappeared. She stepped in. Chase and Switchblade joined her. "That would be Colt. He didn't care what anybody said when Melody got here, even though she's our leader. But they kind of came to an understanding. He takes care of local issues. She connects the world. Well, she *will* connect it. Now that you're here."

The door rematerialized. "Twenty," Finley said. The hyper lift shot up to the twentieth floor in seconds. But the motion was practically undetectable. The elevators in Chicago were antiquated compared to this. Even the lift in NYC that Chase had taken to the top of the skyscraper didn't compare. The technology used in this prototype building never made it into production.

Maybe the WR wasn't as financially sound as their data indicated.

"Very cool," Switchblade said. "But I feel like my brain is still on the first floor."

"You get used to it," Finley told him.

The door that seemed to form out of nothing but light disappeared again, and Finley stepped out onto a burgundy tile floor. A man approached her. Young. Dark hair to his shoulders. Green eyes. Skin as pale as the snow.

Finley stepped forward. "Colt, this is—"

"Well, well. The transhuman. Never thought you'd get this far." The man folded his arms. "And your trusty sidekick—the infamous Switchblade." His glaring eyes quickly softened. He pasted on a smile and extended his hand to Chase.

Chase accepted the handshake and held it to the point of causing this supposed leader a bit of pain. But the guy didn't flinch. Chase let him go before scanning his iris. Colton Peters. Thirty-one. Kid of a preacher who went rogue sixteen years ago. Did that make Colt a charter member of the underground? Chase didn't care.

"I'm going after my wife. If you have any information, tell me now. If you don't, get me a truck and I'll be on my way."

"I was about to send out a rescue party. We were just talking about it." Sincerity oozed from the man's lips.

"*We* can handle it. Just get me a truck."

Colt motioned to the door at his left. "First, come with me. I'm sure there are some old friends you'd like to see."

Chase grabbed his arm. "What have you done

about bringing Mel back?"

"Our communication system is just now up and running after a few days of being shut down. We're trying to contact her."

"Get. Me. A truck."

The man nodded slowly. "Of course. Follow me."

Switchblade sidestepped to the door and pushed it open, as if to take charge over this pasty little man. Beyond the door, a long table waited, covered with antiquated radio equipment. A dozen people circled the table. Some were relaying messages—some simply adjusting dials. Chase looked behind him. Finley had taken off. Probably to spread the word about his arrival.

Chase didn't know any of the people at the radios. But they seemed to know *him*. Some jumped out of their seats to greet him. At the far end of the table stood a woman. Arms pulled tight around her chest. Her eyes filled with worry.

Her eyes. Soft. Dark. Familiar. Chase went to her.

"So you decided to show up." Tears welled in her eyes. "Now maybe something will be done about bringing my children home."

Chase nodded. "You're—"

"I'm your mother-in-law." She relaxed her arms and placed her hand on Chase's shoulder. "I am Sameea."

Lighter than Mel's coffee-and-cream skin tone, she spoke with a hint of an accent. But her eyes were Mel's eyes. And the gentle tilt of her head. And the smile that now lightened the worried lines of her face. Chase pulled her into a hug.

"I'm so happy to meet you, Sameea." He stepped back and grasped both her hands. "And yes, I will go after Melody. And your sons. I just need to gather some information and secure a transport, and I'm out of here."

She snapped her fingers at Colt. "Find my son-in-law a truck. No more waiting."

The man displayed that plastic smile again. "Of course, dear. I made contact with a transport while you and your new family member were making small talk."

Sameea's nostrils flared and one eyebrow went up. Chase nearly laughed. The expression was classic Mel. Switchblade must have noticed too, because when Chase glanced at him, his head was bent and his shoulders shook with quiet laughter.

He extended his hand, and she reached for it. "Switchblade," he told her. "I'm a good friend of your daughter's."

"I know who you are," she said. "You will go and be of assistance to my son-in-law."

Switchblade nodded. "That's what I do. We're an unstoppable pair."

The double doors to the right burst open and a stomping herd filled the room. Little Erin reached Chase first and flung herself into his arms.

"I knew you would come," she cried. "Did you bring me any chocolate?"

Chase laughed. "Not this time."

"It doesn't matter." She let him go and looked him in the eyes. "Just go find Miss Melody. Right now."

Leo grabbed Chase's shoulder, and Chase embraced him. And then a few others from Blue Sky Field. Two dozen more simply stood together, smiling.

"We're so glad you're here," Leo said. "We were about to give up hope."

"Don't ever give up, my friend." Chase met the eyes of every survivor from Quebec. Then he faced Leo. "Tell me what you know about Mel's excursion. In fact, come with us. Let's go get her."

20

A truck arrived in less time than it took Sameea to pack a few sandwiches. Leo knew where Mel and her brothers had gone in another rogue, gas-powered truck. He'd share details once he, Chase, and Switchblade were on the road.

Switchblade disappeared for a few minutes. Probably visiting the high-tech, lavish facilities. Chase had stopped by there himself. But when Switch returned to the radio center, he pulled Chase aside and lifted the edge of his jacket to reveal a pistol. Not a laser gun—an old handgun.

"Where'd you get that thing?" Chase asked.

"Your mama-in-law gave it to me. Along with a box of bullets."

Chase shook his head. "My in-laws are outlaws."

"Well, that much we knew. And the new headquarters is part of the wild, wild West. Sheriff in town seems to sit a bit high on his horse. Don't you think?"

"You mean Colt? There's something familiar about that guy. And I've got questions about the way he's operating. But it'll have to wait."

"They say the truck is in the parking garage under the building."

"Yeah, it's waiting on us." Chase circled the table, where several people still worked to contact other branches. And Mel.

"Any luck?" he asked.

An older woman answered. "Contacting our brothers and sisters in the area—yes. But not a word from Melody. Her two-way is turned off. Or broken." She met Chase's eyes. "I'm glad you're here. We're all worried about her."

Chase rested his hand on the woman's shoulder. "We'll find her."

He joined Switchblade and Leo. A tall, bony man with dirt under his fingernails accompanied them on the hyper lift. In seconds they were two stories under the massive building.

The door vanished and Chase stepped out to find a dark, damp garage. Nothing high-tech. The old truck he'd seen earlier waited twenty feet away. Chase hurried to open the driver's door. The key was in the ignition.

At the rear of the truck, Switch rolled up the door on the bay. "Got two cans of gas. That ought to get us there and back."

"Who left the truck here?" Chase asked. "Who runs supplies?"

"Believers are spread out," Leo said. "The truck belongs to a co-op. The driver will come back for it when we call him. It was one of his trucks Melody took to Ann Arbor. Hopefully, we'll come back with both trucks. And a load of computers."

Leo hopped into the driver's seat. Switchblade waited for Chase to climb in the middle before pulling himself in and shutting the door. Leo fired the engine and pulled onto a ramp that came out at street level. A few other older vehicles and a couple of modern transports passed them.

"Who else occupies the Cosimo?" Chase asked.

"Salesmen," Leo said.

"What do they sell?" Switchblade asked.

"Food. Well, they give away more than they sell. They grow it right in the building. It's pretty amazing. We've promised the other residents some equipment."

"You mean computers?" Chase asked.

"Right. They'll let us have a whole floor to garden on our own if we can set them up."

"A floor of a skyscraper to garden? I don't get it, Leo. The way this town operates," Chase said. "The way that *building* operates. Mel led me to believe Detroit was a ghost town. But..."

"The town runs on willpower. It's a rough place—especially at night. But there are a lot of good people who've made Detroit function virtually free of WR control. As for the Cos—it's the foundation. A government masterpiece taken over by the common people. Half the building is filled with hydroponic gardens. They even grow fish and chickens." Leo laughed. "The higher up you go, the worse it smells. But they do a good job keeping it clean."

"How did the Underground Church end up in a place like that?" Switchblade asked. "And why is it so high-tech but there aren't any computers?"

"It's self-operational. All that stuff you saw when you came—the lifts, the power and water supply—are all internal to the structure. But everything that could be stolen disappeared years ago. And nobody's brought in more equipment for fear of being monitored."

"But the WR doesn't seem to care what goes on here," Chase said. "Why worry?"

Leo pulled onto the highway and headed west

toward Ann Arbor. "They think the people here are backward. Too inept to become a threat. People are wary of computers and high-tech communication because that would show progress. And progress would bring the WR back to town in numbers. But now things are changing."

"What's different now?" Chase asked.

"Seriously, robot?" Switchblade shook his head. "Do you really need to ask that question?"

Chase breathed in. "I'm what's different. The salesmen, the…farmers. They think I'll set them up to go high-tech with no fear of being monitored."

"That's the general idea," Leo said.

"I'm here for the church. Mel and I will set up communication again. But I'm not hooking up every resident of the *Cos*, as you call it, with a worry-free connection to the world." Chase rubbed his hands together. "Who suggested I would?"

"Melody shared the plan with the believers, and Colt shared the plan with everybody else."

"Big surprise," Switchblade said. "Why am I feeling uneasy about that guy? Is he the one who sent Melody off to pick up the hardware? And what about these brothers of hers? They in thick with that scrawny dude?"

"Ridge and Brax were with the group that brought the underground into the Cos. So yeah, I guess they're tight with Colt. But he sure hasn't been in any hurry to look for them." Leo exited the highway and headed down a four-lane road through an old suburban area. "As far as your other question, it was Melody's idea to go. She wanted to be the one to check out the goods."

"Why are we getting off here?" Switchblade asked.

"The highway is patrolled. Farther you get from

Detroit, the greater the WR presence. No sense asking for trouble. This is the path Melody took."

Even as Leo spoke, the exoself surged with information. Cameras on the highway beyond the exit recorded every passing vehicle. Nearby, a WR transport waited in ready mode. The Feds who operated it couldn't be far away.

"I take it Ann Arbor is monitored," Chase said.

"Not like the big cities, but yeah, it's got a WR presence. Like most towns."

"Most—I thought it was all." Chase searched the exoself for other towns where incoming data fell off to nothing. To his surprise, there were a few out there. "How could I not know there were places where the WR had so little to do with…"

"With people?" Switchblade asked. "It's like some kind of free-range human experiment."

"Exactly," Chase said. "But experiments are conducted within a time frame. And then the data is analyzed."

Leo drove on until they spotted a sign for Ann Arbor. He listened to the two-way in the truck and even put out a call for Mel and her brothers. No word.

A warm afternoon had developed. Dirty snow piled along the streets would melt away after another day or two like this.

"Where do we go now?" Chase asked.

"Warehouse district. We're looking for a man they call the Negotiator."

Switchblade rammed his head into the low ceiling of the cab.

"What's wrong with you?" Chase inched over on the seat to give him a little more room.

"Uh…It's nothing."

"I hear he's a real tough sort," Leo said. "Even the crooks in Detroit wouldn't tolerate him. They kicked him out a couple of years back."

Chase raised his brows and studied Switchblade. "You know him. Don't you?" He couldn't stop the irritation from changing his voice. "What's he going to do when he sees you?"

"I'll tell you, Charlie. Blow my brains out. That's exactly what he's gonna do."

21

"You're not making me feel any better about my wife being mixed up in this mess." Chase ran a check on this Detroit criminal's alias. Nothing.

"Wait," Leo said. "You know him, Switchblade? What'd you do to the guy?"

"Broke up his operation. Sent his brother and most of his entourage to Federal prison. Briggs got away. But I guess he lost respect in D-town."

"Briggs—that's his name?" Chase ran another check. This time, he found plenty. Including intel on the shakedown caused by Switchblade. Only it didn't name him, of course. Or even give any indication that an insider had turned on the operation. Seemed odd that the good man Chase knew—as tough as he was— had been involved in illegal drugs, stealing and stripping WR transports, identity changing. Even eliminating some Feds in Detroit. And they let him go? "God sees the heart of a man."

"Well, all right." Switchblade shook his head. "You got anything useful?"

"I've got your back. You know that. Right?"

They pulled to a stop in a tight space between two metal buildings in a rundown warehouse district. A few transports were parked in front of the newest buildings. No indication of WR activity in the area.

Leo eased down in the seat. "I can't see getting out

and asking questions in the middle of the day. Not that there's anybody around to ask."

"How do you know this is the place?" Chase asked.

"Melody sent me her coordinates when she arrived. I was in touch with her the first couple of hours. She had the deal worked out. Had the computers loaded. That's what we need to be looking for—a truck like this one."

Chase reached over and flung the door open. He climbed over Switchblade and dropped to the pavement.

Switchblade practically fell out on top of him. "You just gonna start bustin' locks?"

"You bet I am." He headed left.

Leo stepped out of the driver's side and came after him. "Maybe we should wait. It'll be dark soon."

"I can't just sit here," Chase said.

The three headed to the front of the building to their right. Chase grabbed the lock and broke it. He pushed up the rolling door. Nothing inside but a few dusty crates and filing cabinets.

He marched to the building on the other side of the narrow walkway. This one wasn't even locked and contained nothing.

Switchblade peered around the corner of the building. "Too bad you can't see through walls, Charlie."

"Maybe I can. I'll give it a try."

"I thought you needed Melody's code to hack a satellite."

"Mel never understood how I could use her code for that. Said she didn't program me for it. So maybe there's another data trail I can take." He searched the exoself. It'd all come easily with the code from the Psalms. But not at first. He'd tried worming in over the past few weeks with no success. But with the recent changes, maybe he could do it.

Leo leaned against the metal building and rubbed his hands together. "Mind if I get back in the truck while you work on...whatever it is you're doing?"

Chase nodded. Switchblade went a little farther toward the next row of warehouses. The exoself latched onto a trail from a university in San Francisco. And Chase found the wormhole.

Probably some genius undergrad holed up in a cyber lab, trying to see how far he could go hacking a WR feed. And he chose the place least likely to get him trouble. If the WR didn't care what went on around Detroit, they probably wouldn't notice somebody skimming a view off their satellites.

Chase latched on and soon he was receiving images from in and around the city. Now to pinpoint his own location. He manipulated the feed and zeroed in on the warehouses. The kid—or whoever started this—was hopefully following some other trail and not paying attention to the fact that the hacker just got hacked. Chase zeroed in on his own image. If the Feds happened to be monitoring, they could see this too, but facial recognition wasn't likely from this kind of sat-feed. Chase looked down anyway.

He searched images of the whole complex and tried to find a way to dissolve the walls. But the satellite programmed for nothing but basic surveillance didn't cooperate.

Before he let go of the feed, he spotted it. Three rows to his right, behind the center building. A truck like the one they'd used to get here. And Switchblade was running away from it. Chase broke off his link to the hacker.

Switchblade appeared from around the corner. "I think I got it."

"There's a truck," Chase told him. "Looks like a match."

"Yeah. Thanks, robot. While you're hacking satellites, I'm hoofing it."

"Come on. Let's find out what's in that truck." Chase motioned to Leo, and they headed for the truck three rows down.

"This is it," Leo said.

Chase twisted the lock open and shoved the door up. Boxes lined the bay. Chase pulled himself in and ripped open the first box. A stack of old laptops. He searched the rest of the truck. Boxes of computers. Even an outdated holographic display.

No indication Mel had been in here.

He jumped out and ran to the truck's cab. Not even locked, and nothing inside.

He broke the lock on the nearest roll-up door. Switchblade and Leo followed him inside. No motion detectors. Security cameras in all corners, which Chase quickly shut down. More computers. A few flight packs.

Chase wandered deeper into the warehouse. Boxes of vials. "If this stuff belongs to your old friend Briggs, he's heavy into drug dealing."

"We was never what you'd call friends," Switchblade answered.

Leo called out from the other side of the warehouse. "What would a guy like that be doing with model airplanes?"

"Planes? This must be the place," Switchblade

said. "He likes toys. The real thing too. Built his own airplane for drug runs."

"How'd he avoid the drones?" Chase asked.

"Shot down a couple of 'em. Steered clear of the rest."

Leo appeared from behind a pile of crates. "Where'd he keep the plane?"

"Local airstrip," Switchblade said. "He used to talk about it. Privately owned little dirt runway next to a bar and a motel. Plenty of privacy. I never went there. The Fly by Night—that's what he called it."

Chase drew his brows tight. "Switch, where is this place?"

"Between here and Detroit."

"You drive. I'll search the intel. Come on."

22

Leo wouldn't leave without the truck filled with computers—it was the whole reason Melody took this risk. Chase didn't care. He just wanted to find her. But he hot-wired the truck and told Leo to get it back to the Cosimo. Then he and Switchblade set out in the other truck to find the Fly by Night airstrip.

Chase ran a check, but the place was off WR radar. No surprise. Leo sped up ahead and before long he took the ramp back onto the highway.

Switchblade stayed on the two-lane road heading away from Ann Arbor and into the countryside.

"Got to be a secluded location," he said.

"I'm trusting you," Chase said. "I've got nothing. But we're not just going to stumble onto it. Maybe we should ask locals what they know."

"I'm worried about Leo. They wouldn't have left the truck out in the open unless they were close by. Won't be long before they go lookin' for it."

"Leo will be back at the Cos by nightfall. And he's got the two-way. No point worrying."

"You're right. Let's find us some airplanes. Got to be some connection to…something. Tell Sparky to keep looking. But we ain't stoppin' to talk to nobody."

A rogue airstrip wouldn't have a WR data trail. But there had to be something. Chase ran a check of aircraft parts. Tires. Parachutes.

Liquor.

The WR seemed to have reached into local distribution. Would they overlook unauthorized activity for the sake of revenue? A recent delivery had been scheduled at a local pub.

"I've got it. I think." Chase mapped the location. "Take the next left. Five miles, then right."

"What'd you find?"

"A bar called the Cockpit. Ever heard of it?"

"Nope." Switchblade made the turn and headed west. "But it sounds like what you'd call a bar at an airstrip."

"WR made a delivery there. I can't believe they're dealing with rogue customers."

"You got some notion the WR is upright in their business dealings?"

Chase smirked. "Not anymore."

The afternoon sky dulled. Chase got Leo on the two-way. He was under the Cos. The computers were being moved up to headquarters. At least that part of the mission was done. Now to find Mel and her brothers.

And a guy called the Negotiator. And probably some other thugs. Chase couldn't walk in, ask for his wife, and settle the whole matter with a handshake. What was it this man wanted to negotiate? Mel...for what?

He closed his eyes and breathed a prayer. He wasn't going back to that stupid skyscraper without his wife.

"Two miles to the bar." He opened his eyes to the darkening sky. "And hopefully an airstrip."

Switchblade drove faster. "Place won't be poppin' till late. Maybe we can get in and out before anybody notices."

The rough road ended past a couple of abandoned houses, where a sign marked the entrance to a private landing field.

"Fly by Night." Switchblade veered left toward some buildings. "This is it—we got the right place."

Chase leaned forward and clutched the dash. A crooked placard over the door of a rundown shack identified the bar—the Cockpit. The sign on a small trailer read *Office*. A pink motel looked like it hadn't seen guests since the 1960s, but two self-drive vehicles waited in front of it. A few hundred yards to the north, three hangars met the end of the runway.

A hasty search through the nightspot and the office turned up nothing. And nobody. That left the motel.

It stretched out in a V-shape with six rooms on each side. Curtains hid the view into two units— seemed they were the only rooms occupied. Chase broke the lock on the first one and rushed in.

Switchblade pulled him back and yanked the door shut. "What if somebody paid for this dump to take a nap...or something?"

"Nobody's in there. Bed's made. Curtains are pulled on the next room too."

"All right, but we knock. No sense gettin' the management on us."

"What management? Look at this place." Chase brushed past him.

Switchblade grabbed his arm. "Let me handle this." He stepped to the door and rapped softly.

After a moment, a man in a white T-shirt and boxers opened the door. He rubbed his eyes and squinted. Then he reached behind him to yank the spread off the bed. He wrapped it around his shoulders.

"What the…What do you want?" the man asked with a shiver.

"We're looking for the Negotiator," Chase said.

Switchblade elbowed him.

The man started to laugh, but it came up a wheeze. "First hangar. Office is in the loft. But he's probably out flying. Or murdering. You sure that's who you're looking for?" The man wiped his face and yawned. "Hey, do I know you?"

Chase ran after Switchblade, who was already at the truck, and they drove toward the hangars.

A plane flew in and landed on the dirt strip. Switchblade slowed until the little craft rolled to the third building. No activity around the closest one.

They left the truck behind the hangar. Chase broke another lock, and the narrow door on the side of the big metal structure swung open. He walked in. Four small planes waited in the darkness. One boasted the name *Furious Negotiator*.

"That's comforting," Chase said. "The man, or at least his plane, is furious."

"You ain't lying, Charlie."

"Stay close. We're going up."

In the loft, four doors spread out on the landing. One bore gold letters—*LB*.

"Lance Briggs." Chase broke the knob off.

Switchblade came in behind him and flipped on the light.

Inside, they found a long table covered with boxes and model airplanes. A filing cabinet. A big polished mahogany desk. Chase rolled the black leather chair to one side. The drawers were locked. He jerked them open while Switchblade stood watch at the door.

Papers. A VPad. A gun. A few packets of pills. A small box of microchips. Stacks of WR bills.

And a gold wedding band.

Chase slipped the ring onto the tip of his finger. He exhaled.

"It's Mel's."

23

"Charlie, you sure?"

"Of course I'm sure." He held up his hand. "It's my mother's ring. It matches the one I'm wearing—my father's."

Switchblade stepped closer. "What now?"

"We tear this place apart—that's what."

A truck roared near and stopped. Footsteps. The big door at the front of the hangar squeaked and groaned. Switchblade turned off the light and eased the door shut.

Chase slid the ring into his pocket and joined Switch. Light from below seeped in at the floorboard. Two voices. Both male.

"Who else would have taken the truck?" one voice asked. "I'm telling you they busted open a few doors, got their goods, and left. Their people were expendable—going to heaven and all that. They don't care if they lose a few in a business deal."

"They just want us to think they're gone. Probably sent for backup to search the rest of the warehouses. They want the girl—she's their leader."

Some shuffling of boxes. Heavy breathing.

"They'll be back," the voice continued. "But they won't find the girl. We'll fly her to Chicago tonight and collect the bounty. But get rid of the men she brought with her."

"But, boss, there ain't no bounty. She ain't even on the WR's list."

"I know that," the man yelled. "But if she's really the leader of the Underground Church, the Feds will pay. I'm offering a publicity goldmine. Her public execution will go a long way in squelching that movement."

"What about her man? She talks like he could take us all down."

"Ridiculous claims. The whole husband-to-the-rescue story is a bluff. No man would let himself get separated from that pretty little thing."

Chase pressed his forehead against the wall. His muscles tightened. The exoself surged. Everything inside him wanted to storm down the stairs and bust the man's head open.

"I hear him too," Switchblade whispered. "Stay cool, brother. We got to play this right."

"No promises."

"You just make sure Sparky minds his manners."

Chase took a breath. "What do we do now?"

Switchblade pulled the gun from his waistband. "I say we go down before they come up."

"Makes sense. I guess."

"But we need to make an entrance." Switchblade cracked the door, aimed the pistol, and fired.

Chase peered out the door as the four-foot bay light directly over the Negotiator's plane dropped.

Switchblade readied the gun to fire again and yelled down into the now dimly lit hangar. "We're gonna have a talk, Briggs. Drop your weapons."

"Who is that?" the man yelled. "Do you know what you did to my plane? Windshield's busted. For that, you pay. With your life, punk."

Switchblade fired again. This time at the man's shoulder. "Weapons down! Now!"

The man shrieked before pulling out a laser gun and tossing it across the floor. His partner gave up a pistol.

Switchblade stepped slowly down the stairs.

Chase eased around him. "I'm going for the guns." He shoved the pistol under his belt and stuck the laser weapon in the pocket of his jacket.

Then he set his attention on the Negotiator. Lance Briggs. The man's fingers sported gold rings. His eyes were angry slits. The other guy—the sniveling subordinate—cowered at the back of the Hydraline.

"I'm checking the plane." Chase stepped closer and reached for the cockpit door.

"Identity coded," the Negotiator said, his breath ragged. "My plane doesn't open for anyone but me."

Chase grabbed the handle, yanked the door free, and tossed it. He climbed inside. "Nothing but an old machine gun and two laser rifles."

"Got no use for the arsenal," Switchblade told him. "Do your thing."

Chase bent the machine gun's barrel until it made a U-shape and he threw it onto the floor next to the plane. He did the same with the rifles. Then he climbed out and faced Briggs.

"My mistake," the man said. "Pretty little thing *does* have a superhero husband."

Chase grabbed his arms and forced him around. He shoved the man's cheek into the side of the plane and breathed hard at the back of his neck.

"Where is she?" he asked through clenched teeth.

"Let's talk about this. You want your wife. And I want...your help. I could use a man like you. I'll set you up in a real nice place with your lady. And I won't turn her in. Or you. Chase Sterling."

Chase twisted the man's wrist until he screamed. Blood marked the shoulder of his white jacket.

Switchblade was down on ground level now with the gun aimed at the Negotiator's head.

"You know who *he* is," Switch said. "You remember *me*?"

Chase pulled the man's head up by a handful of greasy brown hair and allowed him a glance.

"Switchblade," Briggs growled as he attempted to wriggle free. "You dare to show your face around here? You won't last a week."

"You making threats? You got yourself in a position where threats ain't gonna get you nothing but more trouble. Now tell the nice man where he can find his wife before he loses his temper."

"And then what? He lets me go? I don't think so."

Chase drove the man's chin into the plane's shiny black metal.

The Negotiator let out a yelp. "Bates, you idiot. Do something."

Switchblade leveled his weapon at the man still clutching the plane's tail. The poor guy screamed as the bullet hit him in the leg. He stumbled a few feet to the wall and slid down.

"He ain't going nowhere," Switch said. "Got any other bright ideas?"

"Where is she?" Chase crooked the man's arm to the point of snapping it in two.

He wailed. "OK! I'll tell you. Just let me go."

Chase let up. But he didn't let go.

"You got your computers, but I didn't get what the girl promised me."

"That's because you kidnapped her," Chase said. "What'd you barter for?"

"Maybe I just wanted a date."

Chase swung the man around and punched him in the jaw. The Negotiator banged the back of his head against the plane before dropping to his knees.

"I'm holding back," Chase told him. "So your jaw isn't shattered. Yet."

Briggs rubbed his face. "I wanted some programming. Intel. WR feed on my organization. That's all."

Switchblade crouched beside the man and inched the pistol close to his face. "So you can cover yourself better. Is that it?"

"Yes. But she hasn't done it."

"And she's not going to," Switch told him. "Here's the new terms of the trade: We get the computers and you get to live. But only if we get the girl and the two men back unharmed."

The man narrowed his eyes.

A shadow passed through the open bay door. And then there were two more men in the hangar—one held at gunpoint by the other.

"Don't need to give her up, boss," the man with the gun said. "I heard you yelling. Went and got this one for leverage."

The hostage had to be one of Mel's brothers. Must be the younger one. Chase met his wide eyes.

The armed man grinned. "I'm pulling the trigger on the count of three. Drop your weapons." He pushed the gun against the young man's temple. "One. Two."

Switchblade dropped his gun. Chase tossed the pistol and the laser gun to the ground before he let go his hold on the Negotiator.

Briggs pushed himself off the ground. "What took you so long?" he yelled at his lackey.

"I had to formulate a plan, boss. Like you taught me."

"Next time, just come in shooting. Got it? Now kill the big one. But don't hurt the other one. He's more valuable than the girl."

Chase rammed into the Negotiator with all his strength and sent him flying into the guy with the gun. And Mel's brother. All three men spilled onto the ground as the weapon discharged.

Switchblade grabbed the laser gun. Chase reached for the pistol. The Negotiator was on his hands and knees. His would-be rescuer lay spread out in the doorway. Mel's brother grabbed the man's gun.

But then another man stole it away from him.

And fired.

The Negotiator dropped. Blood seeped from his head.

"Brax, you OK?" the shooter asked.

Had to be the older brother. Chase knelt beside the Negotiator and touched his arm. Dead. He looked up at the man holding the gun. "You must be Ridge."

"You must be the joke my sister married."

Not the warmest greeting for a new family member. "Where is she?"

"I told her to stay under cover till I got this under control. Didn't know you were the one causing the ruckus."

"I'm getting real tired of asking," Chase said. "Where exactly is my wife?"

"I'm here." The trembling voice came from behind.

Chase rose and swung around.

She stumbled through the side door. Her hair hung in tangles and dirt streaked her face. Red marks circled her wrists. She wasn't wearing any shoes. And she was so beautiful.

He dropped the gun and ran to her. She flew into his embrace, and he held her so close he thought he might break her. But she held on just as tight.

The exoself surged at the touch and Chase opened his eyes wide. He raised his head from her neck and cupped her face with his hands. Tears spilled down her cheeks. His own tears clouded his vision. All he could do was kiss her.

Then with his lips a breath away from hers, he spoke at last. "Mel…you're—"

She quickly rested her soft fingers over his mouth, and he kissed them.

She drew him closer, touched her lips to his ear, and whispered, "Nobody else knows."

24

He wove his fingers through her hair. "I love you. I'm sorry it took me so long to find you."

"I love *you*. Everything's all right now. Take me home."

He held her face again. And kissed her deeply.

"Hate to break this up, but we gotta get out of here."

Chase looked up to find Switchblade beside him.

Mel let go of Chase and hugged Switch, and he kissed the top of her head. "Girl, you need a shower." He let her go.

She laughed and wrapped her arms around Chase once more.

"Must be a story behind you and your brothers showing up the way you did," Switchblade said. "Who else is dead?"

"Somebody's dead?" She looked across the hangar, and then she seemed to go limp in Chase's arms.

"Sweetheart, are you OK?"

She motioned toward Ridge, who stood over the injured man against the wall. The guy begged, but Ridge fired and silenced the witness.

"Two down," Ridge said. "One to go."

Chase eased out of Mel's arms. "The other guy's not even conscious."

Ridge narrowed his eyes. "The last unconscious man you didn't kill turned you in. And got a base destroyed."

"This guy doesn't know who I am. Just leave him."

But Ridge fired anyway. "He saw you. For my sister's sake, we're bringing you in at our base. But I'm not taking any chances. Now let's get out of here before I have to kill anybody else."

Chase found Mel with more tears, her hands over her mouth.

"Come on," he told her. "We've got a truck." He held her close and walked her to the side door. Switchblade followed. Brax and Ridge went out the big door at the front of the hangar.

At a quarter past seven, the bar was still empty. Same vehicles at the motel. No one in sight. Switchblade pushed up the door at the back of the truck, poured the gas into the tank, and tossed the cans.

Brax approached Chase with his hand extended. "Melody's told us all about you."

Chase shook his hand.

Ridge only stared for a moment before climbing into the bay of the truck.

"Oh no," Switchblade said. "Up front, deputy. You too, little brother. These two could use some alone time."

"You're not serious," Ridge said. "Us three up front and my sister back here in a cold truck bed with...him?"

"With her *husband*. They can keep each other warm."

The man jumped out and huffed to the truck's cab. Brax smiled at his sister.

Chase mouthed *thank you* to Switchblade. Then he lifted Mel off the ground and slid her into the truck. He climbed in, removed his jacket, and wrapped it around her shoulders.

"All right, you two," Switchblade said. "We'll see you at the Cos." He slid the door down.

Chase leaned against the metal side of the eight-by-twelve compartment and pulled off his boots. Then his socks. He reached for Mel's foot and pulled a sock over it. He did the same with the other foot. And he pulled her onto his lap.

"Tell me the truth, sweetheart. Did any of those men lay a hand on you? Because if they did, I'm sorry I didn't kill them myself."

"No. The Negotiator made some insinuations. But nothing happened."

"Thank God for that." Chase pulled her closer.

She kissed his cheeks. Then his lips. Snuggled into the nape of his neck, she said, "I know we have a lot to talk about. But right now, I just need you to hold me."

And so for nearly the entire ride back to Detroit, he held her and stroked her hair. He kissed the raw skin on her wrists where she'd been tied up. And he cried. And prayed. "Thank You," he said more than once. But that was all until the truck stopped and the sounds of the city intruded on the sweet silence.

"I think we're at a traffic light," he said. "Must be close."

"Tell me what you're thinking. I know it was a shock when you first touched me."

A tear slid down his cheek as he gazed into her lovely brown eyes. "I'm so sorry. It was only one night. I can't believe I let this happen."

She lowered her brows and frowned. "Well, I'm

not sorry."

"But we don't know how it will...I'm a transhuman."

"You're still a man. And I love you. And we're having a baby." She smiled and kissed him. "I'm not afraid. Please be happy with me."

He nodded. "Your vitals are good, but you're a little undernourished."

"What is it?"

"What do you mean?"

"A boy or a girl?"

Chase laughed. "I haven't got a clue, Mel. That's beyond my ability to know."

"Doesn't matter. It's a boy. I know it."

He rubbed her back and sighed. "You haven't told anyone? Not even your mother?"

"I wanted to tell you first. I'm sorry I didn't get a chance to warn you, but I couldn't just stand there and say, 'Oh, by the way, big surprise coming when you touch me.' I couldn't wait to be in your arms."

"I understand. Are you going to tell now?"

"There'll be a lot to talk about tonight. Let's wait."

"Yeah. It'll take time to get used to the idea." He caressed her cheek. "But, Melody, I'm here now. And we're together. And whatever happens, I'm all yours. And you're mine." He edged sideways and reached into his pocket. He pulled out the little gold band and slipped it on her finger. "I love you forever."

"Our wedding vows." She kissed him softly. "You found my ring. I thought it was gone for good." She held on to him as the truck tilted forward.

"Feels like we're going under the Cosimo. Question number one—what the heck are we doing in the Cosimo?"

"No. Question number one—what happened to my computers?"

"Leo drove the truck back. They're here."

"That's a relief. Tomorrow we use that brain of yours to reestablish communication."

"Yeah, and that brings up the next several questions. How did you shut down your code with nothing but a laptop? And how will you turn it back on? It's not like when we got the exoself back. Is it?"

"Sparky? How is he? Up and running, I hope."

"It's not as efficient, but it works. But how are you going to reinstall the code?"

"*You're* going to do it."

Before he could continue the Q & A, the door flew up. Switchblade raised his brows. "I shoulda knocked."

Mel grinned and slid off Chase's lap. "No problem, big guy." She inched to the edge of the bay, and Switchblade took her in his arms and set her on the ground.

"I'm so glad you two ended up together after that awful raid," she told him. "I thought we might never see you again." She let him go and grabbed Chase's hand. "Do you have any idea what happened after the transport picked us up in Herouxville?"

Chase met Switchblade's eyes. "We have questions about that too. But there'll be plenty of time to discuss it later." He let go of her hand, slid his bare feet into his boots, and jumped out of the truck.

Brax stood near the hyper lift.

"Where's your hotheaded, trigger-happy brother?" Mel asked.

"Already went up. To talk to Colt."

Switchblade slid his hand over the lift panel.

"Your brother tight with that man, Melody?"

"Like glue. And I don't like it." She stepped in when the door disappeared, and she held tight to Chase's arm.

25

In seconds they were on the twentieth floor. The door dissolved before a cheering crowd.

Sameea embraced both her children. "My precious ones. Praise the Lord." She pulled back and clutched their hands. "Your brother ran right past me. Is he all right?"

Brax's nostrils flared. "Mama, he shot some men for no good reason. And he didn't exactly treat Chase like family. You should talk to him."

"He's nearly thirty. He needs no lecture from me. God must deal with him." She looked up at Chase. "Forgive my son. He's young and stupid."

Then she set her attention on Mel and attempted to wipe the dirt off her face. "But as for you, my little one, you take on too much. Your husband is with you now. You must settle down."

Mel laughed and shook her head. "My husband's arrival means that much more work. It can wait until tomorrow, but we have a few things to go over tonight." She clasped Chase's hand and led him into the room with the radios, and she sat at the head of the table.

He dropped next to her, scooted his chair closer, and wrapped his arm around her shoulders. The crowd dissipated except for a few key people. Leo. Brax. Some people Chase hadn't met. Then Ridge and

Colt entered through a side door and joined the group. Sameea stood behind Mel and ran her fingers through her daughter's tangled hair.

"Mama, stop that. I know I'm a mess."

Sameea took a seat next to Brax.

Leo started. "The computers are in the adjoining room. Melody, it looks like you've got enough to set us up almost as well as we were at Blue Sky Field."

Mel nodded. "Two holographic displays, a 3D image table, and six stations. And a few laptops and tablets. Oh, and some VPads. We can clean them out and make them untraceable. Tomorrow we reactivate the code."

"And then what?" Colt asked. "We hook up to the rest of the bases around the world? Is that really necessary?"

"It is if we're going to help each other," Mel said. "I know that's not your primary concern, but—"

"My goal is to take care of the people right here in our own base."

"Like you took care of my brothers and me when we went missing? You didn't bother to look for us until Chase took charge. Did you?"

Colt came out of the chair, his hands on his hips. "Your husband has no rank here. He's not in charge of anything."

Mel crossed her arms. "Well, *he* came and got us. *And* the computers. Sounds like a man in charge to me."

"Mel, what happened back there?" Chase tried to redirect the volatile conversation. "How did you get free?"

Still eyeing Colt, she explained. "We were in the next hangar. When the Negotiator found out the truck with the computers had been stolen, he had his guys move us to a truck, and they left us there. Then one of the men came back. He said somebody had the boss in the hangar and he needed bait. He untied Brax." She shifted her gaze to Chase. "We had no idea it was you and Switchblade. After he cut Brax loose, he looked out the door for a few seconds. And Brax kicked the guy's box cutter back toward Ridge and me. Fool never even noticed. He grabbed Brax out of the truck and pulled the bay door down. Ridge scooted until he reached the box cutter. In a few minutes, we were both free."

Ridge spoke up. "I went after Brax and told Melody to stay put. Of course, she didn't."

Mel leaned forward, her elbows on the table. "I had to know what was going on. So I sneaked to the side door of the hangar. And then I heard Chase's voice." She leaned back and rested her hand on Chase's knee. "And I knew everything would be all right."

Colt dropped back into his seat. "The only reason there's even the slightest chance everything will be all right is because Ridge eliminated the witnesses. Nobody can know we've got this transhuman here at the Cos."

"I was ready to kill the man in charge," Chase said. "But not when he was on his knees. One guy already had a bullet in his leg and the other one was out cold. Ridge shot three defenseless men and it was not only a waste of life, it was a waste of time. A couple dozen people know I'm here. Not in this building, but in Detroit. You can't kill all of them. I wouldn't let you if you tried."

"You couldn't stop me," Ridge yelled.

Chase stared into his brother-in-law's eyes. "I

absolutely could stop you."

Ridge leaned back and glared at Chase.

"That's enough," Mel said. "I am the leader of the Underground Church and I'm telling you believers do not kill unless in defense of others."

Ridge shook his head. "Girl, use your brain. It *was* in defense of others. I was protecting our base. And now I find out this man of yours has not been covering his tracks. God help us."

The debriefing continued into the night as Chase reviewed the last three months. But there was no talk of Switchblade's recent injury or the transfusion that saved his life.

Chase had questions too, and Mel explained the trip across the northern territory in the stolen transport. Chase had avoided going through Toronto, but Mel's group took that route and met some resistance. The few laptops they'd managed to sneak out of Blue Sky Field were confiscated, but not before Mel wiped them clean.

Finley came in with sandwiches and pitchers of juice and milk. Chase poured Mel a glass of milk, and she drank it in seconds. She must have been starving. And exhausted. He made her eat a sandwich, and he ate one as well. Some kind of soy meat product with fresh tomatoes and cheese. This enormous gathering of believers ate pretty well. One less thing to worry about.

At last, Sameea took charge of her children—at least the younger two. She sent Brax off for a shower and told him to go to bed. Then she forced Mel out of her seat and led her to the door.

Mel looked back with anxious eyes. But Chase nodded. She was in her mother's care, and he'd see her again in a few minutes.

The others around the table left for their living quarters. Colt and Ridge were still discussing the best use of the computers when Switchblade grabbed Chase by the arm and pulled him to his feet.

"Let's find out where we're supposed to bed down," Switch said. "I hear it's up a couple of floors."

They met some of the others from the meeting in the hallway. Finley approached them.

"You two must be beat. I have your room assignments," she said. "Switchblade, you're in the men's dorm. Room 2207. Chase, you'll go to Mel's room." She giggled. "2116."

Chase hugged her. "Thank you. And thanks for the snacks. You do a great job running this hotel, my dear."

She stood on her toes to kiss him on the cheek. "I'm so glad you guys are here." She turned to Switchblade, and he bent to let her kiss his cheek too. "I'll see you in the morning."

Chase and Switchblade entered the lift, and Chase spoke the floor number. "Twenty-two."

"That's *my* floor," Switchblade said. "Ain't you getting off on twenty-one?"

Before he could answer, they were up and the magic door was gone. Chase stepped out and leaned against the wall. The exoself had filled him in on the hotel that made up ten stories of the Cosimo. Graphic prints and a few black sofas filled the lobby. Chase dropped onto the nearest one.

Switchblade sat beside him. "You gonna tell me what's wrong?"

"I just need a few minutes. Mama's probably still fussing over Mel. I'll give them some time."

"You're the one who ought to be fussing over her.

So, what're you doing here with me?"

Chase lowered his head. "All this danger. And death. And now there's a…"

"A what, Charlie?"

"She's pregnant." Chase looked up.

Switchblade sucked in a breath. After a moment he said, "I leave you two alone for forty minutes and you—"

Chase punched him in the arm. "Idiot. It happened in Quebec."

Switch rubbed his bicep. "I know. Just trying to lighten the mood. It's not the worst thing that could happen. You and your wife are having a baby and it's a reason to rejoice. God chose to bless you. Don't look at it like it's a burden."

Chase sighed and rubbed the back of his neck. "Thank you, brother. I needed to hear that. I don't know about this place, Switch. That jerk, Colt. And my brother-in-law."

Switchblade leaned forward and rubbed his hands together. "I know it's hard for you. But I come from a different world. I regret what happened back there as much as you do, but he did what he thought was necessary. And he may have saved us a world of trouble. But I ain't telling *him* that. He don't need no encouragement."

"I see your point. But I hate it that those men had to die. Even if they *were* rotten thieves. It hurts my…"

"Your spirit, Charlie. That's what hurts. Say a prayer, go find your wife, and get all the comfort you can. Despite being in a five-star hotel, this life ain't gonna get any easier. Not for a while."

Chase wrapped his hand around Switchblade's shoulder. "I'm going. I'm so"—he closed his eyes—"so relieved to have her back. Baby and all." He met Switch's smile. "And I couldn't have done it without you." They stood, and Chase stepped toward the lift. "Nobody else knows. Don't say anything."

"Uncle Switchblade can keep a secret. Night, brother." He glanced at the digital sign pointing to various groupings of room numbers and headed left.

"Good night, my friend."

26

The lobby on the twenty-first floor stretched out even grander with blue and gold digital prints and ornate furniture. Chase found Mel's room and knocked on the door.

Mama Sameea answered. She stepped to the side without a word.

The room held a big bed, a sofa, and a small kitchen area. A large window was covered by digital blinds. A closet door stood open. Another door was closed.

"Melody is in the bath." Sameea pointed to the closed door. "She will be out soon."

Chase nodded. "I hope you know how much I love your daughter."

"You will stay here now and take care of her."

"I don't plan on going anywhere. Not without Mel. It hurts too much being apart from her."

Sameea barely shook her head. Her eyes seemed unsure. Her smile unconvinced. "I'll leave you now. Good night."

"Good night."

She left, and Chase went to the window. "Open." The blinds dissolved the same as the door on the lift.

The city teemed. Even where the streetlights didn't shine, Chase could see the dealers. Pimps. A man shot the glass out of a storefront. Another threw something—maybe a brick—and busted the windshield on an old car. All this right below the new world headquarters of the Underground Church. Did the citizens of Detroit even know?

Mel rubbed his shoulder.

He let his gaze fall on her. She wore a lacy blue gown. Her dark hair spiraled past her shoulders.

"I love you." He wrapped her in his arms, his face to the window. "Close." The blinds materialized.

"I am a little more lovable with the stink of being kidnapped washed away."

"I didn't notice. You just smelled like home to me. Like lilacs. Why do you always smell like lilacs?" He picked her up and carried her to the bed.

She leaned against the headboard. "You fought so hard to get here."

He sat on the bed, facing her. "At times I wondered if you'd give up on me. I even thought…"

"Tell me."

"I thought it would be best if you forgot me. You'd be better off. Safer. But I couldn't stay away."

She reached for his hand. "God brought you back to me."

He leaned forward and kissed her. "To you and our baby."

"You coming to terms with it?"

"I had a talk…um."

"What did you do?" She smiled. "Let me guess—you told Switchblade."

"Don't be mad. I know we said we'd keep it quiet. But he won't tell anybody."

She laughed. "I'm not mad. I told my mother."

He smiled and kissed the inside of her elbow. "No wonder she looked at me like that when she let me in your room."

"*Our* room." She pushed his hair behind his ears. "You could use some cleaning up yourself. But not right now."

"Yeah, we still have so much to talk about."

"Enough talk." She leaned close, pressed her hands against his chest, and pushed him down onto the bed.

27

Next morning, Chase and Mel savored a long breakfast in bed—compliments of Finley and Erin. Chase showered and dressed in clean clothes. Compliments of the supply chief—a bald guy with a scar running across his head. Mel had gone to start setting up the computers. He nearly refused to let her go down one floor without him. But this was important. Believers around the world were depending on Mel to get them back online.

And Mel was depending on Chase. She told him *he* would reinstall the code. What was he supposed to do? If he could, he'd have done it already. Weeks ago.

He stood in front of the mirror over the sink and trimmed his beard. Mel didn't protest the long hair— she agreed he had to at least try to keep his identity a secret. And he didn't plan on staying inside this monument to the goodwill of the WR forever.

The Cosimo had gotten a lot of publicity when it first went up. For years, the city of Detroit hoped for the boom the WR had promised with the high-tech superscraper—as it was touted by the media. *Change Your Life* had even planned an episode from here, but it never happened. The hype began to fall off almost as soon as it began, though the building didn't empty out completely until about six years ago.

Cold fingers crept up Chase's artificial spine as the

exoself ran a check on the last known tenants of the Cos. He dropped the razor into the sink.

A WR research team had been the last to leave. Over a hundred scientists, programmers, AI specialists, and government overseers had taken up the entire eighty-ninth floor. Their mission was to determine the effect of widespread use of transhuman technology. Chase scanned the list of participants and consultants. Dr. Robert Fiender. No surprise. Intel reported he'd been in on the setup but had pulled out to work for a privately owned laboratory.

"The Helgen Institute." Chase dried his face with a towel and then left the bathroom. He dropped to the edge of the bed. A couple of other names came up that he recognized from the Helgen. No doubt recruited by Robert.

And then another name. Assigned to the team right out of college, she'd stayed only three months before being reassigned to the SynVue entertainment complex in Chicago.

Melody Reece.

The air seemed to drain from Chase's lab-grown lungs. She'd worked here before he met her? Why didn't he know that? Had she been assigned to evaluate him years before the transformation? He laughed. Ridiculous. She wouldn't lie to him. But she'd led him to the building where it all started. And she knew it. And he didn't.

He drew his lips tight and rubbed his hands over his face. Then he rose off the unmade bed that still held the sweet scent of his wife. After dressing quickly, he rushed out the door. The lift delivered him to the twentieth floor in seconds. He scanned the busy workspace.

A crowd of residents surrounded the computers. Mel sat at a station, frantically typing.

The quiet voice inside Chase's spirit made him stop. He breathed in and out. There were so many things he didn't know about her. Family history—her mother was definitely not from Alabama like her father. He knew she'd studied AI but didn't know anything about what she did before she came to work as his assistant. He knew the important things. She was a believer. She loved him. She was carrying his baby.

She could explain this.

At the station, he stopped behind her. She entered code the old Chase Sterling would have never understood. But the exoself explained it as fast as she typed. She was programming the holographic display. The black table set up next to her began to dance with tiny blue beads of light. She leaned back in her seat.

"Praise the Lord," she said. "It works."

He rested his hands on her shoulders, and she jumped.

"I didn't mean to scare you." He let go.

She sprang from the chair and faced him. "It's OK. I'm glad you're here." She leaned close and kissed him. "I missed you." She smiled. "I can't stand being apart from you. Not even for an hour."

"We need to talk."

Her eyebrows rose. "You look serious. What is it?"

"Take me to the eighty-ninth floor."

Her mouth fell open, but no words escaped. Her shoulders sank. Her loving gaze met the floor. But she recovered instantly and looked him in the eyes. She nodded. "All right. Let's go."

28

He walked ahead of her to the lift. She caught up and they stepped in.

"Eighty-nine," she said.

Moving up sixty-nine floors took more than a few seconds. He sensed her eyes never left him, though he didn't look at her until she began her climb out of the secret.

"Chase, I was going to tell you."

"You should have told me already."

"When? When I worked for you? We never talked about what we did before we met. Before *Change Your Life*. Should I have told you in Quebec? Everything happened so fast. But I'm telling you now, baby."

He met her desperate eyes. Doubt flooded his mind. Was this all some elaborate plan? No. She loved him.

He touched her cheek. "I was running data on the building. Imagine my surprise when I found out my wife worked with the team researching transhumanism. You never once told me you'd met Robert. And he acted like he'd never met *you*."

"That's because we never met. After your transformation, I was in the same room with him a few times. But there was never any reason for me to consult him. And as for my time in this place, I never even saw him. I'm not surprised he was here at some point, but our paths did not cross."

The lift stopped and the door disappeared.

Mel held him back when he tried to step out. "I was planning on bringing you here this morning. And I was going to explain everything. You have to believe me."

"I'm not sure what's coming in as intel and what's just my own imagination. Something about this place is..."

She eased her arms around him. "Chase, please. You have to trust me."

He studied the lobby. The graphic prints on the walls were similar to those at the Helgen. Double doors were closed to the right. He stared at them for a moment before dropping onto a leather sofa.

Mel sat beside him and rubbed his back. "Just tell me what you're thinking. I can't stand this silence."

"The Negotiator said you're not on the WR's wanted list. Why is that? You used to be on it."

She shook her head. "I have no idea. If they thought we were together in Quebec, maybe they gave up on tracking me when they didn't find any trace of *you* there. As far as they know, I haven't done anything but drop out of the system."

"Have you? Really?"

She lowered her hand from his back. "What are you saying? That I'm still working for them?"

"You were in on the whole transhuman experiment from the beginning. Did you come to Chicago to evaluate me? To see if I was a good test subject?"

"What? How could you think—?"

"Did you know what they were going to do to me all along? Was it an act—that sweet young girl who didn't even want to touch a lab-grown kidney?"

Tears puddled in her eyes. "Chase Sterling…Redding…whoever you are…" Her voice rose louder and higher. "I never did anything but be a friend to you when you didn't have a lot of friends. You didn't care about anybody except yourself, but I saw something in you. I never misled you about who I was. I just didn't talk about my background in AI. And you know why—I've explained that much. I didn't want to get mixed up in that world."

"But you admit you were here."

"Like I said, I was going to tell you this morning. I'm hoping there's something left here that will help us reinstall the code."

He shook his head and rubbed his eyes. "Why were you here for only three months?"

"I hated it. It was evil and it scared me. Chase, I was twenty-one. The WR decided I was some kind of prodigy, but designing artificial intelligence was not how I wanted to spend my life. I begged for a new assignment. And they sent me to Chicago to work for SynVue. I knew it would be a menial job, but I didn't care. And then I ended up working for *you*. And I was happy."

"Nobody ever told you the plan was to turn me into a transhuman?"

"If I had known, I would have warned you."

He looked her in the eyes and rested his hand on her arm. "Did they do anything to you while you were here?"

"What do you mean?"

"Experiments. Implants. Could something have happened to prepare you for—?"

"For what? You think I was sent to you for a

reason? You think I was programmed to get close to you?"

He didn't answer.

She wrapped her arms around his neck. "I love you, Chase. And I have no secrets. Wouldn't you know if I had any kind of implant?"

He nearly laughed. The idea was preposterous and he wouldn't allow his wicked thoughts to hurt her. He pulled her close. "I'm sorry. I love you. I would do anything for you—I'd die for you. And I don't care what you did here. Just tell me everything you know, sweetheart. Even if it doesn't seem important. What went on behind those doors?"

She lifted her head from his shoulder. "Come on. Let's go in."

He thrust his fingers into her hair and kissed her. Then he let her go and rose off the sofa.

She spoke and the doors swung open. She entered the dark room. "Power on."

He followed her. Multiple recessed lights went from dull to bright in seconds. Chase scanned the place. Empty desks lined three walls. The fourth wall contained a massive computer system built into the structure. It blinked and flashed. Ten screens displayed code. At the end of the wall, a gurney waited, attached to the supercomputer by a web of electrodes. The exoself pulled the protection code—32-7.

Chase walked to the gurney.

"Have you been on this floor in the last few weeks?" he asked.

"A few times. To see if the computer still functioned."

"I thought all the computers were stolen or trashed." He laid his hand on the gurney's soft white cover and ran his finger over an electrode.

"This one can't be removed. And it's virtually indestructible."

"You're going to use this to reprogram me?"

"I told you last night—you're the one who's going to do it. At least you've got to get it started. Then I'll take over." She stepped near a keypad positioned behind a clear shield. With a wave of her hand, the cover rose and she began typing. "They built this into the Cosimo and made it tamper-proof. Only those of us with clearance could get to this floor."

"So, the lift knew your imprint and it let you in." Chase joined her in front of the lit-up wall. "The exoself is sparking code. It senses a threat."

She met his eyes. "Am I the threat?"

He wrapped his hand around the back of her neck and kissed her forehead. "Forgive me. And tell me what to do."

"See if the system is being monitored. If it is, disengage it."

"I don't know if I can." Chase studied the readout on various screens.

"Instruct the exoself to worm in. I think it will be easy for you to communicate."

Chase followed the code the exoself pulled up. "I'm in. Mel, this is odd. It's like Sparky is talking to his ancestor. They know each other."

"Any outside monitoring?"

"No. But just in case, I'm putting up a shield that will cause the system to appear inactive. Like it should be. Now what?"

"Tell me what Dr. Fiender did when he cut the WR off from the exoself. Did he isolate it from your processors?"

"Yes. I could see it. Like a holograph."

She took his hand and led him to the gurney. "Do you trust me?"

He squeezed her hand and kissed her before stretching out on the thin mattress. "I still don't know how I'm supposed to reinstall your code."

"The exoself is designed to change its coding process frequently. I need for you to tell me how to get in."

"Right. I see what you want. Robert explained it. I'm searching for the primary access. Come on, Sparky. Tell me how to get in."

Mel positioned the electrodes on each side of his head. The clear pads she secured to his skin seemed to hold like magnets.

"Roll onto your side." She clutched his shoulder and pulled him toward her, then reached over to lift his shirt and place more electrodes along his spine.

"I've got it. Access programming by seventeen-four." He hadn't slept in two days—not since he woke up from that long nap after the transfusion. Not even in the soft bed with Mel last night. But now his eyes grew heavy. "Why do I feel tired?"

"How long has it been since you shut down?"

"A couple of days."

"What did you do while I was sleeping last night?"

He smiled. "I watched you."

She caught his stare and grinned. But only for a second. "Maybe you just need to rest."

"It's not that. I feel like…I'm being drained. It wasn't like this the last time the exoself pulled out."

"You may be more dependent on the connection now. I'll work as fast as I can. Now that I have the access code, I can reinstall *my* code. And then we'll get you back down to the command center and you can do your thing."

"I still don't get why you can't just program the computers, Mel." His eyes fell shut, but he remained aware of his connection to the supercomputer. "And why on earth did you risk your life to get a bunch of old computers when you had this beast at your disposal?"

"It's designed for one thing—programming a transhuman. As far as I know, this is the first time it's ever been used. When I was here six years ago, it was just being set up. But it was never put into operation. When they were finally ready for…"

"For me?"

"When it happened, the Helgen was the only place with the right people."

"But I was initially programmed in Chicago."

"Fiender brought his team and the equipment from his compound with him."

"I wonder why he left this place to work in the desert."

"Like I said, our paths never crossed."

He struggled to open his eyes. The exoself floated in the center of the room. Mel walked around it. She pulled down figments of coded line and pushed up phantom numbers.

"When I'm done, you should be connected to supporters like before," she said. "Any information passing along the route of the four Ss will be stored in the exoself."

Chase closed his eyes again. He searched his mind for the code. For the Psalms. It was gone, but a verse remained in his memory, and he recited it. "You are my hiding place; You will protect me from trouble and surround me with songs of deliverance."

"I'm done, Chase. I'm putting it back."

The exoself seemed to climb back inside him and spark every processor. But he was ready to shut down for a while.

And he would have if Mel hadn't shaken him. She removed the electrodes and rolled him onto his back. "Come on, baby. You need to wake up."

He opened his eyes wide. The exoself was back, but was his connection to the underground restored? The data trails of the four Ss seemed to be coming in. Only there weren't as many as there used to be.

"I think a lot more people have gone underground," he said.

"But a great number of bases have computers now. The word spread quickly when we got...almost got connected." She pulled his shirt down and gripped his arm as he sat upright on the gurney. "We just have to hope they're watching for us to come back online. Maybe we can even get in touch with some of our people we got separated from in Quebec."

He pulled her close. "We still have a lot to talk about."

"You know something I don't? When were you going to tell me?"

"I was going to tell you last night after we went to your room, but we...didn't spend too much time talking." He ran his hand down her arm. "Then I was going to tell you this morning, but I got hung up on—"

"On the stuff I was going to tell *you* this morning. Well, we got that issue settled. I hope. Now tell me what you've been holding back about Blue Sky Field."

"Nobody else made it, sweetheart."

"But I thought if you managed to get us a rogue transport...We were hoping the others made it out too. Tell me what you know."

"The families were taken to the center north of Herouxville. The elderly people never made it out of the base."

She edged her face into the nape of his neck and he could feel her tears on his skin. He held her tight.

"You must know why," she whimpered at last.

"There are some experiments going on with brain tissue. They only use young brains."

She wept for a moment. "So, that means the families were taken in for...for their brain tissue? And the older ones were worthless, and so they were exterminated."

"That's what the report indicates."

"They used the machine. Bloodless. Didn't they?"

"I've been limited as to how far I could get into the data. I don't have any reports on individuals." He wiped away her tears and kissed her cheeks. "I'm sorry. I know it's a shock."

"We seem to be pretty good at shocking each other this morning." She rested her hands on his shoulders and looked him in the eyes. "Are we OK?"

He brushed her hair back and kissed her. "Of course we're OK. I'm sorry I freaked. I still have questions. But not about your love, Mel."

She exhaled. "For a minute I thought you were considering some kind of conspiracy theory."

Could she read his mind? He had to get out of this room. "It was just a lot to take in. That's all. Let's go get the underground back online."

29

Switchblade greeted them on the twentieth floor.

"Glad to see you two surface from the honeymoon suite," he said. He wrapped his arm around Chase's neck and pulled him forward. "Brother, you look dog-tired." He grinned wide and chuckled.

Mel walked away without a word. Switchblade let Chase go. "Everything all right?"

"Rough morning. I told her about our people in Quebec. After she hooked me up to a supercomputer built to program transhumans."

Switchblade grabbed Chase's arm and pulled him aside. "We got that kind of hardware in this place?"

"Mel was here when they designed it." Chase leaned against the wall and rubbed his face.

"Did you know that?"

"Not until this morning. The exoself filled me in."

"Charlie, she wouldn't do anything to—"

"I know. She was going to tell me. Sparky just beat her to it. I'm afraid my bride and I don't know each other very well."

"You two are on the same page now. Right?"

"I've got questions and I'm not sure Mel has the answers."

"What'd she tell you?"

"She was here for three months. Hated it. Got reassigned at SynVue. Never knew much about what went on in the research lab on the eighty-ninth floor. But she knows how to program me. Long before my transformation, she was my assistant. She was assigned to *me*. And I was the one they picked to become the test model."

"Man, what are you thinking? That woman don't got nothing but love and devotion for you."

"Don't you think I know that?" He stepped to the window and pressed his hands against the thick poly-shield.

"All right, then. Forget about it. You and Melody just need some time. And you'll get it. After you do your robot thing. Come on."

Chase followed Switchblade into the command center, where the leader of the Underground Church would direct hiding believers around the world.

She looked up from a workstation and motioned Chase to join her. The pale runt they called Colt sat next to her. He reminded Chase of...somebody. A dozen others poked at screens and secured cords under plastic guards along the tile floor.

Chase pulled a chair alongside Mel and let his hand glide down her back.

She leaned close until her arm was tight against him. "The system is ready for you. It'll work just like it did at Blue Sky Field. You'll use the code to add every up-top contact. And then bring the bases online." She slid the keypad toward him.

Chase dropped his fingers to the keys. "Why do we need *him*?"

Colt snickered. "You don't want me to watch?"

"Just thought you might have something better to do. Like boxing up some fresh fruit or something."

"Plenty of others running supplies. As head of this

base, it's my responsibility to—"

"To monitor the leader of the underground? Mel is in charge here." Even as he said it, doubt welled up inside him and the exoself sparked 32-7. But he wouldn't fear her. And he needed no protection from her. Why was this happening?

"Melody and I worked this out before your blessed arrival." Colt eyed the screen as Chase began entering the code the exoself seemed hesitant to share. "What is this gibberish? Do you even understand it?"

Mel spoke before Chase could answer. "Anything different this time? Any changes in your processors?"

"Something is definitely different. My communication with WR systems hasn't been as efficient since you activated the killswitch. Now that I'm reconnected, information is coming in scrambled. I can't process it all."

"Has anything happened that might affect the way you function? Injuries you haven't told me about? If so, I need to know."

Switchblade stood on the other side of Colt, and Chase met his eyes.

"Nothing happened, sweetheart. Nothing at all."

30

Chase worked quickly, even though some of the information coming in from WR sources didn't make sense. Maybe it was his fault for throwing out bogus leads about his own location. The two underground bases in Toronto had been ransacked. Most of the believers were listed as detained. So why did the Feds release a truckload of rogues that included a former AI specialist who was a known associate of Chase Sterling?

He couldn't think about it now. People were missing. Probably dead. He exhaled and pushed away from the computer.

"What's the matter?" Mel asked.

"I sent the invitation as far as Toronto, but I can't find any bases ready to come online. Except for the little group in National City. And they were expecting contact. Mel, I'm not sure there's an underground left in Toronto. Thanks to me."

"I don't understand."

"The exoself planted false information reporting I was in Montreal, and then in some other large cities, including Toronto. It happened without my direct input. But I didn't try to stop it." Chase pounded his fist into the workstation and the force left an imprint. "I'm afraid the Feds may have wiped out bases all over the eastern half of the WR."

She rubbed the dent Chase left in the workstation before grasping his hand. "Baby, let's not damage what little equipment we've got. There are at least a hundred people here at the Cos from Toronto. They said they got a warning before the system shut down." She brushed back his hair. "You might have sent out false information, but you also warned at least some of the believers to get out."

"You never told me how you managed to avoid detainment in Toronto. Even if they did think we never met up in Quebec, seems like they would have interrogated you."

She shook her head and shrugged. "They held us for several hours. Took our laptops and searched what little supplies we had with us. And then they let us go."

"No DNA scans?" He watched her eyes. And for the first time, he scanned her iris.

"Well, yes. I can't explain it. God was watching over us."

Everything she'd told him about her involvement on the eighty-ninth floor matched her records. If he'd scanned her months ago, he'd have known. And they'd have dealt with it.

The fact that she'd gotten out of the detention center in Toronto didn't make sense. But if she hadn't...

His eyes flew wide at the thought of her meeting the machine called Bloodless. He sprang out of the chair and pulled Mel from hers.

"I need some air," he told her. "I know this is important, but please...let's take a walk."

Worry filled her eyes. "OK. I'll meet you by the lift in five minutes."

"Where are you going?"

"To see if there's a radio available. And I have to go to the bathroom."

He grinned and let her go. How could he be so paranoid? Maybe because data trails were tying themselves into dead ends inside his processors.

Colt had moved to another station after Chase got at least one chain of up-top believers online. Maybe the guy wasn't useless after all. Switchblade was in the corner of the command center. With a blonde. Chase grinned. At least some things about this life hadn't changed. He left to wait at the hyper lift.

Mel returned and they took the speedy ride to street level.

"You don't need permission from that pasty guy?" Chase asked.

"If you mean Colt, no. Why would I?"

"I can't shake the bad feeling he gives me."

Mel laughed. "Think about it. Who does he look like?"

Chase stopped a few yards from the exit and crossed his arms. The black hair. Green eyes. Pale complexion. He sucked in a breath as the realization hit him. "Oh, Mel, I wish I'd never brought it up."

"That's right. A blast from our SynVue days. He could be the queen's little brother."

The prospect of facing Kerstin again sent a shudder through the exoself. Chase had driven her phantom image from his programming in Quebec, but the real woman was still out there. Somewhere. He prayed he never saw her again.

"Let's change the subject."

Mel kissed him. "Good idea."

"I walked all over the place when I first came into

the city," he said. "Might not have been the smartest thing to do. And maybe it's a mistake now. I mean, we're supposed to be in hiding."

"We'll only go as far as the cemetery. It's pretty safe for believers. I'd have gone out more often if it wasn't for the cold." She took his hand and led him to the big doors in the lobby.

"But not with a fugitive."

"This town is full of fugitives. One more won't draw attention. Even a famous one."

"I can't risk putting you in danger." Chase stalled at the door.

"Then stay behind me." With a pat to her hip, she smiled. "I'm packing." She marched out the door.

He caught up with her as a gush of warming air hit him. "You're...what?"

"No radios were free, but I brought a gun."

"Do you know what to do with it?"

She pulled him across the street. "Forget about the gun. You and I have never just taken a walk. And here we are like normal people, strolling down the sidewalk." She kissed him again. "I love you. And I'll keep you safe."

"I'm here to keep *you* safe." He wrapped his arm around her.

"Chase, tell me what's different? With your transformation, I mean. You're having trouble processing? What else?"

"I'm stronger. And a couple of days ago, I put up a shield that hid us from drones."

"Nothing else? I need to find out why intel is coming in scrambled. It might mean the difference between getting the bases back online or not."

He sighed and looked up at what he could see of

the blue sky between the buildings. He couldn't tell her what he'd done. The transfusion was not the reason for the malfunction.

But how could he know that? And there'd been enough secrets between them.

"Um, sweetheart, I have to tell you something."

Switchblade stepped in front of them. "Robot, what do you think you're doing?"

"It's OK," Chase said. "The lady's packing."

Switchblade met Mel's smile. "Yeah? I guess I'm not needed anymore."

"Don't be so certain," Mel said. "I've never fired the thing. Not sure I want to."

"Melody, you can't go around with a weapon you don't know how to use." Switchblade's arm interlocked with hers and he pulled her forward. "Now, I ended up getting here with three laser guns. Little things. Not like that old pistol your mama totes. You got one of them on you?"

She pulled out the small gun. "I'm not sure what you call it."

Chase forced the .22 caliber back into her pocket. "Put that away."

"Let me teach you how to fire a laser," Switchblade said.

"Sure. Maybe tomorrow. But right now, once this handsome transhuman clears his head, we've got to get back to work."

Switchblade nodded. "I know you two need some time and I guess you're safe enough. I'll go on back to the Cos."

Chase smacked him on the back. "You're more likely to get in trouble out here than I am."

"Why is that?" Mel asked.

"Because this is where he gave up being a thug. And some other thugs didn't approve."

"Who are you calling a thug?" Switchblade punched Chase's arm.

"I said you gave it up."

"Wait," Mel said. "Switchblade, do I need to be worried about this?"

"The biggest threat is gone, thanks to that hotheaded brother of yours. I'll steer clear of certain classy neighborhoods. Nothing to worry about." He stopped at the corner. "I'll go on back now. You kids don't stay out too late."

"Don't be silly. Come with us." Mel grabbed his hand. She reached for Chase with her other hand, and the three went on to the streets around Mt. Olivet.

Believers seemed to know who Mel was. Word still traveled fast the old-fashioned way. But people here and around the world needed the connection Chase could give them. If only he could clear the fuzz from his brain.

The plan to disclose another secret had not played out the way he'd hoped. But maybe it wasn't meant to be.

"So, you're that church lady." A tall black man with a green knit cap blocked the sidewalk.

"Who are *you*?" she asked.

"The WR don't tolerate your kind no more. So, why are you sticking it out? Hang up your halo and join the real revolutionaries. This ain't no place for the international headquarters of the hot and holy." He smiled. "I don't know if you're holy, but…" He twisted a lock of her hair around his finger.

Chase gripped Mel's shoulders and eased her backward. Then he put a little space between the punk and himself. His arms tensed. "We're just out for a stroll. Why don't you move along and we'll do the same. Before one of us is sorry."

"And exactly who are *you*?" the man asked, his eyes glaring.

"Me? I'm the church lady's husband. And I don't appreciate the way you spoke to her. But I'll let it go if you get out of our way."

The man shook his head, smirked, and wrapped his hands around Chase's neck. "I don't take orders from your kind."

Switchblade moved in fast, but not before Chase shoved his hands into the guy's armpits, lifted him off the ground, and threw him twenty feet.

His head slammed into the iron fence surrounding the cemetery. The crowd that had gathered seemed to freeze.

"You must be Chase Sterling," a woman said at last.

"I used to be." Chase met her eyes. "Are you a believer?"

"I am."

Chase scanned the gathering. "Any others?"

Four stepped forward.

"You know where I can find this guy's people?"

Mel grabbed his arm. "Baby, what are you doing?"

"We can't just leave him here. Not a good way to show the love of Christ. Is it? And we're not taking him back to…where we came from."

"You mean the Cos?" a man asked.

Chase sniffed and faced the man. "Not a big secret, huh?"

"The up-tops know where to find the base. But I doubt the guy you just tossed like a rag doll knows about it."

Chase grabbed Switchblade's arm and hurried toward the young man sprawled on the sidewalk. "Get Mel to the base. I'm taking this guy back to wherever he came from."

"Brother, have you lost your mind? You ain't going no place but back with us."

Chase knelt beside the man and touched his arm. "He's not hurt bad."

Mel caught up. "Did I hear you tell Switchblade to take me home? If the guy's not hurt bad, he'll come around soon. Come on, let's go. Don't forget who's in charge here."

Chase stood and grasped her shoulders. "I'm not forgetting who's in charge. I've got to take the man home."

"You really have lost your mind."

"Do you trust me?"

"At the moment...no."

"Do you trust God?"

"I can't let you go again because God is leading you somewhere. The last time that happened—"

"I'm not leaving this city."

"Melody, your man's got a calling," Switchblade said. "This ain't his first mission." He eyed Chase. "But you know I can't let you go on your own."

Chase nodded. "Mel, I'm going to ask these people to escort you back to the Cosimo. We'll be home in an hour."

"Can't be done," Switchblade said. "Two hours."

"I'm coming with you." She crossed her arms.

Switchblade rested his hand on her shoulder. "Our people don't need to lose another leader. And I know about the little bundle. Girl, you've got to go back. No other option."

Her eyes were moist now, but she dropped her arms and nodded. "Two hours." She lowered her brow at Chase. "Don't make me come looking for you."

He kissed her forehead. Then he motioned for the woman who'd recognized him.

"Will you and the others take her back to the Cos?"

"Of course. But what do you plan to do?"

"Get the man home. I'll carry him if I have to." Chase pulled Mel close and then eased her toward the woman. "When I get back, we'll get the bases online."

"*If* you get back," Mel said. And she walked away.

31

She looked back before facing the Cos. Five believers surrounded her. Three men and two women. They'd get her back safely.

Chase knelt again beside the man, who still lay unconscious in front of the iron fence. "He's just a kid."

Switchblade shifted on his feet next to Chase. "You got any idea what you're about to get us into?"

"I was hoping *you* knew. Does the green cap mean anything? Or this tattoo on his arm?" A red dragon with a sword running through it covered the skin from wrist to elbow. Even with a blade piercing its neck, the dragon spewed fire.

"Charlie, you're killing me here. I got the same tat. Only I didn't get it on my arm."

Chase looked up and grinned. "Yeah?"

"I got nothing else to say about it. Slap the joker and see if you can rouse him. You ain't gonna carry him if he can walk."

Chase pulled the man upright and smacked his cheek.

The guy's legs jerked and his eyes fluttered.

Switchblade relieved the man of his weapons—a knife and a pistol.

The kid muttered, and Chase stood and helped him to his feet.

He opened his eyes and groaned. "What'd you do

to me? You got some powerful strength in you."

"Don't you forget it," Chase told him. "Now pay attention. We're delivering you to your people. And then we're going back to ours. No more threats. No more pain. Got it?"

The kid reached behind him. He laughed as he shook his head. "And you're gonna give me back what you stole? Why? We forming an alliance? I don't think my brothers will go for that."

Chase lifted his chin to Switchblade. "Where to?"

The unarmed stranger pushed Chase off. "Why are you asking this bum where we're going?"

"Place we said we was going when we met the druggies in the woods," Switchblade answered. "Eight Mile Road."

The man leaned forward with his hands on his knees. "How do you know that?"

Switchblade pulled out his namesake weapon and poked the guy's arm. "How old are you? Nineteen? Twenty?"

"Close enough," he said. "Why?"

"I was shedding blood on Eight Mile when you was still sittin' on your mama's lap."

The man spit pink-tinged saliva on Switchblade's shoe.

"Got a tooth knocked loose?" Switchblade pushed him forward. "Go on, dragon. Lead the way."

Chase followed alongside Switch, who seemed relaxed in this tense situation. But Eight Mile Road might stir his nerves. Maybe this was a bad idea. Chase shook his head. Only it wasn't *his* idea.

After a few blocks with little conversation, they were in a different kind of Detroit. Even the midday sky seemed to darken. But something about the place was familiar. Chase scanned old brick buildings. Glass littered the street. Shattered windows. Abandoned cars.

Broken asphalt.

He reached down and rubbed his hand over the rough pavement. He'd seen it during the deep sleep following the transfusion. When he looked up, a group of men—no doubt dragons—stood before him.

"Here you go, Charlie. Welcome to Eight Mile Road," Switchblade said. And then he ducked as a bullet raged past them.

"Hold your fire," Chase yelled. "We came to help this young man home." Chase pushed the kid forward and he ran to join his people.

"They got my gun. My blade too," he told his crew.

Switchblade pulled the weapons from his jacket and tossed them to the road.

The kid lunged for his stuff. "That one's not telling you everything." He motioned to Chase. "He threw me fifty feet. Knocked me out cold."

A big man in a black leather jacket stepped forward. "You do that? Puny guy like you?"

"He's exaggerating." Chase tilted his head toward the kid. "But tell him why I took you down. Tell him how you were harassing my wife. A real man stands up for his woman."

"You mess with this man's lady?" the big one asked. "Terrell, how many times I told you to keep your mouth shut and your pants zipped?"

"It was nothing that bad," Chase said. "Or he'd be dead."

"All right, then. But he would've found his way home. So, why are you here, little man? And who's the other guy? That one looks more homegrown. You're smart to bring some muscle with you."

The kid—Terrell—laughed. "Did you hear me say he *threw* me? Last thing I remember, I was flying through the air."

The big guy socked the kid across the jaw. "Fool. You're dazed. That's all."

"Hah! Show him." Terrell circled Chase like a fly on a steak. "Show him what you did."

"I guess you got your marbles knocked loose," Chase told him. "Sorry about that." He stepped forward with Switchblade at his side. "I know the kid could've made it home on his own. But I wanted to see where he came from. And to offer him, and you, something more than life in the shadow of a government that's all but abandoned you. Something better than stealing. And killing. And dying."

The man stepped close and lowered his head to meet Chase's eyes. "We. Don't. Want. Nothing. Now go before I hurt you."

"Believe me when I say I *want* to go. But I need ten minutes. Anybody who doesn't care to listen can leave." Chase studied the seven men encircling him. "But somebody's going to stay."

The man opened his mouth and flexed his jaw. "You think so? All right. Anybody wants to stay, he can stay. I won't make nothing of it." He put his hand to Chase's shoulder and pushed him. Then he walked away. Three men followed. But Terrell and two others remained. Either out of curiosity or the call of God.

Then one of the men eased closer, pulled out a knife, and gashed the sleeve of Switchblade's jacket. He ran after the others, who were now half a block away. But he looked back once and mouthed something to Switch.

Chase started after the punk, but Switchblade grabbed his arm and held on.

"Forget it," he said. "I'm OK."

"You're bleeding." Chase ripped the sleeve loose and used it to bandage the wound.

"Do what you came here to do," Switchblade said. "I don't collect scars for nothing."

Chase shifted his eyes to the two men—Terrell and some other young hoodlum. They were waiting.

"Listen up," Switch told them with a strong voice. "This man's got something to tell you."

32

Two blocks from the Cos, Chase circled back thirty feet. He rested his hand on Switchblade's arm. "The bleeding stopped. Can you make it the rest of the way?"

"Just had to slow down a minute. You think the nano stuff bleeding out will take me down the way it does you?"

"My processors rely on the nanobots. It's not the same for you. But it's only been a couple of days since you were injured. Your body's still recovering."

"My body recovered as soon as the doctor pumped your blood into me." Switchblade threw his shoulders back and stepped up his pace. "Come on. Our two hours is about up. Don't want Melody coming after us. Girl's got a temper."

"I was about to face that wrath when you came up on us today."

"What'd you do, robot?"

"I know we said we wouldn't tell her about the transfusion, but I don't want any more secrets between us." Chase rounded the corner a block from the monstrous building.

"Let me tell her. She might love you more, but she'll yell at *me* less."

Chase laughed. "You're right. Maybe she'd go easy on me if we tell her together."

They entered through the big doors with five minutes to spare. Plenty of time to get to the command center. Chase sucked in a breath. He had to straighten the paths between the exoself and Mel's code. And he had to get the bases back online. The lack of communication between up-top believers worried him.

They exited the lift on the twentieth floor. Switch pushed the door open and entered the command center first. And it took Mel only seconds to react to the sight of his mutilated jacket and bloody arm.

"I knew something like this would happen." She ran to Switchblade and grasped his hands. "How bad are you hurt?"

"It's nothing. Just a cut."

She eyed Chase. "Tell me the truth."

He nodded, and she let go of Switchblade and threw her arms around Chase. "Are *you* all right? I've been so worried. You've got to get the screen communication working again so we won't be out of touch." She let him go and lowered her brow. "Better yet, don't go off like that again. Do you understand?"

Before he could answer, she had Switchblade by the arm, dragging him back to the lift.

"Mel? Where are you going?" Chase called after her.

"Clinic on the tenth floor. Come on."

Chase followed, and the lift headed down at Mel's command.

Switchblade leaned against the opaque wall of the lift. "Melody, we was gonna have a talk with you about some things that happened on the way to Detroit."

"First, tell me what the two of you have been doing out there *today*." She stepped close to Chase as the lift door opened. "I know you want to help people. But it's too dangerous. Please, for my sake, tell me you won't make a habit of this."

He sank into her brown eyes. But he couldn't make her any promises.

"We'll talk about this later." She walked ahead and pushed open the door to reveal a small medical facility. Several people—presumably from the underground's high-rise base—waited in blue chairs. Or maybe the place was open to everybody. Mel rushed past them and pulled Switchblade through double doors.

A woman with a stethoscope around her neck hurried toward them. "What happened?"

Mel let go of Switchblade and pushed a swinging door open. "Where's Mason?"

"The doctor's with a patient. It might be a few minutes, but I can get this man cleaned up." The woman tossed her long red braid behind her and went to work loosening the ripped sleeve. "Tell me what I'm looking at. Gunshot? Knife?"

"The latter," Switchblade told her. "It ain't bad."

She pulled the bloody tourniquet off. "Well, you're right. Lot of blood though. You'd think it'd at least need a few stitches. It's almost like…"

"Like what?" Mel asked.

"Like it's healing at a rapid pace." The nurse shrugged. "I'll tell the doctor to come take a look when he's able." She swung the door open and left them.

Mel looked from Chase to Switchblade and then set her stare on Chase. "Is that what's happening? Do I even need to ask why?"

"Mel, I was going to tell you earlier."

"We seem to be falling into a pattern of getting

caught in our secrets." She crossed her arms. "Well? Tell me what happened."

"Drone got me," Switchblade told her. "The doctor who carried us down here in her transport operated, but I kept bleeding. I wasn't happy with him when I came to."

"Mel, he was dying," Chase said. "I had to do it."

She lowered her head for a moment. "What kind of man would you be if you could save your friend and didn't?"

"I'm glad you understand." He held his arms open, and she fell into his embrace.

"But, Chase, you're pushing the limits," she said. "No more."

"Understood, boss." He rested his finger under her chin and pulled her gaze up to meet his. "Sweetheart, have you told this doctor about the baby?"

She shook her head. "Maybe while we're here together…"

Switchblade cleared his throat. "I don't need to be around for that. And since I'm self-healing, I think I'll just excuse myself." He pushed off the counter.

"Not until the doctor sees you," Mel said.

"I agree." Chase grabbed Switchblade's arm to pull him back.

The doctor entered—a rugged young guy who looked more like a cowboy. He glanced at Chase, then went straight to examining Switchblade's wound. "I heard the long-lost superhero husband and his sidekick had arrived."

"Look, doc, I'm fine," Switchblade said. "Just clean me up and I'll get out of your way."

"My nurse seems to think you don't waste any time healing. You want to tell me about it?"

"Got me some of the transhuman's blood. Not my idea, but it saved my life."

The nurse with the braid tended the wound, which now appeared to be nothing more than a scratch. Switchblade thanked her and the doctor.

"Going up to find that supply guy and get me a new jacket. And some lunch." He wadded up what was left of his old jacket and tossed it into a receptacle. "Charlie, you be OK without your sidekick for a while?"

"Yeah. But catch me later."

Switch nodded. He rested his hand on Mel's shoulder for a second before he left the room.

"So you're Chase Sterling," the doctor said. "I would have never recognized you."

"Celebrities tend to look different in person." Chase settled into a chair and pulled on Mel's hand. She sat beside him.

"Especially when they're no longer groomed for stardom," the doctor said. "You want to tell me what your friend was talking about? What's so special about your blood?"

"First, I want you to examine Melody. She's pregnant."

The doctor lifted his brows as he looked at Mel. "How long?"

"Almost three months," she answered.

"You're sure?"

She grinned. "About the timing? We were only together one night before we got separated. So yes, I'm sure."

"Well, let's get you checked out and talk about your care for the next six months."

Chase leaned forward. "Doctor—"

"Call me Mason."

"Mason, my wife probably hasn't told you everything about me."

"I know you're the government's prototype transhuman. Are you concerned about what that might mean for the baby?"

"*And* for the mother."

"I wish I could tell you. Has anything been altered other than certain internal organs and the assimilation of processors?"

"As you just found out, my blood is different—enhanced with nanobots. That may have affected other…stuff. But I can't be sure." Heat rose up Chase's neck and spilled onto his cheeks.

Mel seemed to swallow a laugh as she grasped his hand.

"I see," the doctor said. "Well…we'll just treat this like any other pregnancy. And pray."

33

Back in the command center, Chase sat next to Mel, attempting to concentrate on the task of bringing the bases online. And not on the unknowns of the baby inside her. Or the exoself's nagging about her involvement in the government's plan to unleash transhumanism. Or the fact that she seemed to be a non-issue with the Feds.

He watched her working. If Amos had recovered from his cancer, would he expect Mel to give up her post? It'd be fine with Chase. He fixed his eyes on the screen and tried once more to bring up the base in Gagnon. Chase's mother, and Amos, were likely still there.

Mel reached for him, and he took her hand and met her eyes. Her trusting, loving eyes. The Spirit inside him offered peace. Chase hoped it was enough to wipe away the exoself's mistrust.

She smiled. "How's it going? Did you reach anybody yet?"

"The trail still seems blocked." He studied the code. "It's the fourth S."

"The one that provided the most help in Quebec. It took you way beyond the scope of my initial programming. What's it getting you now?"

"Safe houses. Not much more."

Mel sighed and tapped her keypad. "Which is

what I programmed. But the exoself isn't taking you beyond the starting gate. Is that right?"

"Mel, you don't think it has anything to do with me giving blood. Do you?"

"Your processors may be readjusting. Any physical changes? You told me you've gotten stronger and I know that hasn't diminished—I saw you throw that guy fifty feet."

He titled his head in her direction. "It wasn't more than twenty feet. And no, nothing has changed as far as that goes. But..."

She swiveled in her seat and rested her hand on his arm. "What is it?"

"I feel at odds with the exoself. It's feeding me data I don't understand. It's like I've got some kind of computer virus or something. Is that possible?"

"I'm afraid so. And the loss of blood is likely the cause. I think you'll be able to compensate for it. I just don't know how long it'll take."

He let his hands fall from the keypad and drop to his lap. "I'm sorry, sweetheart. I know you were depending on me."

She combed her fingers through his hair. "Don't look so worried. I'm not."

He kissed her hand. "You need to eat something. Your blood sugar is a little low."

"Oh, OK, doctor." She grinned as she stood and pulled him out of his seat. "Come with me."

They took the lift down to the massive kitchen and dining room. It'd once been the operations floor for the conference facility that now housed the command center. They found fresh bananas grown right in the building. Mel spooned peanut butter onto hers.

Chase shook his head. "If you're going to do that, I

don't think we can keep our secret much longer."

"So let's make the announcement. In fact, I'll call a meeting tonight, and we can go over some business too. But we'll tell my brothers first."

"I talked with Brax this morning, but I haven't seen Ridge all day. Or your mother."

"Mama has laundry duty today. Ridge is probably off cavorting with criminals."

"Can't hold that against him. I did the same thing a couple of hours ago."

"Yeah, about that. How did it go?"

"The guy I *didn't* throw fifty feet answered the call, along with another young man."

She nodded. "That's wonderful. But…"

"But you don't want me to become a street preacher."

She drew her brows tight. "It scares me to think what might happen."

"'Be strong and courageous. Do not be afraid or terrified because of them, for the Lord your God goes with you; He will never leave you nor forsake you.' Deuteronomy thirty-one, six."

She dropped her spoon into a sink, leaned against the counter, and crossed her arms. "Bible-head."

He laughed and embraced her. "You're the one who put the Bible in my head."

"And now you're using it against me. You're going back. Aren't you?"

He wiped a spot of peanut butter from her bottom lip. "Probably. One day."

She eased out of his arms and lowered her eyes to the floor. "Let's go find Brax and Ridge. And Mama."

He followed her to the lift and they returned to the command center.

Chase scanned the crowded room. He'd gotten some of the up-top believers back into the system, and several people were now coordinating deliveries of supplies with groups around the world.

Ridge and Colt huddled in a corner. Mel joined them. She pulled Ridge by the arm and left Colt with a scowl on his face.

"Brax is on a run to the shelter with Finley," she told Chase. She leaned close and whispered, "He likes her."

"You're not telling him anything the rest of us don't already know," Ridge said. "They'll be back any minute. What's this about?"

"Go get Mama and wait in the lobby on the twenty-first floor. We'll bring Brax and meet you there."

Ridge huffed and headed for the lift.

"If this is a family meeting, I think we should invite Switchblade," Chase said.

"You mean your blood brother? All right. Might as well include a few old friends and let them know before the meeting tonight."

"You stay here and wait for your brother. I'll go find Switch and Leo." He kissed her softly and then took the lift to the men's dorm.

The door to Switchblade's room was cracked open, and Chase pushed it wide to find his friend kneeling at the foot of his bed.

"You OK?" Chase asked.

"Just staying prayed up."

"Mel and I are going to share the big news with her brothers and few other people. And even though you already know, we want you there. You're family."

Switch nodded as he rose off the floor. He grabbed

a glass of water from the dresser. "I'll be there. Might need me to pull Ridge off of you."

"You think he'll have a problem with it?"

"He don't like you, Charlie. Or me, for that matter."

Chase sat on the edge of the bed. "That man on Eight Mile Road—did you catch what he mouthed after he knifed you?"

"Yep. He said, 'Welcome home.'" Switchblade set the glass down.

"I'll go alone next time."

"Man, your brain needs rewiring." Switchblade paced across the room. "Where you go, I go. You ought to know that by now. Don't matter if the enemy is plotting against me. I ain't afraid of the hoods."

"Yes, you are."

"OK, I am. But I'll go afraid. You got that, robot?"

Chase smiled. "Got it. Come on, we need to find Leo. Maybe some of the ladies from Blue Sky Field."

"Anyway, can't nobody hurt me now that I've got transhuman blood."

"Yeah, about that. Earlier, when I touched your arm, I got a read on what's going on with your blood."

Switchblade lowered his brow. "Bad news?"

"Depends on how you look at it. The nanobots in my bloodstream were activated by my processors. And they're sustained the same way. But—"

"I don't got no processors. So what does it mean?"

"The nanobots in your blood are dying off. Like regular blood cells. Healing that cut ended the lifespan for most of them. The rest won't last long. I suggest you don't put yourself in a drone's sites again."

Switchblade smiled. "No plans for that, brother. I got to admit, I'm relieved. I been thinking how it is for you, knowing your blood can heal, and knowing you can't give it up. I don't want that burden."

"I understand. But I'm sorry you won't hang on to the benefits."

"We'll just go on like we have been. I watch out for you. You watch out for me."

Chase headed for the door. "You got it. Come on."

Leo was an easy find in the men's dorm. He and Chase and Switchblade braved the women's floor to find Erin and a couple others Mel could trust to help her through the next few months.

Back on the twenty-first floor, they joined Mel, her mother and brothers, and Finley. And Colt.

"What's *he* doing here?" Chase asked Mel.

"Ridge went back down for him. He thinks Colt should be included in any and all meetings."

Chase eyed Ridge, who stared back at him from a plush chair.

"People, listen up," Mel said. "Chase and I have something to tell you. We'll make an announcement at a meeting with the whole base tonight, but we wanted you to know first." She reached for Chase's hand.

"We haven't really talked about it, but I think my husband was surprised by the color wheel of my family. That's what happens when a black man from Alabama marries a brown woman from Sudan. Now Chase is part of our family."

Ridge pushed out of his chair. "Girl, did you call us all here to tell us you married a white man?"

"No. But thanks, Ridge, for pointing that out. What we wanted to tell you is that in a few months…we're going to add new shade to the wheel."

It seemed to take a moment for the colorful proclamation to settle. Finley got it first, and she squealed and threw her arms around Mel.

The other women joined the celebration. Leo slapped Chase across the back. Brax shook his head, but he smiled. Colt stood in the corner and rolled his eyes.

And Ridge plowed his shoulder into Chase's stomach and pushed him into the wall.

"Stop it!" Mel beat on her brother's back.

Chase picked up the guy, lifted him three feet off the floor, and pinned him against the wall. Chase needed only one hand against Ridge's chest to hold the jerk.

Ridge flailed his arms and kicked his legs. "Put me down, you fool, and let me finish beating the crap out of you." He clawed at Chase's arm. "Let me go!"

Laughter filled the room. Even Colt seemed to find his cohort's predicament amusing. But Mama Sameea was not happy, and soon Mel put on a more serious face.

"OK, baby, put him down," she said.

"Not until he apologizes. This was supposed to be a happy moment and he ruined it."

"Seriously. Put him down." She pulled on Chase's free arm. "Nothing was ruined. We all had a good laugh." She chuckled again.

"Not until he apologizes," Chase said. "Say you're sorry."

"I'm not sorry," Ridge yelled.

"I can do this all day." Chase pushed a little harder into Ridge's sternum.

Ridge's eyes opened wide as he pried at Chase's hand. "I'm sorry!"

Chase let go, and Ridge fell to the floor. Mel knelt next to him as laughter filled the lobby.

"We accept your apology. But don't mess with my husband." She looked at Chase and grinned, and he helped her up.

Ridge pushed off the floor and flexed his arms. "Congratulations," he said with a tone that denied the sentiment.

"Thanks, brother." Chase held out his hand, but Ridge only huffed before he got on the lift with Colt.

"I think that went well," Chase said, and they all laughed again. Even Sameea managed a gentle smile, and her brown eyes sparkled.

34

Mel spent a frustrating afternoon at her station. Chase sat across from her, anxious for the day to end. Despite the joy of being reunited with some of the believers from Blue Sky Field, what Chase needed now was a reconnection to the elusive program designed to bring the Underground Church together. But the exoself seemed hesitant. And accusatory. And uncooperative. Because of a computer virus?

He surveyed the command center. All these people had one mission—to live in safety. Even if it was practically in plain sight in this ridiculous building. Was he the only one who felt the call to forget about safety and remember the people on the outside? They needed the ultimate transfusion.

"What people?" Mel asked.

Chase met her questioning eyes.

"You said something about the people who need a transfusion."

"I did?" Chase tapped his fingers on the workstation.

"You can't even think about that," she said. "You are not the answer to the world's health problems. If it's meant to be, Fiender and his kind will advance the technology and make it readily available. But I won't let you sacrifice yourself."

"That's not the kind of transfusion..." He shook his head. "I was just thinking about the people here in

Detroit and all over the world who need the blood of Christ. He's the One who made the sacrifice. I might not be able to share my blood, but I can share His."

She stared into his eyes for a moment. "You're right, of course. But my job is to lead this base—all of the bases—to a safe existence. Maybe when I've accomplished that, I can think about the rest of the world. For now, *this* is my world."

"This will never be a safe world, Mel. You and I might be able to bring it all online, but safety is no guarantee. I gave up on that when they wiped out our people in Quebec."

Her chin trembled, and Chase reached for her hand.

"There's a lot I can do," he told her. "And even though I know I'm called—and programmed—to serve the church, there's a greater calling."

"To reach the lost?" She squeezed his hand.

"Yes." He wiped a tear from her cheek.

"Then you won't mind if I come with you on your next little mission trip."

He'd been had. He pushed back in his rolling chair and crossed his arms. And smiled. "I'll just get back to work on reestablishing the code."

She grinned. "You do that."

He returned his attention to the computer at his side. But he didn't need it. Data flowed through the exoself from church houses around Detroit. "Mel?"

"What is it?"

"Things are coming together. For a town that purposefully went dark and rid themselves of technology, there seems to be a lot of computer activity going on around us."

She rolled her chair near Chase. "When I told the

people to get ready to utilize the program, they pulled out old equipment they'd turned off. I was surprised so many of them kept their computers. It's old technology, but it'll work." She tapped a few keys on the pad in front of Chase. "This is great—the program is reconnecting."

"I've got the group in National City connected to several others nearby. As far as Toronto—a base is still functioning there after all. It's happening quickly now."

She grasped his arm and smiled. "See—nothing to worry about. But are you OK? You're a little pale."

"All of the Northwest Territory is on now. I don't think it'll be long until…" Chase opened his eyes wide and reached for Mel.

"Baby, we can take it slow."

"I have no control." Data crammed his head with so many information trails that he couldn't follow them all. He pressed his fingers into his temples. "I can't…"

"The exoself will do as you instruct it. Tell it to stop."

Chase came out of his chair. Others in the room were now watching him. He couldn't allow the thoughts attacking him to be spoken in this room. He grabbed Mel's arm and pulled her from the station and out of the command center. Then he pushed her into the lift. And he spoke the command that a few hours earlier would only respond to *her* voice. "Eighty-nine."

The lift began its ascent.

"Chase, how did you do that?"

"The exoself and the supercomputer are interacting. It knows me now. It'll tell me what I want to know."

"What do you want to know?" She pulled away.

Was she afraid of him? At the moment, he was afraid of himself. The exoself shared data with the computer of the eighty-ninth floor, as well as with a number of bases around the Western Republic.

The lift door disappeared. Chase stepped out. Mel followed. He grasped her trembling hands. "I want to know why you are not considered a threat. I want to know how you got away in Toronto. And I want to know why you set up the world headquarters of the Underground Church in a building where you once designed the components for...for what they did to me." He was aware of his tone, and he drew a breath and spoke softly. "This place is not safe. It's a trap. And I need to know if you're the reason we ended up here."

She bit her bottom lip as tears streamed down her face. "I told you what they were doing here made me sick, and by the grace of God I managed to get out." She did not try to control *her* tone. "I didn't have a clue you were the one they'd practice their technology on. They didn't put us together, Chase. God did. I didn't put us in this building. The base was already picked and occupied when I got to Detroit. As far as not being on the WR hit list...I don't know. *You* tell *me*. You're the one with data in your head." She backed away, arms crossed, eyes filled with fire. "After everything we've been through, I can't believe you'd question me like this. I'm calling off the meeting tonight."

He breathed hard, staring at her. The Spirit was calling him away from this anger and confusion. But the exoself was leading him away from *her*. No reason to question which voice he should trust. "Something's wrong with me, Melody. I love you. Fix me. Please."

35

The door between them and the massive computer opened at her command. The anger that had nearly overtaken him subsided as he prayed aloud. "God, You made me. Even the manmade parts came about by Your hands. And the love of this woman came by Your good will. I pray she'll forgive me."

Mel stopped and drew him into her embrace. And even though he couldn't let go of the questions bombarding his mind, he held her close.

"Come on," she said at last. "Up on the table. I'll try to adjust the sensors, but I really don't know what to do. Keep praying."

"I am. I trust you. I hope you know that."

She drew her brows tight and attached the magnet-like electrodes to his temples. But she didn't meet his eyes.

"Mel." He grabbed her arm until she looked at him.

"I know. Just lie still."

He relaxed his shoulders. Code flashed on the nearest monitor. More bases came online. He sent a message to the leader at the base in Gagnon: *If my mother is still there, tell her I'm alive.*

A code traveled through his sensors and he determined the number of bases in the EU had declined. And the number of believers taken into custody had increased. He closed his eyes and left the trail of Mel's programming to catch a line from the WR. He hadn't been able to touch this information before. Even now it came encrypted, but he quickly unlocked it and found the number of dead sacrificed to Bloodless. And the names. Over half the believers brought in during the most recent raids were dead. Their bodies discarded, their brains sealed inside their heads and sent to laboratories for research that would lead to more godless technology.

Chase had not been allowed to carry the world into a transhuman future. God would deal with this too. He breathed in and let peace wash over the doubts still pulling at him. "Death, where is your sting?"

Mel brushed the hair back from his forehead. "Stay with me. I need you. Our son needs you."

"You don't know if it's a boy or a girl." Chase grabbed her hand and kissed it.

"Yes, I do. You'll see. Now I don't want to hear any more talk of death."

"I wasn't speaking of my own death. Although it no longer scares me. People are dying. I'm getting reports from all over the world. Bases are being overturned and believers are—"

"I don't want to hear this right now."

Chase closed his eyes as orders sent out by his own processors lined up with WR data. He'd kept the men at Ep's compound from being discovered. He'd erased any suspicion of a base in National City. But farther back—weeks ago—the exoself had achieved tasks Chase knew nothing about. Everything was clear now. The connection to the underground spread far and the intel flowed freely. This beast of a computer had made sense of the tangled code inside the mind of a transhuman. He opened his eyes wide and yanked the electrodes from his temples.

"Chase, what are you doing? If I can't read your output—"

"It was me. I'm the reason you're not on the list. The exoself wiped your record clean. You're not an issue with the WR because I took you off the grid. I even concocted a release for you and the others in Toronto."

"But you didn't know we'd been picked up."

"The exoself never gave up on tracking you. When your DNA scan went into a data feed, I—the exoself—cleared the way for you. As far as the WR is concerned, you've been transferred from your office in NYC to a roving support system. You're still working for the Feds. The report stated the people with you in Toronto were in your custody to be delivered to the center in Grand Rapids."

"All this happened without your knowledge? I don't understand. What about the fact that I never showed up in Grand Rapids?"

"The exoself changed the report. It's like you never got stopped at all."

She shook her head. "That's impossible."

"It's a relief; that's what it is. I'm so sorry I didn't trust you. Please tell me you forgive me. I have to know you—"

"There is nothing to forgive. It wasn't your fault."

"The confusion in my head is clearing. The entire underground—what's left of it—is online. And the doubts are gone." He dropped his feet to the floor and held his wife. "But there's one thing."

"Tell me. Don't hold back."

"When I said this place isn't safe, I meant it. The WR has big plans for Detroit."

36

After an evening spent hacking the intel of an increasingly hostile government, Chase and Mel left for their room. The announcement about the baby could wait. Others stayed in the command center, latching onto WR feeds. And planning. And praying. As for Chase, the awful day had worn him down. He'd sleep tonight.

Except that he'd mentally and verbally attacked the woman he loved. Practically called her a traitor. How could they go on with this between them?

She remained silent on the quick trip up a floor. He pushed the door open, and she went in and simply dropped at the edge of the bed. Her feet on the floor, her hands on her knees. Her head down. She must be exhausted too. And so hurt. Even though she said she understood.

But how could she? Within twenty-four hours of their reunion, he'd accused her of horrible things. Then taken it all back when his processors lined up. When he recovered from...a computer virus? How could any woman tolerate that kind of drama? Chase had hesitated in the snowbound woods so Mel wouldn't have to live like this. Now here he was hurting her again.

He fell to his knees at her feet and brushed the hair back from her face. Then he slid his arms around her hips and dropped his head to her lap. And wept.

"Baby, you can't fall apart," she said. "I know it looks bad, but we've got some time before the Feds move in. We'll be OK." She combed her fingers through his hair. "As long as we're together."

"That's what worries me—the being together. I can't believe the way I treated you. I'm so afraid…"

"Afraid of what?"

"Of everything I touch turning to disaster." He lifted his head and searched her eyes. "Tell me you forgive me. That you still love me."

She clutched his biceps, and he came up on his knees. She kissed him again and again. "I told you there's nothing to forgive."

"Just tell me."

"I forgive you." She ran her hands down his back and whispered, "And I'll show you how much I love you. But I won't let you leave me, Chase. Never again."

Part II

37

"Listen up, people. This man's got something to tell you." Switchblade stepped back.

Chase faced the crowd on Eight Mile Road. Over a hundred today. The largest number in the four months he'd been speaking here. Men and women. Old and young. They packed the street, the walkways, and the abandoned storefronts. A girl no more than eighteen stood in front of Chase, holding a baby close to her chest.

What kind of place was this awful city for bringing up children? Soon he'd find out for himself.

A band of supporters waited with Switchblade. Leo and Brax. Terrell and a few others from the neighborhood who'd joined the family of believers inhabiting the Cos. Like he always did, Chase knelt to rub his hand over the broken pavement he'd first seen in a dream. Or whatever it was. And then he spoke.

"My first time on Eight Mile, I faced a group of seven men. Five walked away. Two believed. Today most of you will walk away. But some will believe. I don't know when my last trip to Eight Mile Road will be. If not today, then soon. It won't be long before I leave this city. And listen to me when I say that *you* need to get out too. The WR is luring the ousted, people from all religions, and dissenters to Detroit. Rumors carry promises of safety. Of relative freedom from Federal forces. But it's an illusion. And I can't stop what's coming."

Chase faced the cloudy sky. How could he tell these poor people they were about to be exterminated? They had no place else to go.

"But that's not why I'm here. Today I want to tell you—"

The exoself sparked, and Chase looked up again. A drone flew within a quarter mile. No, it wasn't one but four drones moving in on Chase's crime-ridden, impoverished mission field.

"Everybody run. Get inside," Chase yelled. "Now!"

Switchblade grabbed Chase and dragged him into an alcove. The rest of their team followed. People in the street scattered as the drones came into view.

"We're under the shield, but I can't cover all these people," Chase said. Before the drones could fire, he brought them to the ground. Right into the crowd. He pulled away from Switch and rushed into the chaos.

A young Asian man cried out, his leg pinned by a length of smoking poly-resin. Chase pulled the shard loose. The poor kid wailed as Chase came out of his own shirt and wrapped it around the wound.

Brax rushed in, blood on his hands.

"Are you hurt?" Chase asked.

"Nope—not my blood. Don't think anybody's hurt too bad."

"We let the crowd get too big."

"How'd they know?" Brax asked. "And how'd

they get here so fast?"

"I wasn't monitoring satellite feeds. Guess I should've been. Feds saw a crowd and sent the drones to break it up. As for how they got here so quickly, they were obviously close by. Which can only mean one thing."

"They're moving in."

"We've got to get back to the base. But I can't leave these people like this."

The man with Chase's shirt wrapped around his leg spoke up. "If you want to help us, you need to keep yourself out of danger. Go. Before more drones show."

"He's right, Charlie," Switchblade called from the middle of the street. "We'll send a team back with supplies. I'm getting you out of here."

With his hand on the injured man's head, Chase prayed. Fast. Then he rose and followed his people away from the failed mission. Except for Terrell and his buddy, who stayed behind to help.

"Won't be any more drones," Chase told the others as they hurried back toward the Cos. "I hacked the feed. Long story short, nobody will miss them."

"How many more times can you lie us out of trouble?" Switchblade asked.

Chase's spirit sank. He was a liar. A good one. If there was such a thing. But what choice was there? "As many times as I have to." He attempted to wipe the blood and dirt from his bare arms, but it only smeared. Mel couldn't see him like this. She couldn't know.

Too late.

She'd entered a message into his processors through her computer.

Chase, we know about the drones. Report is they left the area. Is that true, or did you take them down? Tell me you're all right.

"Sometimes I wish I hadn't reconstructed the screen communication for my bride." Chase slowed a bit.

"She comin' down on you already, robot? Might as well talk to her. I mean…think at her. Or whatever you do."

"Yeah. I'm thinking."

I'm fine, sweetheart. No one seriously injured. But send a med crew their way. I didn't expect this. I got sloppy.

Just get home. I'll send the crew out.

"Mel's sending help," Chase said. "We'll meet them on the way."

Brax stopped at a spigot near the cemetery and washed his hands. "I can't believe the way you brought down the drones. Never thought I'd get a chance to see that."

Switchblade watched the street. And the sky. "You ain't seen nothin'. He can blow up a man's brain if there's an NP in his ear."

Brax reached up and scratched his ear. "A what?"

Chase bent and cupped his hands beneath the spigot. "Neuro-prosthesis. WR is planting them in cops and Feds to control their behavior. I've got one myself, but nobody can program it but me. And Mel, maybe."

"Don't think I want to see you blow up a brain," Brax said. "Leo and I will go back with the med crew. No reason this day has to be a total waste."

"You're right," Chase said. "In fact—"

Chase Sterling, don't you dare think about going back. You get to the Cos ASAP.

"That's a good idea," Chase said. "I'd go with you, but your sister says I have to go home now."

Brax laughed as Chase washed himself with the

tepid water.

Before they got too much farther, a crew with medical supplies approached. The nurse with the long red braid slung a towel at Chase, and he dried his arms. Then she threw him a T-shirt.

"Thanks, Dani."

"Yep." She didn't even look at Chase. But she circled Switchblade. "You OK, big guy?"

"Good as gold. I'd come with you, but…"

"I know. Get him back to the Cos so his wife's blood pressure will go down. It's not good for the baby."

Chase popped his head out of the top of the tight shirt. "Mel's…I've gotta go." He ran ahead.

"Hey, slow down," Switchblade yelled after him.

But he didn't. He was in the lobby at the Cosimo in less than two minutes. His best time yet. Before he could get to the lift, Switchblade called after him.

"Charlie, for cryin' out loud."

Chase swung around to find Switch bent over and huffing.

"I know your evolution's got you running like the wind now, but I can't watch out for you if I can't keep up with you."

Chase bounced on his feet. "Sorry. Come on."

They entered the lift. "Twenty," Chase said.

"You sure there ain't gonna be no more drones today?"

"I don't think so. But I'm not sure of anything."

The door dissolved, and Chase hurried into the command center. Mel sat at her station, a crowd circling her. Some of them were new at the Cos—up-top believers from the city who'd moved in to help prepare for what was coming.

Mel jumped from her seat when she saw Chase. Her eyes had that look—hellfire and brimstone. She grabbed Chase by the hand and pulled him from the room.

He hoped to find people in the hallway. She wouldn't yell in front of them. Good—two men. Newcomers. But they wasted no time stepping into the lift when Mel crossed her arms over the top of her round belly.

"Mel, I—"

She threw her arms around him and held on tight. "I know. You didn't expect them to be so near. Just tell me you're OK. And tell me you won't go out there again. Please, Chase."

He wove his fingers into her hair and kissed her. "I'm OK."

"And?"

"One more trip to Eight Mile Road. Just one. Then I won't leave this building until we're prepared to leave for good."

"And when will that be?" She pushed away. "I've been running data from your WR feeds. They're still throwing out bait to lure people in. They've got drones so close they can break up an impromptu meeting. And they're taking a census. How long are we going to stay here, Chase? And when we leave, where are we going?"

"I know they're counting. Categorizing."

"People are coming into Detroit daily. Not so many believers, because we've warned them. But we can't—"

"We can't save everybody." Chase grasped her hands. "We can't save *anybody*. Molly taught me that. And you told me too." He pulled her to his chest, closed his eyes, and breathed in her sweet scent. "Your blood pressure is one-forty over ninety. Come on, you're taking a nap. I'll stay with you." He led her to the lift.

"No. I've got so much to do."

"Plenty of people taking charge in the command center. Nobody will miss you for an hour."

"Chase, I am the leader of the—"

"And I'm your husband. And you're taking a nap. The world's not going to end in the next hour. If it does, you can just sleep through it." He pushed her into the lift.

She crossed her arms again. And grinned. "Oh, yes, sir. I submit to your authority."

"Smart lady." He kissed her and ran his hands down her arms. "Twenty-one," he said to the lift.

"You'll stay with me?" She returned the kiss.

"Yes, Mel. We're going to our room for a *nap*." He lost himself in her eyes.

He didn't tell her the exoself just reported a caravan of WR transits had stopped in Ann Arbor. On their way to Detroit.

38

Three days later, the Feds hadn't progressed past Ann Arbor. Alone in his bed before sunrise, Chase tried to determine the WR's next move. They had set up a temporary center in the same industrial complex where the Negotiator stored his model airplanes. No report they'd brought the Bloodless execution device with them. Three scouts who'd entered Detroit didn't stay long. Their vague reports gave little information, except to note the WR wouldn't carry out their plan until a larger number of dissenters had established operations in the city.

Dissenters were arriving by the hour.

Recent entries gave no indication the Feds had a clue the international headquarters of the Underground Church filled several floors of the Cosimo. The scouts had checked the people-mover stations. The cemetery. They'd shut down the shelter on Division. But they didn't come near the superscraper. Was the exoself planting false information again?

"Or are we hiding by the grace of God?"

Rising from the tangled sheets, he stretched his arms. Another sweet night with Mel curled up at his side made it hard to believe this wasn't paradise. He'd discovered her rhythmic breathing and the warmth of her skin against his enabled him to power down, to be lulled to sleep. And he functioned better with more sleep. Like any man would.

But this morning, when he opened his eyes, Mel wasn't beside him. He pulled on jeans and a shirt, straightened the hair that had grown nearly to his shoulders, and brushed his teeth. A message to Mel's screen com got no reply, so he headed for the lift.

He found her alone in the command center, studying a holographic display of the city. The computer at her station still blinked his message. Coming behind her, he eased his arms around her waist, rested his hands on her stomach, and kissed her neck.

She reached up and wrapped her hand around the back of his head. "Don't do that unless you want to go back to bed."

"Maybe I do."

Her soft laugh filled him with promise. With a deeper sense of belonging than he'd ever known.

"How's he doing in there?" Mel asked with a pat to her belly.

"He, or she, has a good right punch. That's about all I know."

"You know it's a boy." She swiveled in his embrace.

"Even if I knew, I wouldn't tell you."

"Oh, you're a bad transhuman." She lifted up on her toes and kissed him.

"Your enzymes are a little high. Do you feel all right?"

"I feel great. I'm sure it's nothing."

"I'm sending a message to Mason's computer."

She rested her hands on his shoulders. "Don't do that. If it keeps up, I'll let him know."

"I already did."

She shook her head. "Can you really access every system in the building now?"

"The progression of—"

"Of the transhuman. I know. The student surpassing the teacher and all that."

"Oh yeah? Come on. Teach me something I don't know." He pulled her closer and kissed her deeply.

The door swung open, and Chase met the timid smiles of two women and a blushing young man.

"Good morning," Chase said. "We were just..." He took Mel's hand. "We're going to get some breakfast." He pulled her to the door. "Carry on," he told them as he pulled Mel into the hall.

She laughed again and wrapped her arm around his waist.

"I saw you picking at your oatmeal yesterday." Chase stepped into the lift. "Morning sickness?"

"No. But nothing tastes good."

The hyper lift took them down, where a warm breakfast waited. Chase force-fed Mel eggs and toast. She seemed to struggle swallowing each bite.

But when he touched her, he found the enzyme levels had already returned to near normal. Must be the pregnancy messing with her body. And her appetite.

He'd dismissed the matter until Dani came by their table with a small white bag. She sat beside Mel.

"Mason sent me to draw some blood," she said.

Mel rolled her eyes at Chase. "See what you've done?" She turned to Dani. "I'm fine."

"Do as you're told," Chase said.

"Oh, all right, but not at the breakfast table." She kissed Chase on the cheek before standing. "At least I won't have to eat any more of those bland eggs."

He kissed her hand before she followed Dani out of the dining hall. Switchblade entered as the ladies departed, and he brushed against Dani's arm before sliding into the seat Mel had left empty.

"What's up with the medical bag?" Switch asked. "Melody ain't sick. Is she?"

"No. Just some bloodwork. What's with you and Dani?" Chase smiled.

"Too soon to tell, brother. But we might be spendin' some time together."

"Good for you. Remember what you told me a few months ago?"

"What's that?"

"You said, 'Grab all the comfort you can.' So take your own advice. And court the pretty nurse."

"Pretty, huh?" Switchblade's eyes seemed to light. "I'm surprised you noticed. I ain't never seen you take your eyes off Melody since you first got to Blue Sky Field."

A strange combination of gratitude and fear met in Chase's heart. "I still can't believe she's mine. I couldn't handle all this madness without her. If I had my way—"

The exoself sparked, and Chase jumped out of his seat.

"I know that look," Switchblade said. "What's wrong?"

39

"Bloodless." Chase headed out the door.

Switchblade followed. "Here?"

"Ann Arbor."

"Close enough."

The lift took them back to the command center, where Chase activated the holograph, and in an instant the warehouses in Ann Arbor rose up from the black table.

"I'm dissolving the walls." Chase walked around the display. The white and gray buildings appeared to break into bits of code and fall away like rain.

Four of the warehouses teemed with activity. Computers. Men and women in blue and green WR garb.

From a truck, the device came down a ramp. Lined up in the alley between the warehouses were six prison transports. And an odd-shaped, oversized self-drive marked Cryo-Eugenics. Super-cold storage for brain tissue to be used in the improvement of the human race.

Chase scanned the area, locking on to Vpads and catching the Feds' communication. They'd isolated an organized group of Dissenters of the Republic in Ann Arbor and they were bringing them in.

"No underground base there," Chase said. "Fifty-two up-top believers. I'm sending out a call. They need to get out."

"To where?" Switchblade asked. "You bringin' 'em to the Cos? We're trying to get people *out* of Detroit."

"For now, I don't see that we have any choice."

"I'll get us a couple of trucks. But Melody ain't never gonna let you near that place."

Chase looked up from the display. "I've already got the trucks coming. We'll let Mel decide who should go. You and I will sit this one out."

"Girl's got you wrapped tight. Thank God." Switchblade shook his head. "Maybe she'll send Colt."

Chase grinned. "Leo knows the route. But yeah, it might do the Cosimo king good to face a little danger. I think Mel would agree—he's been driving her crazy lately. Thinks she needs a six-month maternity leave. Starting yesterday."

"Send Ridge along too. That boy needs some humblin'."

"Not sure Mel would go for that." He circled the display again. "It shouldn't be too hard to get the trucks in and get our people out. I only wish…"

"You wish you could get the dissenters out. They're in God's hands, brother. You gotta let 'em go."

"I know. We've got to keep the believers safe for as long as we can."

Others joined them to view the events unfolding in 3D. Mel entered and rushed to Chase's side.

"What are we looking at?" she asked.

"Warehouses in Ann Arbor," Chase told her. "Where you met Briggs. I'll explain later. Right now, we need to send a rescue team. Got two trucks coming to bring in fifty-two believers."

"Chase, you are not—"

He grasped her hands. "It's your call, boss. I suggest sending Leo. He knows the town. And three others. Two men in each truck. But like I said...you decide."

She exhaled. "All right. Leo can pick himself a tag-along. And...Colt can drive the other truck. He needs a trip out into the real world."

Chase glanced at Switchblade. "He'll want Ridge to go with him."

Mel drew her brows tight. "I won't stand in the way. It'll do him good. But don't tell Mama I approved."

The trucks arrived within half an hour. Leo secured a Vpad and a laser weapon. And a guy named Sam, who'd been at the Cos for nearly a month. He knew some of the up-tops in Ann Arbor. Colt balked, but when Chase insulted his pride, he agreed to go. Of course he called on Ridge, who didn't hesitate.

Chase took Ridge aside in the parking garage. "Your sister wasn't sure about this but decided you'd do a fine job bringing our people in." Chase grabbed Ridge's hand and shook it firmly. "Don't let her down."

"I'm surprised the all-powerful Chase Sterling is staying behind."

"I'll be monitoring. Keeping you a step ahead of the Feds."

Ridge slung a satchel over his shoulder. "Don't bother. I'm armed and ready. We got this."

40

The trucks rolled out. With both prayer and data flowing through him, Chase returned to the command center.

"They're meeting behind an abandoned campus on Huron River Drive," he told the support team surrounding him at Mel's station. "Looks like the word spread to all the up-tops in the area. Turns out there were a few more than we thought—sixty-seven will join us."

He found Finley in the crowd and motioned to her. "We'll need another floor for space. I know it's a lot to ask—"

"I'm on it." She smiled and rushed out of the room.

Sameea waited against the wall. Her arms crossed. Her eyes moist.

Mel sat next to Chase, typing on her keypad. She slanted her eyes toward him. "We're out of beds. I'm afraid our hotel is overbooked."

"We'll make do. Plenty of blankets and more than enough food. And we won't be here long."

"How long?" She dropped her hands from the keypad and faced him. The warrior glow seemed to fade from her eyes. And fear took its place.

He touched her cheek. "Don't be afraid."

Even as he said it, panic flooded his mind. The

exoself reported her enzyme levels had spiked again. Deep inside, the Spirit repeated his own words.

Don't be afraid.

He managed a smile and brushed his thumb across her cheek. "Ten minutes to the rendezvous point."

With no screen communication in the trucks and the old radios retired to storage, Chase relied on VPads programmed to come through the speaker at Mel's computer.

"Leo, Colt, listen up. Four WR surveillance vehicles are posted at the next intersection," he said. "Take a right and then drive two blocks before you get back on Huron River."

"Will do," Leo answered.

"I don't see anything," Colt said.

"Trusting your limited view of what's ahead will get you caught," Chase told him. "Take the next right."

A pause. Then, "I'm turning."

"Follow Leo," Chase said. "And try to keep up."

Fifteen minutes later, the displaced believers were loaded into the trucks. "Take the same detour back," Chase told the drivers. "Feds are still parked."

With both trucks headed out of Ann Arbor, he breathed a sigh. Ten minutes passed as those gathered in the command center celebrated the victory. He joined Sameea, who'd relaxed a bit now that her son was on the way back.

"Whose idea was this?" she asked Chase. "Yours, or my daughter's?"

Chase smiled. "It was Colt's idea." He lowered his eyes. "But I knew Ridge would be his pick. And Mel knew too. So, I guess we're all to blame."

"I cannot blame any of you for his comings and

goings. This life is filled with danger and my son runs straight into it."

"He'll be home soon." Chase squeezed her hand.

Leo's voice came through, and everyone hushed.

"We got separated. Colt's not responding."

Chase rejoined Mel at the computer. "I'm tracking his VPad," he said as the exoself marked the location. "Three blocks back. Not moving. And the Feds are coming up behind them."

"Should I—?"

"No. Continue to head east. I'll see what I can do."

Mel sprang out of her chair. "They'll get picked up. All those people. My brother."

Chase redirected the connection. "Colt, what's your status? Answer me."

A long pause. "I...ran a light trying to keep up with Leo. And I hit a car."

"Is the truck operational?"

"Front end is smashed. We're stuck."

"Emergency vehicles have been dispatched. Along with Federal agents. You've got three minutes. Get those people out of the truck and tell them to scatter."

"You're kidding. I can't—"

"Now, Colt. Don't waste time thinking about it."

Dead silence.

Ridge's voice came over the speaker. "He bolted." His voice grew louder, his breathing heavy. "There's a wooded park just ahead. I'm getting people out of the truck." He stayed on the VPad while shouting directions. "Go! Go!"

"Got a few injured from the crash," he yelled into the VPad. "They'll never make it."

Mel leaned on her station. "Ridge, you need to get out of there. Run."

"Not until I've got these people off the street."

"Ridge!"

WR sirens blasted though the speaker. And then the connection dropped.

"Dear God, help them," she prayed aloud. "I sent my brother off to get caught."

Chase pushed out of his chair and eased Mel into hers. He knelt in front of her.

"Listen to me. I will find him. I'll bring him back."

"You didn't tell me what was going on at the warehouses. Tell me now." Her breath came in short gasps.

"Melody, you need to stay calm."

"Tell me!"

He grasped her shaking hands. "They've got prisoner transports. They're bringing in dissenters."

"And?"

He couldn't lie. Not to her.

"And they've got Bloodless."

"And my brother just got picked up." Tears filled her eyes.

"We don't know that. Either way, I'm going after him."

"So I can lose you too? No. You're not leaving me."

"If I had gone to begin with…This is my fault. I'm going."

She closed her eyes. "God, help me. Show me what to do." Tears streamed off her cheeks and found Chase's hands. At last, she nodded.

41

Mel's mother led her from the command center, and Chase let her go. He'd find her before he left the Cos. When the truck returned, he and Switchblade would drive it back to Ann Arbor.

No, it'd be too conspicuous after recent events. They needed to blend in. Chase messaged the truck's owner through the four Ss. The guy wasn't too happy to hear he'd lost a vehicle. But after some convincing, he agreed to send Chase an old car.

If the scattered believers could be rounded up again, the truck would return after dark to retrieve them. For now, Chase and Switch needed to meld into the city. Plenty of old cars in the area. And they'd have enough space to bring Ridge home. Maybe Colt, if he surfaced.

"Nah. Let him find his own way back."

"You havin' second thoughts?" Switchblade sat beside him. "We was foolish to trust this job to amateurs. Now we gotta go clean up their mess and find your bro-in-law. Can't leave him out there alone."

"I was talking about Colt." Chase moved to the holograph. "But it was just a thought."

"Not a bad thought."

"Yes, it was. We'll try to find him. Hopefully, we won't have to go anywhere near those warehouses."

"Amen to that, brother."

"I've got a car coming. Less attention that way. Should be here about the same time Leo gets back. I'll go find my wife before I go. If she'll see me."

"Hah. I'll see you in the garage if she lets go of you."

Chase headed for the lift. "Twenty-one," he said.

No sign Mel had been in their room. He passed Finley in the hall.

"Have you seen Melody?" he asked.

"Just saw her in the kitchen when I went to check our food supply. We've got plenty of—"

Chase was down the hall before she could finish. He took the lift to the kitchen. But no Mel.

He returned to the twentieth floor. Before he entered the command center, he received a message through the exoself. Not from Mel's screen com—Chase knew the imprint when she contacted him through her computer. This was different.

Chase, respond if I'm getting through.

I'm here, sweetheart. Where are you?

Eighty-nine. I wanted to be alone. I can't say goodbye to you again. Go with my love and prayers.

Mel, what is this? I feel like you're in my head.

Switchblade came out of the command center and slapped Chase across the back. "We need to get moving. Leo's in the garage with thirty-five new residents. And our car is ready to roll."

Chase hesitated.

"Now, Charlie. Come on." Switchblade was in the lift.

"Yeah, OK. I'm coming."

Mel, I wanted to see you before I left. To hold you. But I've got to go. I love you forever. I'll be back before you know it.

I love you forever. I'll go back down to the command center in a few minutes and get on the screen com. And I'll see you soon.

"Charlie, what's with the glazed look on your face? You all right?"

"Uh…yeah. Mel's in my head."

Mel, can you hear…sense everything I think and say?

No, baby. I'm intercepting thoughts you direct through the exoself into this data feed. I'd stay with you like this if I could, but they'll need me downstairs.

"Yeah, I know she's on your mind," Switchblade said.

"No, you don't get it. She's on the eighty-ninth floor. I'm guessing she's hooked herself to that monster computer. And we're communicating through the exoself without using the screen com."

Switch shook his head. "Bible says you two are one flesh, but…I hope she can handle it."

"What do you mean?" Chase stepped out of the lift into the garage.

"I mean we're driving an old coupe into a hornets' nest. And we don't know how bad we're gonna get stung."

Chase and Switchblade greeted the refugees from Ann Arbor. A few families with small children. Some older people. But there was no time for getting acquainted.

A 2014 blue sedan waited next to the truck. Keys in the ignition. Full tank. Chase took the driver's seat. It'd been a long time since he'd driven an old car.

Mel, are you still there?

Yes. Are the new folks here?

Headed up now.

Then I'd better go. Redirect to the screen com program.

OK. I hope you haven't stuck wires in your pretty head.
No, I decided to go wireless.

Chase laughed as he drove out of the garage.

Switchblade loaded a pistol. "What's so funny?"

"I love that girl."

"Is she still in your head?"

"Not anymore. She's on her way to meet the new residents."

"You know which road to take to get us to the highway?"

"Yeah. I've got a computer in my brain." Chase eased into the right lane and turned at the corner.

"Right. Sorry. Little nervous, I guess."

"Hard to believe you'd be scared of anything after you faced your demons on Eight Mile. They respect you now."

Switchblade let down his window and breathed in. "Didn't say I was scared. Still got one demon eyeing me though."

"The one who knifed you. I saw him on the fringes of the crowd the other day. I wonder what he's thinking."

"Don't much care as long as he keeps his distance." Switchblade let his arm hang out the window. "Anyway, we got enough to worry about today."

"Yeah. Pray through it. I need you to stay sharp." Chase sent a message to the screen com. "Mel must still be with the new people. She's not answering me."

"Girl can get inside your head, but she can't shoot straight. Fourth lesson a couple days ago and she still couldn't hit the side of a barn."

"Doesn't matter. I don't want her firing a gun anyway."

"Might come a day she needs to protect herself. Or somebody else."

The conversation waned as they headed out of the city. Chase slowed as he took the exit for Ann Arbor.

The town seemed deserted. Chase followed the map in his head to the street where Colt crashed the borrowed truck. Somebody'd hauled it off. Plenty of broken glass remained on the pavement. A wooded area skirted a park. This would be where Ridge sent the believers running for their lives. Chase scanned the place for heat imprints. No sign of life. Nothing but silence in Mel's programs.

"The up-tops aren't communicating. I don't know where to look." He scanned the nearest buildings. Movement in a window on the second story above a storefront caught his eye.

"Data indicates that building's been empty for years. But somebody's in there. I'm going up." Chase headed across the street.

"Probably transients. They won't have nothing to say."

"We've got to start somewhere. Come on."

They found a dark staircase in the back of the unlocked old store, where a few dresses still hung on racks. Shoeboxes littered the floor.

Chase followed Switch up the stairs and through a doorway. "Hello. We mean you no harm."

No answer.

Switchblade circled the empty room before stopping at the window. "People 'round here got to be scared to death with the Feds moving in. I don't see how we're gonna find Ridge. He ain't gonna be walking the streets."

Chase spotted a door and eased it open. Inside the

small closet, a child sat on the floor. Knees pulled up. Head down.

Chase knelt and touched the child's auburn hair.

The little head jerked up as the child backed against the wall. And screamed.

"Hey, hey, it's all right. I'm not going to hurt you," Chase said over the cries.

"I want my mommy!"

Short, unkempt hair. Tattered clothes—a little boy's clothes. Chase held his arms open. "Come out and I'll help you find her."

The boy hushed. He swiped his hand across his nose and stared. And then he crawled forward and let Chase scoop him up. His legs dangled as Chase rose off the floor.

"Charlie, we ain't got time for helping no kid who lost his mommy."

"What are we supposed to do? Leave him alone?"

Switchblade shook his head and huffed. "See what you can find out. I'm checking the rest of the place." He headed out the door.

Chase found an old chair, dropped into it, and stood the boy in front of him. The exoself reported the child's malnourishment. "What's your name?"

Hazel eyes seemed to study Chase. "Eli."

Chase scanned his iris, but children born and raised outside WR regulation had no identity implant. This boy was one of them. "You must be about six. Am I right?"

"Next month." Eli sniffed and wiped his nose again.

Chase grasped the boy's hand. "When was the last time you saw your mom?"

"When the man got us out of the truck."

Chase sucked in a breath. "The truck that crashed? Was the man about my size? Dark skin?"

"Uh-huh."

"Do you know where he went?"

"He got picked up."

Chase lowered his head. "Are you sure?"

"Yep. The people who was hurt got picked up too. But Mommy ran to the woods."

"Why didn't you run with her?"

"She told me to go in the store and hide."

"Did she tell you to wait here?"

"Yep." Eli's chin quivered. "Do you know how long I'm supposed to wait?"

"No. But I need to go find the man who got picked up, and I can't leave you here."

Switchblade stomped into the room. "You find out anything from the kid?"

Eli stepped closer to Chase and frowned. "Don't worry," Chase told him. "He just looks mean." Then to Switchblade he said, "I think Ridge got taken in. I'm scanning recent data from the warehouses, but it doesn't indicate any prisoners were delivered yet. The Feds are just getting organized."

"So where would they send him? Local jail?"

Chase met Eli's eyes. "Can you tell me what kind of vehicle you saw?"

"The rescue kind."

"You mean the hurt people got put in an ambulance?"

"And the black man. After the bad man shot him."

Chase looked up at Switchblade. "Hospital. I'm pulling the data now." The exoself supplied the information. "Four injured in the crash. Two shot. Ridge is listed in fair condition."

"They scanned him?" Switchblade asked. "Then they know he's rogue. Why treat him? Why not just waste him?" Realization showed on Switch's face. "Sparky covered for him."

"Looks like it. We've got to get him out of there before—"

"Before they find out the truth." Switchblade headed down the stairs. "What do we do with the kid?"

"We'll take him with us. The others taken in—the injured ones—will know him." Chase picked the boy up and hurried down the stairs.

"Feds gotta know some injured rogues were brought in. Might be fixin' 'em up to send 'em to the warehouse to get their—"

"They're going to fix them up and send them home. That's all."

Switchblade lifted his brows.

Chase shook his head.

"Right. Sending 'em home."

With Eli buckled in the back seat, Chase reclaimed his driver position.

Switch climbed in. "Kid keeps staring at me."

"Talk to him. And be nice. Uncle Switchblade needs the practice."

Switch faced the boy. "So...how you doin' back there, Eli?"

"I want my mommy."

"Uh-huh. Where's your daddy?"

"In the other truck."

Chase nearly ran into the curb. "Your father was on the other truck?"

"Yep. Me and my mommy had to take care of Rufus. So we got in the second truck."

"Who's Rufus?" Chase asked.

"My cat. I had to give him some food. Daddy said we couldn't take him."

Mel, are you there? I need some information.

"Charlie, you think we ought to tell—"

"I'm contacting Mel's screen com right now."

I'm here, baby. Are you all right?

Got a little boy with me. He says his father was on the first truck.

You've got Eli? Oh, Chase, that's wonderful. This man is beside himself. He and his wife got separated. You and I know how he feels.

I haven't got the boy's mother. I don't know where she is. But I've got a location on Ridge. He's at the hospital. Bullet wound, but not too serious. I'm going after him. Tell Eli's father I've got his son. Finding the rest of the people from the truck might be impossible.

Nothing is impossible. I'm praying.

Me too.

"Eli, your dad is safe. And when we're done here, we'll take you to him." Chase searched for communication among believers trying to get out of Ann Arbor.

"Is my mom with him?"

With a sigh, Chase looked at Switchblade. "No." He pulled into an alley behind the hospital. "Not yet."

42

Switch pulled out his blade, flipped it open and shut, and stuffed it back under his belt. Then he grabbed the gun he'd slid under the seat and stuffed it into his pocket. "No point taking the kid inside. He'll be safer out here."

"Which one of us is going to stay in the car with him?" Chase asked.

"Kid, get down behind the seat and don't make no noise," Switchblade told him.

"Don't be ridiculous," Chase said. "We can't leave him alone."

"His mother left him."

Chase shifted in the driver's seat and eyed Eli.

"I can do it," the boy said. "Been hiding since I was little."

"You sure?"

"Yep. I won't move. I promise. But when you get back, can we go see my dad?"

"You bet. We'll hurry. Now get down."

Eli dropped to the floor, pulled his knees under him, and placed his hands over the back of his head. Like he'd done it a hundred times. A lump rose in Chase's throat. What an awful way for a kid to have to get through life.

"OK, Eli. I'm locking the doors. You stay put." Chase opened the door and climbed out.

Switchblade rose out of the passenger's side and pushed the door shut, and they headed for the rear of the small hospital. "Kid kinda got to me back there, Charlie."

"Yeah. Not the first time recently I had to think about my own child coming into this crazy world."

"Don't be lettin' it trouble you." Switchblade eased up to a glass door. Lettering indicated the entrance was for authorized personnel only.

Chase ran data on the place, latched onto the security system, and relayed a code to open the door. He and Switch slipped in. The emergency area took up most of the back of the building. The exoself quickly revealed Ridge's location, and Chase headed left. In the direction of two cyber-guards.

"What now?" Switchblade asked. "You shuttin' 'em down?"

"Already done. Cameras off. Real, live people might be a problem though."

"We just gotta look like we belong."

Chase tugged on the end of a gurney as he hurried down the corridor. "Hop on. I'll take you for a ride."

Switchblade propelled himself onto the rolling bed in one smooth motion. He settled back and stared at the ceiling. "If anybody asks, what's wrong with me? And who are you? Ain't nothing about you that says you belong on the doctor side of a gurney."

"I'm a med-tech from out of town. Found you on the street near the accident scene and brought you here in my car. Found this gurney about the time your legs turned to jelly."

"You like making up this crap, Charlie? You sure are good at it."

"No. I'm tired of lying. Pray nobody stops us and I

won't have to say a word."

Switch closed his eyes and mumbled something.

And Chase did exactly what he was so tired of doing. He planted a report in the hospital's main data output calling all available staff to the main emergency entrance for incoming wounded in multiple transports. Soon a dozen doctors and nurses hurried out double doors twenty yards ahead. Not one so much as glanced to the side to see the stranger pushing a patient toward them. They headed one way. Chase went the other way.

He pushed Switchblade into a processing area, which was empty except for an old man in the corner leaning on a cane.

Chase searched the signs at the front of the nearest hall for cubicle numbers. Ridge was listed as being in number four. Just steps away. "Here we go. Come on."

Switch jumped off the gurney. "Where?"

"Four." Chase pulled the gurney up to the cubicle. He swung the curtain back. "For once, something might be easy." He let go of the gurney and grabbed hold of Ridge's arm. "Wake up." He shook his brother-in-law until Ridge opened his eyes.

"You came after me?" Ridge blinked a few times. "They're not letting me walk out of here, you know. They've got to know by now I'm rogue." He squeezed his eyes shut and grimaced.

Switchblade pulled the curtain shut. "You in pain? You gotta bear it. We're takin' you out."

"You shouldn't have come. I messed up bad. I deserve whatever happens to me."

"Shut up, idiot," Chase told him. "I never heard anything so stupid."

Switchblade smirked. "Ever listen to yourself,

Charlie? Days past, you were the *king* of stupid."

Chase glared at the man who'd just spoken the truth. Then he shook his head and grinned. "Come on, brother. You're not hurt too bad. Bullet went straight through your arm."

Rolling Ridge into the hall, Chase told Switch to push the other gurney into the cubicle. After stuffing a couple of pillows under the sheet, Chase yanked the curtain closed.

"What about the others who were injured?" Ridge asked.

"No room," Chase told him. "We're in a car. Already got one other passenger waiting in it."

"So, what'll we do about the others?"

Chase knew the answer. He'd accepted it. But it'd be hard.

"We got some people to safety, Ridge. The rest will have to wait. Maybe we'll be able to help them. Maybe we won't. They're in God's hands."

Ridge closed his eyes.

Switchblade glanced at Chase and nodded. "Ridge, you done all right today. You didn't run like Colt. You stood by the folks in the truck to the point of gettin' shot. You got no reason to feel bad about it."

"He's right," Chase said. "You did your best. I'm proud of you."

Ridge opened his eyes and glanced at both men. "I surprised myself."

"Well, I wasn't going to say that." Chase smiled. "You surprised me too. Showed me what kind of man you really are."

They came to the door where they'd entered. Chase started to lift Ridge off the gurney.

"I can walk," Ridge said.

Chase let him go, and he sat straight and dropped his bare feet to the tile floor. Once out of the building, they hurried down the alley to the undisturbed car. Chase pushed the button on the key and the doors unlocked. He climbed into the driver's seat.

"Eli, you OK?" he asked.

Ridge eased into the back seat. "Where'd you get this kid? He was in the truck."

Before Chase could answer, three people ran toward the car. Well, two ran. The other hobbled—the old man with the cane. Chase jumped out of the car as a middle-aged woman and a younger man reached him.

The woman spoke first, her breath ragged. "We saw what you did and followed you. Please, take us with you. They're going to send us to some kind of processing center they've set up."

Her arm hung in a sling. The man next to her seemed more seriously injured. A bandage wrapped around his head and blood trickled from beneath it. The old man caught up. Chase looked at Switchblade.

"We can't leave 'em here, Charlie. I take up the most room—I'll stay here and wait for somebody to come back for me."

"Pile in," Chase said to the three. "Switchblade...just get in the front and let Eli sit in your lap."

"You've got Eli? Praise God," the woman said. "What about his mother?"

"No sign of her," Chase said. "Hopefully..." Before he could finish, the exoself streamed data about the new detention center in the warehouse. And Bloodless. "Switch, you're right. You should stay. But I'm staying with you." He eyed Ridge. "Pain meds wearing off, brother? Because you're driving these people to safety. Switchblade and I will catch up."

Ridge nodded. "I can drive. But you do that thing in your head and tell my sister you're staying. I don't want to be the one to give her the news."

"Yeah, I'll tell her. Probably hear her yell all the way from the Cos."

Switchblade came around the car as the others slid in. "You got intel? Why are we staying? And how are we supposed to get back with no wheels?"

"The Lord will provide. I'll fill you in when we get them out of here."

Ridge gripped the steering wheel, but he didn't turn the key.

"Go on," Chase told him. "And hurry."

"I don't want to leave you and Switchblade here. Let me stay too. I won't do anything stupid."

Chase knelt to peer into the car's open window. "I need you to get them to safety. That was your assignment earlier today. Follow through. It's the best thing you can do right now."

Ridge exhaled. "OK. If I need to come back for you, I will. Stay in touch. And if you see Colt…"

Chase lowered his voice. "Colt got caught. Maybe some of your runners from the truck too. I'm going to see if there's anything I can do."

"I was going to say take him out." Ridge turned the key. "But I stopped myself. Get him home and we'll deal with him."

Eli had been scooped up onto the woman's lap. Chase reached in and clutched the boy's small hand. "You're going to see your dad now. I'll be there soon."

Eli nodded, and Chase rose and slapped the roof of the car as Ridge pulled forward.

Switchblade crossed his arms as the car drove away. "All right, robot. Tell me what you're getting us into this time.

43

"We're going to the warehouse. They're processing people for...I don't know if there's anything I can do. I just need to know I tried." Chase closed his eyes. "God, help me. And keep Mel calm when I tell her."

Switchblade headed toward the street at the south end of the alley. "You stopped short. Processed for what? Execution?"

"Yes. We've got to walk six blocks, and it'll take us past a Federal checkpoint. Walk a little ahead of me. Or behind."

"So it don't look like we're together. Got it. I'll stay ahead." Switch stepped onto the sidewalk when he reached the end of the alley.

Mel, Switch and I stayed behind. Ridge is driving four people back, including the boy. We need to check on some things here. Nothing to worry about. If I can't secure transportation back, I'll let you know and you can send the car for us. I love you.

Nearly a full minute passed.

I can't say I'm surprised, but don't tell me it's nothing to worry about. I'm reading your data and I know where you're going. Please be careful. I'll secure a VPad so I won't be tied to the computer. Please, please don't be out of touch.

Let me know when Ridge gets there.

Will do. God be with you.

"You know where you're going?" Chase asked.

"Yeah, I got it," Switchblade answered. He slowed his pace but kept a few feet ahead of Chase. "How far to the checkpoint? Why don't we detour around it?"

"Whole area surrounding the warehouse is cordoned off. We either get through the checkpoint or we get picked up for walking into a restricted area. Two more blocks."

"You got a plan?" Switch asked.

"I'm still the dead guy whose identity I stole months ago. No reason for them to hold me. And you're still a free prisoner. Not sure how they'll handle that. Maybe you should wait for me here."

"We go together or we don't go. Let me get picked up. Then don't waste no time getting me out."

"I'm not taking that kind of risk."

"Might not have a choice. Be the robot God made you to be." Switch laughed. "You can make them let me go." He ran ahead.

Chase started to yell after him, but two Feds waited at the next corner. Time for some cyber manipulation. And it had to happen fast. He hunted for free-prisoner files.

"Dummy, there aren't any. That's the point." But the glitch showing Switchblade's one job assignment was easy to access. From there, Chase blossomed the error left by an inept WR programmer and rebirthed Leslie Honeywell. Now Switch had not only one assignment but four. Including a current post with security at the new prison compound in Ann Arbor. "Thanks, Sparky. I don't know how you do it."

Chase could have made it happen sooner—given Switch back his identity. Since no record existed of his deal with the Feds, slipping him back into the system was easy.

Maybe.

Switchblade approached the checkpoint, and Chase held back to watch and listen from thirty feet away.

Stepping forward, Switchblade met a short woman with a DNA scanner.

"Leslie Honeywell," the woman said.

Switchblade nearly fell backward. But he stood straight and crossed his arms.

"Why are you out of uniform?" the woman asked. "Report to your post and suit up."

Switchblade tilted his head. "Yes, ma'am. On my way. To my post." He headed on past the checkpoint, but he looked back and made eye contact with Chase.

Chase shook his head, and Switch faced the street and kept going. Chase fell in line to pass through the checkpoint.

Mel, I just made Switch a security guard. Cushy job. Good pay. He might like it here.

Oh, baby, stay out of trouble. Why did you have to mess with the system?

To get in. Almost there. Don't plan on staying long.

Chase's turn came, and the short woman waved the scanner in front of his face. She frowned and looked from side to side. Was she making sure backup was nearby?

"Is there a problem?" Chase asked.

"You don't look forty-eight."

"Good genes. And some bio-med anti-aging drugs. I've got connections."

"You're a washed-up cyber-guard tech. Where'd you get that kind of drug?" She ran her hand across her wrinkled cheek and pushed her graying hair behind her ear.

"Designer-drug industry is booming in Detroit. What do you think I've been doing since I stopped oiling squeaky robots?"

"You're a runner?"

Not exactly the truth, but close. Not exactly legal either. "Yes."

"You look familiar." She stared. "But DNA doesn't lie." She moved out of his way.

A grin settled into worry as he caught up with Switch.

"You dropped me back into the real world?" Switchblade's brows were low, his breathing heavy. "How am I supposed to get back out?"

"Sparky will take care of it. Right now, it's the best thing that could happen."

"People working this gig will know I don't belong."

"Feds don't get attached to coworkers. You're a number. Security officer forty-two thirty-nine zero zero. That's what's on the unassigned badge they've got waiting for you. Find out where to get it."

"This is worse than anything on Eight Mile."

"It's better than waiting in line to get your head severed. Stay calm. I'm stealing a transport."

"You're gettin' too bold, Charlie." Switchblade hurried ahead toward the warehouse with prisoner transports surrounding it and WR uniforms trailing in and out of it.

Chase got that all-too-familiar sensation of a pounding heart, even though it wasn't possible. "Protect him. Please." He latched onto the system of one of the mid-sized vehicles. A self-drive. Room for ten. Variable-tint windows. Bullet and laser proof.

He walked to it and programmed the cab door to open. Inside, he found an official WR cap and armband. The kind subordinates like drivers and other support-team members wore. He quickly put them on. Now he'd blend in. And he'd wait.

But he couldn't expect Switch to locate a group of people neither of them had ever met. The believers who'd gotten caught when they ran from the accident scene were nameless. Only person they knew was Colt.

Chase searched recent arrest data and found fourteen people arrested near the park. They were all in one holding area. Only a few had names. A quick search indicated the names represented rogue citizens. Colt was one of them. The rest were just numbers—likely kids and teens raised outside the system.

Chase had to get inside. He spotted two cyber-guards at the side entrance. Shutting down their main programs, he kept basic portability active in one of them. Then he made it follow him right into the warehouse.

A flesh-and-blood Fed quickly stopped him. "What are you doing with the guard?" the man yelled. "Return it to the outer perimeter."

"No can do," Chase answered. "Got to rework the circuits. Sun's too bright outside to see what I'm doing."

"Hurry it up. Space is tight in here." The uniformed man walked toward the center of the warehouse. Ten laser-banded areas lined the walls. In each section, a group of people. None too old. Mostly under thirty, it seemed. Must be about a hundred total. Not much room for this kind of operation.

A walled-off area blocked the view of whatever waited behind it. But Chase knew. Rolling cryocontainers were lined up between the wall and the prisoners.

Chase scanned the rest of the building. Another area divided off by more movable walls took up a front corner. It even had a door. A real, live security guard kept watch in front of it.

No sign of Switchblade. Chase worked the exoself to reassign a whole group of prisoners and have them moved to the transport now under the control of a rogue transhuman. But the order stalled. The area holding Colt and the believers who'd run from the Feds was marked in the data as number one. The first group to go behind the wall.

And meet Bloodless.

Chase could only watch as the laser band dissolved. Four guards directed the prisoners to line up. Colt was fourth in line. This couldn't happen.

Chase dove deep into WR programs and pulled out the manual for the death machine. He'd read it before, at Blue Sky Field when Amos made him explain the device to the people. Now he rushed through the file, hoping for a way to shut the blasted thing down.

And he got it. He wriggled into the coding and reworked the start-up to safety mode. Technical difficulties would prevent the laser blade from dropping down.

Chase breathed a prayer and smiled. But he shuddered as the exoself seemed to sink into a spasm. The code—32-7—sparked. He dismissed the dread as an irate guard announced the machine was inoperable.

"We're saved!" The shout was followed by others exclaiming relief. Did they know what waited for them behind the wall? And now they knew it wasn't going to happen. Chase backed up behind the cyber-guard as chaos filled the warehouse.

Then Switchblade, dressed in WR garb, exited the walled-up area in the front corner. He slinked along the outer wall. Away from Chase. But he stopped and watched along with everyone else.

The first in the line of prisoners dropped to the floor. The guards who'd moved them from the holding area were now aiming their laser guns. One down. A woman. Then two. A teen boy. Three. Another woman.

And then Colt.

A scream rose up in Chase. But his mouth remained shut. *Be still.* The Spirit filled him. Two more believers dropped. The others waiting for death made no sound.

But the rest of the prisoners filling the warehouse cried out. Before another one met the laser, a high-ranking uniform flew into the center of the warehouse and blew a whistle. The chaos ceased.

"This group was scheduled for relocation," he shouted at the Feds with the laser weapons. "If you stop killing them now, *maybe* you'll keep your jobs."

The four men stared at the officer, at each other, at the dead on the floor. And then they holstered their weapons.

"Get security to move the ones still on their feet to transport number nine," the man in charge yelled. "And no more killing until the device is operational. We were not sent here to waste human life for no good reason."

From the corner of his eye, Chase saw the door of the office swing open a bit, then pull shut. Again, the exoself seemed to quiver.

Switchblade stepped in line with other guards.

Real ones. The side door was opened, and Chase quickly led the cyber-guard out before the weeping believers filed through. Two guards in front of them. Two—Switch and one other—in back.

At Chase's command, self-drive transport nine pulled forward and opened its doors. He disabled the tracking device and shut down the cameras. The eight surviving prisoners from group one climbed in.

Chase motioned to Switch, who held back as the others headed for the warehouse. No one questioned his hesitation. A guard would accompany the group to their new location. Switchblade climbed into the cab. A driver would also ride along, in case of a malfunction. Chase still wore the assigned driver's cap and armband. Where the real driver was, God only knew.

Chase took the seat behind the steering bar, and the transport headed away.

Mel, I stole a transport. It needs to go dark and so do I. I know I can't be tracked, but it's best if I shut down the screen com for now. God willing, I'll be home in forty minutes. Don't worry—this is my last mission, rescue or otherwise. I've had enough.

44

Chase didn't wait for a response before he closed the program allowing communication from his wife. For her own good. For the good of the base. That's what he told himself.

He turned to the passengers clinging to prayer and to each other. Five men, three women. Well, two of the females were teens. That left one who might be Eli's mother. Chase touched the control to lower the glass separating him from the believers.

"I'm taking you all to the base in Detroit. I don't know how long any of us will be there. But for now, you'll be safe. I sent a few ahead of you already. Including a boy named Eli. I was hoping to find his mother."

One of the men spoke. "Beth Jenkins was killed by the guards. Third in line."

Chase lowered his head and closed his eyes. How could he let her die? He should've stopped the shooting. Blown the guards' NPs out of their brains. "I'm sorry," he said. He faced the road as the self-drive sped out of Ann Arbor.

The shaking, fragile voice of a girl interrupted his despair. "You saved us, Mr. Sterling. And Miss Beth went home."

"To die is gain," Chase said. He turned back around.

The girl, no older than Finley, nodded. A tear slid down her cheek. "Thank you for coming after us. Did you break the machine?"

"You know who I am and you know I can...break machines. Do you know what's happening in Detroit?"

One of the men answered. "We should be moving out, not in. Right?"

"Yes. Even now, plans are forming to set up a larger center in the heart of the city."

"Inside the Cosimo?" the man asked.

"Yes."

Switchblade spoke for the first time since climbing into the transport. "How long you known this, robot?"

"About fifteen minutes."

"You tell Melody yet?"

"Indirectly. I sent the report to her computer, but I cut off the screen com. Might be a hidden tracker I can't detect in this transport. Forwarding a report wouldn't attract attention, but a conversation might."

"No other reason you disconnected?"

Chase studied Switchblade's expression. "We witnessed something awful back there. You OK?"

"Yeah. You?"

Chase let his gaze meet the road. Few other vehicles passed by. Maybe the stream of refugees flowing into Detroit had slowed. "No. I'm not. And I won't be until I get our people out of harm's way."

As the transport took the highway and entered Detroit, the survivors in the back sang quietly. Switchblade remained unusually silent.

Until the shooting started.

Residents of Detroit quickly filled the street, pulled out their old pistols, and opened fire on the WR transport. Bullets bounced off the armored vehicle.

"Drop the tint, Charlie," Switchblade yelled. "We ain't strangers to these people. Let 'em see us."

Before Chase could alter the black tint to clear, protesters jammed the street and stopped the transport. The tint came down then, and Chase held his hands up in front of him.

The shooting stopped, as well as the riotous language. A few people laughed. Most simply shook their heads, holstered their weapons, and walked away.

Chase lowered the window. "Yes, I stole it," he yelled. "For a good cause."

A few looked back and waved. Nodding heads smiled. A man gave him a thumbs-up.

"Listen," he said to those who'd lingered. "You need to get out of town. Feds are moving in."

"Where we supposed to go?" a man asked.

Chase pursed his lips and huffed. "Anywhere. Just go." He raised the window and took over the steering bar.

Pulling into the dark garage, he spotted Mel leaning against a barrier. Leo stood on one side of her, Ridge on the other. Chase eased onto the brake and stopped the transport. He pushed the control to open the side door in the back and let the people out before swinging open his own door.

Mel had her arms around him before his feet touched the ground.

"Thank You, thank You," she cried. "Are you all right?"

"Yes, sweetheart." He held her tight and stroked her hair. Thank God, no indication of those spiked enzyme levels remained. "But we've had some losses."

Turning her gaze to the eight people climbing out

of the transport, she sucked in a breath.

Then she met Chase's eyes. "Colt?"

"He's dead. Along with a few others."

"Eli's mother?"

"I couldn't save her." He drew Mel closer. "I can't bear to tell the man I let his wife die." He pulled back, then rested his forehead against Mel's. "I'm not leaving you again. I'm through breaking promises."

Ridge gripped Chase's shoulder. "I'll tell him, brother. He's up in a private room with Eli."

Chase looked up. "Mel, you can be proud of your brother."

Mel let go of Chase and reached for Ridge's hand. Then she faced the people waiting for instructions. "I'm Melody," she said. "The ones who arrived earlier are all up in our headquarters. People are waiting to show you to your rooms. Rest now, and pray. We'll keep you informed about our plans."

"You got a debriefing planned?" Switch asked her. "If so, can it wait half an hour?"

"We'll make it an hour. Meet us in the command center. Ridge, you too."

"Yeah, I'll be there."

The new people joined him as he headed away, some offering to help him with delivering the sad news. He wouldn't have to go alone. Leo went with them.

"An hour." Switch followed the crowd to the hyper lifts. Chase hadn't seen him this shaken since the day of the raid in Quebec.

Mel took Chase by the hand and led him to the lifts. And Chase instructed the exoself to program the self-drive. And run it into Lake St. Clair. No point in holding on to the WR vehicle. They had to know by now it'd been stolen.

Chase prompted the lift. "Twenty-one." He leaned against the cold wall and closed his eyes.

"Bad day," Mel said.

"One of the worst days of my life."

She eased her arms around him. "I have some news. I didn't want to tell you while you were out there."

"Good news?"

"I hope you'll see it that way. They weren't supposed to come, but they want to help us."

"Oh no, don't tell me. My mother and Amos? I told them a month ago to wait for instructions."

"Yeah, I think that's when they headed this way. They'll be here tomorrow, God willing." Mel stepped out of the lift and headed for their room. "Your mama and your new stepdaddy will be joining us, and I believe there's a good reason for it."

Chase nearly smiled. If anyone could lighten his heart, it was this woman. "I hope nobody minds if I just call him Amos."

Mel swung around and wrapped her arms around his neck. She kissed him before pushing open the door to their room. "Come and rest. You should try to shut down. I'll wake you in time for the meeting."

He didn't argue but fell onto the bed, pulled her down beside him, and closed his eyes.

45

Chase managed to sleep twenty-four minutes. He opened his eyes to find Mel lying next to him, her face close to his. Her arm around his waist.

"Hi," she said.

He eased into a smile.

She ran her fingers through his hair. "You said some tough things when you cut me off earlier."

"What do you mean?"

"Last mission? What about your final trip to Eight Mile?"

He rolled onto his back. "I can't think about that anymore. I've got to find a way to get I-don't-even-know-how-many people out of this city. And soon."

"I know. I read the report you sent, and I won't pretend like I'm not terrified. But you sounded so…"

"Beaten? Broken? Ready to give up?"

"Yes."

"Don't worry. I'm not going into self-pity mode. Just reality."

Mel pushed herself up and dropped her feet to the floor. "God is in control of our future, whatever it brings. I hope you know that."

He reached for her as she rose off the bed. "I know. But we need some guidance."

"We'll get it." She combed her fingers through her curls. "Come on. Your leader's having a meeting."

"Coming, boss." He sprang off the bed and followed her into the hall.

When they reached the lobby, whatever resolve Chase had latched onto slipped away. Eli ran toward him. The man who must be the newly widowed father sat on the end of a loveseat.

Chase knelt and opened his arms to the boy.

Eli wrapped his small arms around Chase's neck. He leaned close and whispered, "Mommy went to heaven."

Tears puddled in Chase's eyes and he blinked as he rose and picked up Eli. The man stood and came near.

Chase swallowed hard. "I'm so, so sorry. I tried to…"

The man held out his hand. "I know. Beth is safe now. And happy. Eli and I will be…We'll be fine." He sucked in a breath and nodded.

Chase shook the man's hand and scanned his iris. "Brian, you and Eli can stay as long as *we* stay. I don't think it will be long. I see you've got some experience on the rail system. I'm thinking about—"

"Hijacking a train?"

"Something like that."

Mel interjected. "OK, I think we have a lot to talk about. Brian, you're welcome to attend the debriefing. We're on our way there."

"Fill me in later. I need to spend some time with my son." He scooped Eli from Chase's arms.

They looked alike. Unruly auburn hair. Fair skin. Chase watched them walk away. A man and his child. Alone. He shuddered.

Mel prompted the lift. "Come on, baby. Let's figure out if what we learned today will get us through tomorrow." The quick ride delivered them to the command center.

The room filled with more newcomers than could fit into chairs. But Mel's seat at the head of the table waited for her. Chase simply stood behind her.

Switchblade came near as chatter filled the room. He'd shed the uniform and replaced it with tattered jeans and a blue shirt.

"Have you been to the nurses' station?" Chase asked him.

A grin eased up the side of Switch's face. "What makes you ask?"

"Because you look a whole lot better than you did an hour ago. Like you got some comfort. A good woman will do that for you."

A twinkle remained in Switchblade's eyes as Mel called the meeting to order.

"All right, people, we've got some things to go over," she said.

The crowd settled.

"First of all, thank you to those who went on mission today. We met some trouble, but we came away with a good number of believers rescued. We've suffered loss too. Our base lost one of its leaders. Others were lost as well. A few are unaccounted for. Hopefully, they'll find their way to safety." She leaned back in her chair, and Chase rested his hand on her shoulder.

"But there won't be another retrieval attempt. I've been analyzing the data Chase latched onto today. The Feds plan to start revamping this building in three weeks."

The crowd responded with reasonable fear. A few at the table stood. "What are we supposed to do now?"

a woman asked.

Mel straightened in her seat. "We pray. And we plan." She tilted her head upward and looked at Chase.

He squeezed her shoulder and met the eyes of those around him. "We need to evacuate in large numbers," he said. "Some of us will stay as long as we can. But most of you will go. I've secured four locations to our north. We'll divide the people into groups of about two hundred each."

Switchblade stepped forward. "How we gettin' them north? And what's happening, besides the Feds taking over the Cos?"

"They plan on cleaning out the revolutionaries," Chase said. "They'll get as many dissenters and disgruntled rogue citizens in one place as possible, and then wipe them out." He folded his arms. "But they have no idea we're here inside their future headquarters. None. No indication they know about the gardens or the infrastructure. As far as they know, the Cos is in a state of disrepair. And it's empty. It's almost like…"

"What is it, Chase?" Mel asked.

"Like there's a shield over us. Showing old images as real-time."

Switch met Chase's eyes. "Sparky?"

"Who's Sparky?" one of the newcomers asked.

Chase reached into the inner workings of the exoself. "As long as we can keep the Feds from knocking on our front door, they won't see us. They can't see us at all."

After talk of trains and cargo ships, and a few rantings about fighting alongside the people on the streets, the meeting wore down. The crowd retreated to overfilled living quarters. Chase remained in the command center with Mel and Switch.

He sat next to Mel and rubbed her hands. "You didn't tell them about the impending arrival of their former leader."

"What?" Switchblade slapped his hands against the table. "Your new stepdaddy is coming? I assume your mama is with him. Thought you told them to stay put."

Chase grinned. "I did. But they'll be here tomorrow."

"You going out to meet 'em?" Switch asked.

Chase set his gaze on Mel. "No. I'm not leaving the Cos until Mel and I are ready to leave for good. We still have some up-tops in the city. They can meet them and bring them in."

"Charlie, we got through today by the skin of our teeth. Don't mean we got to fear stepping outside again."

"I'm not scared. Just not willing. And I don't want you out there either."

"Maybe in a day or two we'll feel different. But right now, staying inside the Cos is all right by me." Switchblade walked to the window and prompted the shade to close. "I had enough today. Can't believe the way it went down for Colt. I know none of us was too keen on him, but I feel bad about it just the same."

Chase felt it too. "I've learned not to beat myself up over the losses we take. But you're right. I think we'd all be glad to see Colt back here tonight."

Mel sniffed and wiped tears away. "I wonder how Ridge is handling it."

"Now, *that* boy showed his stuff today," Switchblade said. "But I'm glad it's over. Don't care if I never see Ann Arbor again. Or that old head machine. Or that crazy woman. She kinda reminded me of Colt."

A spark rose up inside Chase. "You didn't mention a woman earlier."

"She was runnin' the whole operation. Had herself an office set up in the warehouse. That's where I went to get my uniform. And she looked me over something fierce. Green eyes staring at me."

Mel's hand slid into Chase's, and he could feel her blood pressure rising.

"Weirdest thing," Switch said. "Had a bobblehead Jesus on her desk. What would somebody like *her* be doin' with something like *that*?"

46

Mel jumped out of her chair and backed against the wall. "She's here." Her voice seemed to shatter into a hundred cries. "Will she never stop?" Her frantic eyes met Chase. "Why can't she just let you go?"

Chase rose and embraced her. "Calm down. She doesn't know where to find us."

Switchblade's hand gripped Chase's shoulder. "I don't need to be told who she is. I'm sorry. I didn't know. Never saw Kerstin Bennett before."

Chase eased Mel back into her chair. "I'll take care of this. I'll get her reassigned and she'll be gone."

"Charlie, I need to tell you about the way she was—"

"It won't be a problem." Chase stared at Switchblade.

Switch nodded. "Right. No problem."

Mel met his eyes. "Tell me everything, Switch. As your leader, I need to know."

Switchblade looked from her to Chase and back again.

Chase barely shook his head. He'd sensed the presence of...something in the warehouse. Was it something, or someone, transhuman?

"I didn't think about it right then," Switch said. "Later I wondered how she was communicating with the lackeys in the warehouse. Spoutin' off stuff. Just thought she must've got some new kind of inner-ear device. Thought she was real smart. But maybe…"

"Maybe she's got some new hardware," Chase said.

"You think she's transhuman?" Mel asked. "If she is, and you try…anything… she'll know it's you. She'll know you're nearby." She pushed Chase's hands off her arms and rose out of the chair. "What am I thinking? She already knows. That's why she's here."

"Mel, please stay calm. I will protect you."

"Who's going to protect *you*?" she yelled.

Switchblade cleared his throat. "Ain't nobody gettin' inside the Cos. We got this, Melody."

Chase added the return of a nightmare to the list of other issues he'd deal with. Tomorrow. "Come on, we're going to get some dinner, and we're going to bed. This day needs to end." He slid his arm around Mel's waist and led her to the lift.

Switchblade followed. "Tell me one thing. You two seemed to know who I was talking about when I brought up the bobblehead. What's *that* about?"

"Used to be on my desk," Chase said. "Kind of a joke about how I could change lives. But I don't know why she brought it with her."

"I do," Mel said. "It's her talisman. She knows you belong to God now. And she plans on one-upping Him and taking you back."

Chase blinked. The surge he'd felt in the warehouse had been a warning. Did Kerstin feel it too? Did she have an exoself of her own?

Was *she* the transhuman Robert said he was being forced to build? He promised to make the next one…What did he say? Inept. Chase exhaled. If Kerstin *was* the one, he could break her. "I need to talk to

Robert."

The lift door dissolved and Chase stepped out, pulling Mel along beside him.

Switch followed. "What about that stuff up on eighty-nine? Can you use the supercomputer to contact your doctor?"

"Could be. Mel, what do you think?"

With her gaze to the floor and her steps slowing, she seemed to be barely breathing.

Chase gripped both her arms. Racing pulse. The oxygen level in her blood was not right. Her lips had a gray tinge.

"Sweetheart, you need to see Mason. Right now. Come on."

"Chase, I'm fine. Just shocked. And a little scared."

He scooped her up in his arms. "No, you're not fine." He stepped back into the lift. "Switchblade, I'll take her down to the clinic. I already messaged Mason's computer, but it says he's away. Go to the mess hall and see if he's there."

"Got it." He ran toward the dining area.

Mel laid her head on Chase's shoulder. "Is the baby all right?"

"I'm sure the baby's fine."

"Tell me the truth, Chase. What's wrong with me?"

"Seems like you're not getting enough oxygen in your blood."

"Don't give me *seems like*. Diagnose me."

"Could be a number of things. Most likely, it's just the stress of this day, topped off by the news of…"

"Of the queen's arrival? I've got to be strong. I'm gonna take that woman down."

Chase couldn't help but smile. "Oh, you are, huh?

My new bodyguard."

"Don't you forget it. Nobody's coming between me and my man."

The lift opened on the tenth floor, and Chase carried Mel to the clinic. Dani ran toward them.

"Oh no, what's wrong?" she asked. "Melody, are you in labor?"

"No. I'm fine. Chase is just overreacting to my body's response to a really bad day."

"Lay her down in here," Dani told Chase. She headed for a cubicle. "A lot of us have felt the overload of stress today." She grabbed a stethoscope as Chase eased Mel down onto the bed. "But we're not all seven months pregnant."

Dani listened to Mel's heart, but Mel pushed the stethoscope away. "The baby—please make sure he's OK."

"Is Mason in the dining hall?" Chase asked. "I sent Switch to look for him."

"Yeah, he's there. I wish we had better equipment. Can't you do your thing and check the baby?"

"Wish I could. Seems I can't get a read without touching skin and I can't touch the baby. Maybe I should try to contact Dr. June and see if she can bring in some high-tech equipment."

Dani lowered the stethoscope to Mel's abdomen. After a moment she said, "Well, the baby's heartbeat sounds fine. And he's moving."

Chase rubbed Mel's stomach as he met Dani's eyes. "I know you've done this before—we've got five babies here. No problems with any of them?"

"No. But we..."

"I run this place," Mel said. "I know about the ones that didn't make it."

Dani nodded. "Four miscarriages. One pretty far along. Not much we could do to save them."

Mason hurried into the cubicle. Switch stopped short and pulled the curtain closed.

"Everybody all right in there?" he asked.

"It's OK, Switch. I'm decent," Mel told him.

"Well, I'll just wait out here."

Good thing he did. Mason pulled Mel's blouse open to listen to her heart. And then the baby's heart. "Dani, draw some blood." He looked at Chase. "What can you tell me?"

"Low oxygen level. Rapid pulse. And the enzymes are high again."

The doctor smiled at Mel. "How about you stay here with me tonight? I'm sure it's nothing, but we'll check you over real good."

She huffed. "You're the doctor." She turned to Chase. "Will you go and get me a few things from our room?"

"We can get somebody else to do that. I don't want to leave you."

"But you know my favorite gown. Please go get it for me. And my toothbrush."

Chase sighed. "I'll be right back." He stepped to the curtain and slid through the opening. "Switch, come with me."

But Mel's voice stopped them. "Switchblade, stay here. I had one chore left tonight. I'll fill you in and you can take care of it for me."

Switchblade eyed Chase.

"She's the boss. I'll be back." Chase headed for the lift, went up to their room, and rummaged through Mel's drawer. Pink gown. Very short, lacy white gown. "My favorite." No blue gown.

He pushed the drawer closed and opened another. Blouses and T-shirts. She'd just have to settle for the pink gown. He pulled it out, grabbed the robe hanging on a hook in the bathroom, and reached for both their toothbrushes—he wasn't coming back here tonight.

He'd gotten to the room and accomplished this task for his wife without thinking too hard about why he was doing it. Without facing what the exoself had revealed. Without losing his grip on denial. But before he made it back out the door, the weight of truth knocked him down. He dropped to his knees and closed his eyes.

"Dear God. No. Anything but this. Please."

47

Regaining the use of his legs, Chase made his way back to the clinic. He found Mel sitting up in the bed, a pillow behind her. A VPad in her hand.

"Put that new guy—Timothy—on the feed to the EU," she said. "Make sure the group in Brussels got to the safe house."

"Mel." Chase dropped the pink gown and other items on the bed.

"And tell Leo we need to get that shipment of supplies to the new base in United Arab Territory. He'll know what to do."

"Mel."

She shushed him.

He grabbed the VPad. "Who have you got on here?"

"It's Ridge, but—"

He lifted it to his ear. "Ridge, your sister is off duty. And you're on. Can you handle it?"

"What's wrong with her?"

"Just needs a little rest. I'll keep you posted."

"Got it. I'm praying."

"Me too." Chase ended the call and slipped the VPad into his pocket. "No more tonight, Mel."

"Yes, sir." She smiled. "I feel better." She drew her knees up and backed away from Chase.

He sat on the edge of the bed. "Please don't be

afraid to let me touch you."

Guilt showed in her eyes. "I'm sorry."

He grasped her hands and kissed them. "You're right. You are doing better."

"See, I told you. Mason gave me something. I want to sleep in our own bed."

"You'll do as you're told. I'm going to find Mason. I'll be right back." He rose off the bed.

"No. Stay with me."

He bent to kiss her. "I'll be back and I'll stay the night." He left her there behind the curtain.

Mason sat in his office twenty yards away. No sign of Dani or Switchblade. Chase walked in, closed the door, and dropped into a chair.

"Go ahead and take my blood before she talks you out of it."

The doctor crossed his arms and closed his eyes. Then he met Chase's stare. "Too late."

Chase jumped from the chair and paced across the small room. "Is that why she sent me on a menial task? So she could forbid a transfusion? She included Switchblade in this little meeting. Is that it? And he's duty bound to preserve my life."

"Sit down and let's talk about this."

Chase fell back into the chair. "You could cut out my organs and give them to her. It'd work just as well as a transfusion."

"Do you know how ludicrous that sounds? Even if it weren't, I'm not qualified and we're not equipped."

"Then we'll get her to…" Chase inhaled. "There is no option but to pump my blood into her."

"I just promised her it wouldn't happen. Switchblade promised. Dani promised." Mason leaned forward and rested his elbows on the desk. "She is our leader and we will do as she deems best. And *you* are the only hope of getting a thousand believers out of Detroit. *You* are the reason the Feds don't know we're holed up in this stupid building. Now tell me what you didn't say in front of her. I need to know exactly what we're dealing with."

"Beginning stages of liver failure. And heart failure." The words didn't sound real. Were they coming from his mouth? "Her other organs are functioning, but one thing leads to another. Heart failure is rare among vaccine recipients but the liver isn't a surprise. Kidneys can't be far behind."

"I didn't know about the link between the cancer vaccine and organ failure until Melody told me. It explains more than a few deaths I've witnessed in the underground. I had the vaccine myself."

"You're healthy."

"I wasn't asking. My only concern right now is Melody. Heart failure doesn't mean her heart is going to stop beating. It's just not working properly, but we've got a month's supply of the right drugs to keep her stable. She'll need to stay calm. Others will have to take over for her."

Chase pulled data trails until he knew more about drug therapy for heart patients. And where to get the drugs. "OK, but the liver is a problem. Isn't it?"

Mason nodded.

"You need to deliver the baby."

"I'd like to wait a week or two. He'll stand a better chance if he gains a little more weight."

"The baby is the reason she's sick. Her body couldn't handle growing a transhuman." Chase clenched his jaw. "This is my fault."

"Do you know that, or are you making unfounded

assumptions? Because as far as I can tell, this is organ failure due to the vaccine. It's happened to thousands of people. Pregnancy may bring it on a little faster but you can't blame it on transhumanism."

Chase only stared at the blank white wall behind Mason.

"Listen, you need to be careful what you say. Don't be too hard on her for not allowing a transfusion. She needs to—"

"I know. She needs to stay calm. I won't bring it up." Chase rose from the chair and left the office. The nightmare of Kerstin's unexpected presence seemed a distant memory. The unfeasibility of relocating the population of the Cos no longer concerned Chase.

He entered the small space in the ill-equipped clinic where his pregnant wife had fallen asleep. And he stretched out on the narrow bed beside her. She didn't stir, but the baby inside her kicked. Moments ago, he'd harbored resentment toward this little unborn person.

He rested his hand on Mel's stomach and whispered, "It's OK, baby. I'll keep your mama safe and well. Nobody can stop me."

48

In the morning, Mel moved to her own bed. Mason would be in to check on her often. He'd given her a handful of pills before allowing her to leave the clinic.

Chase sat on the end of the bed. The breakfast he'd brought Mel remained untouched on her nightstand, but the laptop resting on her belly had her attention.

"Mel, I don't think it's good for the baby to have that thing on top of you."

She rolled her eyes. "And all the drugs I'm taking aren't an issue?"

Chase reached for her bare foot and rubbed her toes. "You seem like you're handling this well."

Her hands fell from the keypad. "My organs are failing, and I've got to deliver a baby before I..." She pushed the computer off her lap and threw her arms around Chase.

He held her close and wove his fingers into her tangled curls. He could hardly speak. But he managed to breath out the only words he knew to tell her. "I can save your life."

She pulled away. Tears streamed down her cheeks. "No. You can't. Please don't be mad, but I already talked to Mason. I won't allow it and neither will my doctor."

"Yeah, it didn't take me long to figure out why

you sent me out of the room last night. I'm not mad. But I'm not convinced."

She stared into his eyes. Her breathing steady. "Chase. I will not allow it."

He met her resolve. And refused to agree. A knock on the door broke the tension. Chase rose off the bed and pulled the door open. Finley waited in the hall.

"I'm sorry to interrupt. Switchblade says you need to come to the command center."

She'd been crying. Had the news spread already? "Go tell him I'll be there in five minutes." He touched her cheek.

She nodded and hurried away.

"I moved the screen com to my laptop," Mel said. "Go on. I'll be fine."

He sat on the bed and wrapped his arms around her. "You just don't want to talk about this." He lifted his face from her neck and kissed her. "I love you more than life."

She held his face and returned the kiss. "Then we have a problem. Can we agree to disagree?"

"For today. No promises about tomorrow."

She shook her head. "Chase."

He rose off the bed. "Gotta go. Eat your breakfast."

She frowned as she picked up dry toast and bit off a chunk. Chase looked on for a moment before leaving her. He'd convince her. Or he'd do it without her even knowing.

Sameea stood in the hall. She went in as Chase came out, and he clasped her hand for a second. Surely Mel's mother would be on his side. He headed for the lift.

One floor down, he found chaos had overtaken the command center. Switchblade yelled at some poor kid working on the holographic display. Ridge sat at Mel's station, a blank stare on his face as others crowded around him, shouting demands.

Chase placed two fingers against the corners of his mouth and whistled.

The commotion ceased. Until they all ran at him with questions about their leader.

"She's resting. But she's got a laptop with her in bed and she's trying to work. All of you need to get this room and the whole underground running smoothly. What I witnessed when I walked in was the opposite. Please try to make it work."

The room quieted, but a real leader was needed. Chase pulled Switchblade from the room and into the lobby near the lifts.

"I know about your promise to Mel last night. I'm not surprised. But I don't—"

"We been through this, Charlie. She's in God's hands."

Chase's jaw tightened. "I know that. But what if it's God's will for me to give her my blood?"

"You're reaching, brother. Look, I don't want to be against you. You're my best friend. But as long as I'm alive, I will stop you." Switch gripped Chase's shoulders. "I'm sorry—I don't see how it can be God's will for you to do what you're thinkin'. Now go on and take care of her. But quit this foolishness."

Chase stared up at the big man. "Who's meeting Mom and Amos?"

"I'm going."

"Thank you. I'll be with Mel." Chase headed for the lift.

"Don't be holdin' this against me. I gotta do things Melody's way."

Chase faced his friend. "Bring them up to our room when you get back."

"Will do. I'm praying, Charlie. God'll work this out. You'll see."

Chase stepped into the lift as Switchblade headed back to the command center. But he didn't go up. He went down to the clinic.

Too many people there to scope out the supplies. And Dani spotted him right away.

"What is it?" She came toward him. "Is Melody all right? Do you need something?"

The Spirit welled up inside him. *Truth.*

"I'm going to save her."

She crossed her arms. "She's in—"

"She's in God's hands. I know. And I'm going to do this. Help me."

Dani breathed in, staring at him. "I can't make you any promises."

He smiled. "Thank you." He headed back to the lifts.

"For what?" she called after him. "I didn't agree to anything."

49

Mel slept deeply that afternoon. Chase left her to meet Mom and Amos in the main lobby. The exoself reported a few Federal agents were scouting the people-mover stations. And they'd roped off the cemetery. But they hadn't approached Eight Mile Road. Or the Cosimo.

But getting around town now wouldn't be easy. Chase stayed on a VPad with Switchblade. The newlyweds had come into town in one of the produce trucks the co-op used to ship out goods from the upper floors of the Cos. Before that, Mom and Amos used multiple transports to get from Gagnon to Detroit.

Now Mom was on Switch's VPad. It'd been weeks since Chase spoke with her and she seemed determined to catch up even before she arrived.

"How sick is Melody?" she asked.

"She's not feeling too bad yet," Chase told her. He ached inside but remained positive. "She's so glad you'll be here for the baby's arrival."

"Me too, son. I know you're being strong for her. For all of us. But you don't have to pretend with me."

"Mom, let me talk to Amos." Chase paced the empty lobby. No one came in or out without permission now. And Mel was still in charge of requests. But she needed to step down.

"Chase, tell me how the evacuation is

progressing." Amos didn't even say hello first.

"We're moving along pretty well with the plans. Of course, people are still coming into Detroit when they should be staying away."

Amos laughed. "Point taken. I'm just following God's lead."

"I know you are. I'm hoping you'll take over for Melody. She's got to rest and I think she will if she knows you're in charge."

"Have you talked with her about it?"

"I was hoping we could do it together. But we'll let her be the one to bring it up."

"I'm on my way, son."

"Watch out for the patrol at the next intersection. Tell Switch to detour around it."

"Will do." Amos ended the call.

Chase continued to track the VPad. "Did he just call me son?" Amos had done that before, but now it seemed odd. Chase missed his dad. The only person close to him that he'd ever lost. Until now. He closed his eyes. "I'm not going to lose her."

Within minutes, Mom flew through the glass doors and rushed toward him. She threw her arms around his neck and covered his cheeks with kisses.

"I'm so glad you're here," he told her. "But I told you not to come."

"Since when does a mother have to obey her son?" She tousled his long hair before letting him go.

Amos embraced Chase and patted his back. "This is quite a place you've set up here. But the Feds are three blocks away. We need to be getting people out."

Chase let him go, sighed, and shook his head. Amos simply smiled.

"You're cancer free," Chase told him. "In case you

were wondering."

"I figured as much. What about those little warriors you pumped into me?"

"Gone. Just like the ones in Switchblade."

Amos put his arm around Chase's shoulder as they headed for the lifts. Mom and Switch followed.

"You must be thinking about what you could do for Melody," Amos said.

Mom interrupted. "Oh no, you mustn't, son. You know you can't do that again. There has to be another way."

Chase continued forward but looked behind him. "Mel says it's not up for discussion. So we're not discussing it."

"Good for her. Amos, don't bring it up again."

"Yes, dear."

Chase smiled. They were a couple. If Dad was looking down, he was smiling too.

Mel jumped from the bed when Mom and Amos came in. Sameea moved out of the way.

Mel and Mom hugged and cried. And laughed a bit as Mom rubbed Mel's stomach.

Then Amos picked Mel up off her feet. "How's my girl? I've missed you so."

She kissed his cheek. "Me too. I can't believe you're here. It's an answer to prayer."

He gently set her down, and Chase led her back to the bed. The reunion had her out of breath. She crawled in and covered her legs.

"What was your prayer, my sweet girl?" Amos asked.

"I took your place when you were sick. Now I need you to return the favor."

Amos lifted his brows. "Oh. I see. Well, I'll give it

some thought." He smiled.

Mel laughed. "Don't tell me you're surprised. This is the reason you're here and you know it."

He sat next to her and rubbed her arm. "We'll tag-team this job. When you're feeling better, I'll gladly go back into retirement."

She smiled but didn't hold it long. "We'll see."

Amos rose off the bed. "Chase, come and show me where to find the heart of this operation. I hope people remember me."

"They're all waiting for you. Believe me, they'll be glad to have you back in charge."

"Hey," Mel said. "Was I that bad at my job?"

Chase bent near and kissed her. "*You* are a great leader. But until now there wasn't another person in this building capable of running things." He headed for the door. "Come on, Amos. Mom, you stay here with the ladies. I'll be back in a while."

"All right, son. The mothers-in-law can help Melody decide what to name the baby."

From the corner nearest the window, Sameea gave a gentle smile. But it didn't hide the pain in her eyes. She stepped close and held her hand out to Mom. Mel introduced the grandmothers as Chase and Amos left the room.

A solemn quiet met them as they entered the command center. Definitely not the out-of-control room Chase had visited earlier. Leo greeted Amos with a hug. Others did the same. Finley and Erin. And the rest of the group from Blue Sky Field. Even people who'd never met Amos in person showed their gratitude to him. *This* was most certainly God's will. Was it the reason Chase had been led to save Amos? So he could resume his role when Mel...

A shudder crawled up Chase's spine. He'd find no such assurance of God's will in allowing his wife to die. Turmoil filled his mind. Then his spirit. If he'd just let Amos die...or Switchblade...

No. He wouldn't allow this evil to build up inside him. By God's grace, he'd saved the lives of loved ones. And he'd do it again. If he never regained consciousness—if it killed him—*that* would be God's will.

50

Days went by as groups of believers made the arduous journey from the Cos to an old train station west of town—the only station in the area the rail system still used. Didn't take much cyber manipulation with the cargo trains delivering goods to the growing number of Feds. Empty cars pulled out twice weekly. Eli's father provided information about guards and schedules. Chase took the trains off WR return trips long enough for some supposed maintenance. But the trains weren't at the station as the reports indicated. They were headed north with two or three hundred Christians on board.

Turned out to be easier than expected. Not one human manned the station. Once the transports hauling food and supplies headed out, only a few cyber-guards remained. Chase shut them down when needed, set the cameras to show false real-time shots, and programmed the empty train.

Getting the groups on board meant using the tunnel system under the Cos. One extension went nearly all the way to the station. Now three successful missions of getting people out the Cos and away from Detroit had been accomplished. The farmers, the salesmen, and all who tended the gardens were gone. They'd left behind prepared chicken and fish in cold storage. And some vegetables and grain. And then they left with the others. Less than two hundred believers remained. Fifty would leave today. And then no more.

It'd been Amos who made the decision. Chase agreed. Everyone who remained had volunteered, knowing it could mean death. They'd meet the WR head-on.

No families. Erin had left with most of the teens, who were moved to safer locations in Ontario. There'd been some hard goodbyes. Finley insisted on staying. She was old enough to make the call. Now she was the youngest resident at the Cos.

Except for one child. Eli remained with his dad. Brian's valuable knowledge of the railways had served the underground well. But the believers were done with the trains.

Today Eli and Brian joined the last group of refugees heading out in a rogue truck driven by one of the last up-top believers to escape Detroit. They'd move to a good-sized base in what used to be Pennsylvania.

In the hallway near the lifts, Chase knelt down to hug the little boy he'd rescued in Ann Arbor.

"I'll miss you, Eli," he said. "Help your dad take care of things at the new base."

"I wish you and Miss Melody could come. She was real nice to me before she had to go stay in her room. Is she gonna get better?"

Chase smiled. "Yes. She is." He tilted his head. "You know, Miss Melody is having a baby. If it's a boy—and she says it is—I think his name will be Eli. Would that be OK with you?"

The boy smiled. "*My* name? For real?"

"For real." Chase rose and shook Brian's hand. Then he reached out and hugged the man. A single dad escaping the grip of the powers that killed his wife. "God be with you."

"And with you," Brian said. He walked away with his son's hand in his. Forty-two others went with them. They'd have to get past checkpoints to make it out of town. And Chase would make sure it happened.

He leaned against the wall and prayed. In two weeks, the Cosimo would be overrun with Feds. So the reports indicated. But for now, they didn't come near the place. The data offered nothing to tell Chase why. "Thank You for keeping them away," he prayed.

But sooner or later, they'd come right in the front door. And they'd reestablish ownership of their superscraper.

He needed to get to the command center. But first he went to check on Mel. She pushed up in the bed when he entered their room. No one was with her.

"You shouldn't be alone," he said quietly. "Where's your mother?"

"I sent her to take a nap. I'm fine, but she's been hovering over me to the point of not taking care of herself."

"I'll stay with you. I need to run data while the last group heads out of town, but I can do that from here." He sat next to her and pulled his legs onto the bed.

She laid her head against his chest, and he slid his arm under her. Ragged breaths escaped her mouth. The whites of her eyes were dull yellow, her skin cold.

"I've been up on eighty-nine again this morning. If I carried you up there, do you think we could reconnect the trail I used to reach Robert? Or do you think the computer virus wiped it out?"

"I wish you'd let that go. What do you think he could do? There's nothing anybody can do."

He pulled her closer and buried his face in her hair. "Mason will be in later. I think he wants to talk about delivering the baby."

"Chase, once the baby's—"

"Don't you dare tell me you're leaving me to raise this baby on my own. I can't do it." He rose off the bed and walked to the window.

"Of course you can. You're his father. And God will be with you."

"It's his fault you're…"

She pushed up. "Come here."

He returned to her side. Tears filled his eyes. "I'm sorry. Sometimes I can't help but feel like this wouldn't be happening if you weren't pregnant."

"But you know better." She stroked his cheek. Then his chest. "Please don't blame the baby. Or God. This is nobody's fault."

Chase grabbed her hand and kissed it. "I have to run data on the checkpoints." He moved to the sofa and rested his elbows on his knees.

Mel lay back, seeming to stare at the light over her head. Before long the sound of her rhythmic breathing filled Chase's ears.

The transport had made it safely past the checkpoints. Now only one hundred fifty-seven people remained at the Cos. Able men and women. Strong and smart. Ready to take on the Western Republic.

They'd try to subvert the government's plan to wipe out dissenters and other groups lured into Detroit. Getting the entire population out of town wasn't possible, but the believers remaining would do what they could to protect the people who had no place else to go.

Mel stirred. "Chase?"

He hurried to her side. "What do you need, sweetheart?"

"You wanted to go back to Eight Mile one more time. I think you should go."

He kissed her forehead. "I'm not leaving you."

She huffed. "But it was your mission."

"My mission has changed. I've got a band of people left here who plan to fight the WR. We have to prepare. And I've got a wife who needs me."

"All right." She closed her eyes. "But if I could, I'd go back there with you. We could be missionaries together. The way it was meant to be."

Hope flooded his spirit. It'd be wonderful. But it would never happen.

Sameea entered with Mason, and Chase stood.

"I've got your medicine," the doctor said. He sat on the edge of the bed and helped Mel with a glass of water. Then he checked her vitals, even though Chase could have told him what he needed to know.

"How do you feel about having a baby tomorrow?" he asked Mel.

Panic nearly knocked Chase down. Tomorrow? She'd give up once the baby was born.

"I'm ready," Mel said. "Do you think he'll be OK?"

"I'm sure of it," Mason said with a smile.

Mel seemed to perk up. Sameea joined in the excitement. Chase leaned against the wall, a weight holding back his enthusiasm. He prayed tomorrow would never come. Finley once told him the Underground Church had been brought to Detroit to wait for the Lord's return. Now most of the believers had left. But Chase prayed the Lord would return anyway and take them away from this nightmare.

Before Mel left without him.

My plans are not your plans.

The peace he loved flooded in. And he admitted what he couldn't quite accept. "It's Your show, Lord."

"Baby, what did you say?" Mel asked.

He went to her and grasped her hands. "Is there anything you'd like to do before the big day?"

She smiled. "Since you asked, yes. I'd like to go on a date."

Chase met her request with a laugh. "A movie? A walk along the riverfront?"

"Maybe just a quiet dinner. Do you think we could do that?"

"I'm on it. I've got to go check on things in the command center. And then I'll arrange the best date we've ever had."

"Shouldn't be too hard, since we've never had a date." She laughed softly and it filled Chase with joy.

He left her with her mother and her doctor and took the lift down to the command center.

"The last group is on their way," he told Amos. "And the rest of us are insane. We can't fight the WR."

"We can and we will. But we're going to need every bit of transhuman power you can muster."

"My wife is having a baby tomorrow."

Amos lowered his gaze. "I wish we could have sent her away from here."

"No more wishing, old man. We hope and we pray."

Amos grinned and shook his head. "You remember."

"I remember everything you taught me. But I'm not sure either of us knows enough to get these people through what's coming."

51

Amos had fallen back into his role as leader with determination. The young would-be soldiers gathered around him. Chase left them to strategize a battle. A cyber war. Would it go beyond that? Flesh and blood? He needed to be part of the planning.

But right now, he had to plan a date for his dying wife. And after their special evening...

He shuddered. He could save Mel or save everybody else. Now was the time to choose.

"I can't save anybody."

He grabbed Switchblade's arm as he passed him on the way to the lifts. "Come with me."

"What're you pulling on me for, robot? I got work to do." Switchblade kept on toward the command center.

"Melody's not going to live much longer."

Switch spun around. His eyes met Chase's and he let out a breath. "What do you need? Just say it."

"She wants me to take her on a date tonight. Tomorrow Mason will take the baby. And she'll give up."

"You don't know that. She's strong." Switchblade came close. "You gotta have faith, brother."

Chase managed half a smile. "Right. Will you help me?"

"With date night? Not if you're planning a last

meal. But if you just wanna spend some time with your bride before the blessed event, I'm all yours."

"OK. Follow me."

Chase spent half an hour with Switch, Brax, and Finley. The kids would plan the menu and set the table. Switchblade would get the table in place once he determined the plan was even doable.

The next few minutes put Chase in the clinic with Mason and Dani. The doctor explained the procedure. Delivering the baby wouldn't provide much relief to Mel's failing organs, but she could rally for a few weeks. And the baby might live.

"Might?" Chase asked. "You don't think the baby's strong enough?"

"As far as the baby's health is concerned, Melody's blood is poison. I'm surprised he's still active. His vitals are good. But he can't live much longer if we don't take him. Even then, he may not survive."

"You have no way of knowing it's a boy." Chase sat in Mason's office and stared at the floor.

"Sounds better than *it*. And Melody seems sure. I want you to bring her here later tonight. We'll do the C-section first thing in the morning."

"I think it's time we start moving below. I want to take her to a safe room eight floors under. In a week, we'll move the command center down too. But I want to make sure Mel and the baby are safe. I don't want to have to move them if they're not doing well."

"It's a good idea—I can get everything ready. Who's left in the building besides our group?"

"No one."

"And the city?"

"Full of dissenters. Maybe even a few up-top believers. And the poor people who can't leave.

According to the data, about three thousand people are still here."

"A few weeks ago, it was thirty thousand. You did a great job getting people out. But what's happening in Detroit—"

"Is just the beginning. The plan to round up society's bad element in one place failed. But they won't stop."

The doctor shook his head. "You must feel like you've got to save the whole world."

"I'd rather save my wife." Chase cocked his head.

"She knows, and I know, you are here for a much bigger role. I'm sorry. It can't happen."

Chase sprang out of the chair and faced Dani. Fear lit her eyes, but Chase thought she gave him the slightest nod. He hurried past her. "I'll bring Mel to the safe room at ten tonight," he said without looking back.

Now for one more chore in planning Mel's date. Chase rummaged through drawers in the supply room near the kitchen. At last, he located a pair of sharp scissors. Then he found the storeroom with enough clothes remaining to take care of an army. He smirked when he found what he was looking for. The one thing nobody needed in the underground. A designer suit. Yet here it was.

Next, he visited his mother, who'd been on a secret mission of her own. Chase didn't ask her to explain the coy grin.

He simply handed her the scissors.

52

Chase knocked on the door of his own room. Sameea opened it. Her eyes flew open wide and she nearly laughed. Was it that funny?

She stepped to one side, and Chase caught sight of Mel. She stood by the window, her hair hanging in loose ringlets across her bare shoulders. She'd obviously sent someone to shop for her in the same storage room where Chase had been. The sparkling black gown fell in waves around her ankles. The bulge in her middle stretched the fabric tight, but she was stunning and Chase could only stare.

Until her surprised expression matched Sameea's.

"Who are you and what have you done with my husband?" she asked.

He smiled. "Chase Sterling has never been on a date without first visiting his personal presentation assistant." He spread his arms and walked toward her.

She seemed to study him. Look him over. "You gorgeous game-show host. I've missed you. I always wanted to kiss that well-groomed, blazing-hot man."

"Miss Melody, how shocking. At one time, that would have been inappropriate. But not anymore." He grabbed her and pulled her close. And kissed her until Sameea cleared her throat.

Chase eased his face away from Mel's to find his mother-in-law shaking her head.

"Such foolishness," she said. "But you do look better without the long hair and the beard. Blazing hot."

Heat rose from Chase's neck to his ears as he laughed. "Thank you. And don't worry. I'm not planning anything foolish. I know Mel's not supposed to get too excited."

"Too late for that," Mel said as she ran her hands down the front of his deep gray blazer.

Chase met her eyes. "You look pretty hot yourself. I think we'd better get on with this date."

"After this, I can't wait to see what else you've done."

They headed for the hyper lifts. Mel walked slowly, leaning against Chase. Once in the lift, Chase spoke the number. "One twenty-four."

"We're going to the top floor? But it's empty. What are we—?"

"You'll see."

The ride up took nearly a minute. And then the lift door dissolved. A dark, empty space greeted them. Chase lifted Mel and carried her up a narrow staircase. He pushed open a metal door. And set his wife down under the stars.

She gasped. A small table waited for them, complete with tapered candles. A large silver dome covered their dinner. Chase wasn't sure what he'd find there, but it didn't matter. All that mattered was the look on his sweet wife's face. The candlelight in her eyes.

"It's perfect." She fell into his arms. "Thank you."

The edges of the superscraper didn't allow a view of the city. High walls surrounded the massive rooftop. Several pyramids emitting golden light shot up from the flat surface around them. Beyond that, the top of the Cos stretched out much wider than the auditorium and stage where Chase once changed lives.

Stars shone bright above. Chase slid a chair from the table, and Mel took her place. He sat across from her and lifted the cover and peeked at their dinner. But Mel put her hand on top of his and eased the lid back down.

"Pray with me," she said.

Her words nearly broke him. He'd been praying for days. But he hadn't allowed her to take part in the conversation. She wouldn't approve. Now he had to be careful what he said.

He clutched her hand and bowed his head. "Thank You for this beautiful woman. She's the best part of my life in this crazy world. I—" His voice shattered.

"Father, bless this man. Keep him strong. Give him courage. Save our baby and let him be a blessing to his sweet, loving daddy. Thank You for this night. For this meal and the ones who prepared it. For the time we have. For whatever tomorrow brings. Protect Your people. Prepare them. Rescue them. Show us the way, Lord. In the name of Christ, our Redeemer. Amen."

He squeezed her hand and looked up to find her smiling. How could she be this strong? "I love you."

"And I love you. Now let's see what we've got here." She removed the dome from the platter.

No surprises. Chicken and fish. Some carrots and potatoes. And a small loaf of bread. "Looks great," he said. He spooned dinner onto her plate and set it in front of her. She pressed her lips together and picked up her fork.

Chase fixed himself a plate and took a bite of the

fish. "Not bad. Try some."

But she only pushed the food around on her plate. At last, she broke the bread in half and bit off a small piece. "I'm so happy to be here with you. Just the two of us. But forgive me if I don't eat too much."

"I know you don't feel well, sweetheart. You don't have to pretend."

"Do you remember all the nights we had pizza delivered to your dressing room? That was the best pizza in the world." She picked up her fork and nibbled on the vegetables.

Chase laughed. "See, we *did* have a few dates before this one. You and me and a pizza from Mario's. Those were the days. You kept me going. Did you know that? You were the only one who treated me like a person and not a commodity."

"But date night was for the queen. Do you think she's still in Ann Arbor?"

"Yes. The exoself keeps track of her."

Mel dropped her fork. "You're not communicating with her. Are you?"

"No, of course not. Whatever she's got installed in her doesn't function like what's in me. She hasn't latched onto my presence. Sparky won't allow it. You don't need to worry about that."

"All right. But you know she'll be coming in with the rest of the Feds. I can't stand the thought of her being here. Being near you. Taking you away." She shook her head. "Funny things go on in your mind when you know you're about to…"

"Melody, she's one among many. I hope I never see her, but if I get the chance, I will end her. Now, can we change the subject?"

"Yes. Let's talk about the baby. And about you. If

it seems this existence is going to continue much longer, I want you to find someone to share it with."

Chase sprang out of his chair. "This is not good date-night conversation, Mel. I don't want your blessing to be with another woman. You are the only woman in this world for me. And it's completely in my power to save your life."

"You know how I feel about that. It would kill you. Or at the very least, put you in a coma for…forever. Even if I didn't love you too much to allow it, *you* are more important to our people than I am. What would happen if you died?"

She stood and her voice grew louder. "The exoself would be gone. The shield over this building would be gone. Our source of intel would be gone. And then we'd all die. So the way I see it, I can go now and leave you to save our baby. Or the baby and I can die when the Feds come in and kill everyone in Detroit. Is that what you want?"

"You don't know that I would die, or even stay unconscious for more than a few days. I woke up last time and I'll wake up again. Just trust me. I can do this."

"No, you can't! I want you to promise me. Right now, Chase." Tears streamed down her cheeks.

He stepped around the table and held out his hands. She turned away and ran toward the high wall surrounding them.

"Mel, take it easy. You shouldn't be—" Chase looked up as the exoself reported drones in the area.

"Chase, I see them. What should I do?" Mel had stopped twenty yards away from him. The drones hovered directly over them.

"It's OK. They can't see us. The shield is up and

we're safe. I'm coming to get you. Just stay right there."

"I'm not leaving this rooftop unless you promise."

He started toward her, but she backed away.

"Promise me."

A small device dropped between them. An old remote-control drone with a camera attached. Like the ones used twenty years ago, long before S-drones filled the skies. Then another dropped. And another.

"Chase, do something. Blow them up."

"I can't. Old technology. They're taking pictures. There's a door twenty feet behind you. It's a maintenance closet. I'm unlocking it through the building's security programs. Go inside and wait for me." Chase stared into the lens of the fourth little drone floating down onto the Cos. "Mel. Now. Go!"

She did what he told her and the door opened for her. She went in and pulled the door shut.

Chase couldn't blow up the old drones, but he could scramble the camera feed. And he could smash the little things. He grabbed one and crumpled it like paper. Then another. The other two flew away. The surveillance drones hovering over the Cos headed back in the direction of Ann Arbor. How did they know there was activity on the roof?

He hurried to the closet and flung the door open. Mel lay crumpled on the floor. He knelt beside her.

"Promise me," she whispered.

He slid his arms under her and pulled her close. "I'm sorry. I'm sorry, Mel. Whatever you want, I promise. Just don't leave me."

But she didn't answer. Her blood pressure dropped. Her liver, and now her kidneys, were failing fast. He rose and carried her back to the staircase. They wouldn't be ready in the safe room yet, but he held her all the way down into the parking garage. Then he took another lift and went down farther.

Switchblade stood before him when the lift door dissolved.

"We picked up on the drones," Switch said. "I figured you'd bring her straight here. What happened up there? Why is she out?"

"It was too much for her," Chase answered. He hurried to the room where Dani and Mason were setting up the bed and the equipment they'd brought down.

Mason dropped the blankets he held. "Put her down."

Chase gently lowered her to the hospital bed and backed away. And Mason listened to her fading heartbeat. "She's not going to make it till morning. I'm taking the baby tonight."

"I have to do something," Chase said. "Can you wait?"

"We've got to get the rest of the equipment moved down, so yeah, it'll have to wait. But not long. What do you mean you've got to do something? Are we under attack?"

Chase could hardly comprehend the words. "What?" He caressed Mel's face. "No, we're not under attack. The drones are gone. No intel about…anything."

Switchblade gripped Chase's shoulder. "Then what have you got to do that's more important than being here for Melody?"

Chase rushed for the door. "Fifteen minutes. That's all. It's for her. Get her mother and brothers down here to…tell her goodbye." He headed for the lift. Switchblade followed him.

"I know you got something up that transhuman sleeve, robot. I told Mason not to bother locking up nothin' 'cause it wouldn't stop you. So the stuff you need to do what you're thinkin' is hidden. Not a needle or an IV bag left in the clinic."

"I'm not going to the clinic." Chase stepped into the lift.

"Then where—"

"Brother. Trust me." He looked up. "Lobby." The door materialized and the lift headed up.

But Chase didn't exit in the lobby. If Switchblade followed, he'd never find him. "Eighty-nine," he said. And the lift climbed high.

53

"Open." The doors hiding the supercomputer let Chase in. The massive thing blinked and flashed. He didn't know what to do. Mel had started at a control panel. He walked up and waved his hand over it.

"Dear God, show me the way."

The exoself plunged into communication with the system, and in only a minute Chase was able to enter the right code. He pulled the gurney closer to the panel. The magnetized electrodes gripped his head.

"Sparky, I'm leaving you here. Keep the shield up. Send all data to Amos's computer. Allow him to interact with you and to feed information into WR programs."

Chase's muscles tightened. He fell onto the gurney. Before the exoself pulled away, he took the data trail to Robert's old laptop. It might not go anywhere, but he left a message.

Hey, how's my favorite mad scientist? I'm in a tough spot. There's about to be a war, and I'm leaving the exoself on the eighty-ninth floor of the Cosimo building. You know the place. If you can, please help me make this work. Unplug the WR.

The cyber power he'd come to rely on slipped out of Chase. "Thank You, Lord. I'm not trusting a computer program to save Your people. They're in Your hands. But if You can use Sparky, well, he's all

Yours. Now I'm going to save my wife. Don't let them stop me."

He yanked loose the electrodes and tried to push himself off the gurney. But he fell to the floor. "Come on, you can do this." He got up on his hands and knees. Then he stood and grabbed the side of the gurney. "Pull it together. You've got a long way to go."

He faced the exoself, which hovered in the center of the room. "Do what I told you. And don't talk to strangers." He headed toward the door. The exoself surged. Blaring light filled the room. Chase stepped back. "If I can come back for you, I will. If not, trust the ones I trust. You know who they are." He hurried to the lift.

"Garage," he said. When he arrived, he moved to the lift going deeper down. "Eight." He stood straight and brushed off his designer suit. "Show time."

No one in the hallway. He marched to the safe room and found the door open. Sameea wept over her daughter. Brax and Ridge leaned against the wall. Mason sat in a chair, his head down.

Ridge looked up. "Dani and Switchblade went up to bring more stuff from the clinic. After they spent a few minutes looking for *you*. What's going on, man?"

Chase fell back against the wall and breathed in. "Mason, how long until you deliver the baby?"

"As soon as Dani gets back with the equipment. We've got an incubator. And a ventilator if we need it."

Chase nodded. He couldn't lift himself off the wall. Had he become so dependent on the exoself? He exhaled as Dani and Switch came in. His mother and Amos were right behind them.

Mom already had tears in her eyes, but she calmly led Sameea out of the small room. Brax and Ridge followed. Amos said a prayer before going back into the hall. Switchblade hugged Chase and followed the others. Did he notice Chase could hardly move? Dani and Mason were left at Mel's bedside.

"I need a minute," Chase said.

Dani slid by him, grasping his hand for a second before she left. And from her hand to his, a tubular object passed.

The doctor stood in the doorway. "One minute, Chase. We're running out of time." He stepped into the hall.

With every bit of strength he had left, Chase pushed the door closed. He slid the safety lock into place. No one but a transhuman could bust it down. But before he'd given up the exoself, he'd gone into the security system of the safe room and programmed the door to release ten minutes after a manual lockdown. That's all the time he needed.

He fingered the hypodermic in his hand. The banging on the other side of the door started. Throwing off his blazer, he pulled the chair close to Mel and dropped into it. He rolled up the sleeve of his white shirt.

"Sweetheart, I've broken every promise I ever made to you. Except one." He kissed her soft lips. "I love you forever." Then he rubbed her stomach through the hospital gown they'd put on her. "Daddy's got this." He picked up the syringe.

And jabbed it into his arm.

Losing the exoself already had him going down. How long could he stay conscious with the nanobots streaming out?

"Keep it together." The oversized barrel filled with blood. He eased it out of his arm. And thrust it into

Mel's. Then again. And again. A fourth time, he drew his blood and gave it to his wife. Would it be enough? His eyes fell shut and his fingers grew weary. Again. Five, six, seven. It was all he could do.

The needle dropped to the floor. And Chase dropped too. He stared at the white light over his head.

Until all went black.

54

"Charles Redding."

"Here I am."

"What do you see?"

Chase pushed himself up. "Nothing but clouds. Am I in heaven?"

"You won't find clouds in heaven."

"Then where am I?"

"Get on your feet."

Chase rose as though a hand had come up through the clouds and thrust him upright. "I'm not going back again. Which way do I go to get home?"

"You know the way."

The smooth surface beneath him became warm. And wet. The white haze that had hidden his feet was gone. In its place, a river of red. He headed toward the hill at the end of the flatland. "Is this the blood that saved me?"

"Walk in it."

"It's flowing from the hill. Can I go there?"

But the hill was gone. And the blood washing over his feet became clean water.

"Is Mel in heaven?"

"She's mine."

"The baby?"

"Mine."

The river's flow took him. He sank into the rhythm

of the water lapping against the shore. "I don't want to go back without them. I gave my blood to—"

"You couldn't save anyone."

Chase eased closer to the river's bank. "I know. What do You want me to do?" And then he fell headlong into a field of color and sound. The color lifted him upward. The sound let him fall into a blissful place. Over and over. He laughed out loud and lifted his arms over his head.

And then he found himself again in the clouds. "Take me home." He reached down to touch the ground. Cold stone. The clouds parted.

He stood among the pyramids of light on top of the Cos. The high wall surrounded him. "Is this where I'll speak?"

Rushing wind like the wings of angels swept over him. He lifted his eyes to the cloudless sky and prayed for the return of the indescribable color and sound he knew must belong to heaven.

And then a baby cried. Long and hard.

He stared at the cold stone rooftop. "Babies don't cry in heaven."

55

"Chase? Wake up. What did you say? Tell me again. Open your eyes!" Somebody was shouting. And there was that crying again. A baby.

Chase's eyelids were surely glued shut. A rock must be lodged in his throat. He groaned and let out a rattled whisper. "Babies don't cry in heaven."

The soft weeping of a woman joined the loud wail of an infant. "You hear that? Open your eyes. I'll show you the baby."

"Mel?" Chase forced his eyes open. His clouded vision slowly cleared. And he saw who spoke to him.

"Mom."

"Yes, son. I'm right here. And your baby is here."

"My baby lived."

"The baby is strong and healthy."

Chase blinked. "Mel's gone."

"I'm afraid so."

Her words nearly threw Chase back into the dream world. But he held on.

"I don't like it, but she goes off almost every day. Your wife says she has to continue your mission." Mom moved away and became a blur. She bent over. Did she pick up something?

"She's…" He closed his eyes. "Oh, God, thank You," he whispered. "Thank You." He tried to push himself up, but he had no strength.

"Chase, I'm going for the doctor." Mom moved closer.

"Not yet." He reached for her and she grasped his hand. "Mel's better?"

"Yes." She smiled. "Completely."

"And she had our baby? Let me see him."

Mom laughed softly. "Well, son, Mel was so sure about it. Turns out she was wrong. You have a little girl."

"A daughter?" The crying had ceased.

"Here she is." Mom sat on the bed and raised the edge of a blanket. "She has Melody's hair. Don't you think so? I've never seen a baby with so much hair. But look, she has your eyes."

Gazing into the tiny girl's blue eyes, Chase managed to push up on his elbows. "She's beautiful."

"Chase, I haven't even got a VPad in here with me. I've got to go get Amos. And you need to see the doctor." She seemed to laugh and cry all at once. "This is a miracle."

"Mom, where is Mel? I've got to see her."

"She's gone to Eight Mile Road."

The news gave Chase's voice a surge of strength. "She's what? That's no place for Mel, especially not with the Feds moving in."

"Now, don't panic. She didn't go alone. Switchblade's with her. And Mason and Ridge. And some others. As for the Feds...well...they can't exactly move in."

"What are you talking about? How long have I been out? Where am I? And you just said you were going to get the doctor, and now you're saying he's with Mel? Mom, what has happened around here?"

The baby let out another cry. Mom's eyes were

wide.

Chase fell back onto the pillow. "Start at the beginning."

"The beginning? We got back into the safe room. You were on the floor. Melody was already stirring. Mason said her vitals were good, but he wasn't at all sure she'd recover, so he did the C-section as planned. The baby was healthy. Amazingly healthy. By the next morning—the next morning, Chase—Melody was healed. You saved her."

"I didn't save anybody." Chase smiled. "How mad was she?"

Mom chuckled and shook her head. "You know what she's like. But she loves you, son. She spends most of her time in here with you. I can't believe you picked now to wake up, while she's out in the city."

"The city—what's going on out there? What did you mean about the Feds? How long have I been out?"

"Nearly a month. We thought you'd never wake up. In fact, the doctor said even your manmade parts were dying. I really think I'd better go get him."

"A month? The Feds planned to take over the Cos two weeks ago."

"The exoself stopped them."

"About Mason—is he here? Or is he on Eight Mile?"

Mom tilted her head. "I'm going to get *your* doctor. Robert Fiender is here. He's in the command center with Amos."

Chase forced himself upright in the bed. "Robert is here? How on earth?"

"I know you have a lot of questions. I'll be back in a few minutes." She hurried across the room and lowered the baby into a small crib.

Chase studied his surroundings. Things were getting clearer, at least about his location. He was in his own bed. In the room he shared with Mel. "What's her name?"

"Melody hasn't named her. She said *you* would name her when you woke up. She never gave up hope." Mom faced him and smiled. "The baby's sleeping. I won't be long. Will you be all right?"

"As long as she doesn't cry again. I'm not sure I can get out of bed, much less take care of a baby."

Mom hurried toward the door. "Oh, Chase, this is wonderful. Everyone will be so happy." She rushed back and kissed his cheek. "Three minutes."

She left him, and he lay back in the bed. He rubbed his face. An IV fed into his left wrist. Clear liquid dripped from the bag on a pole next to him. He almost checked his vitals but remembered he'd left the exoself on another floor. The lights were dim. No sound except the soft squeak of his daughter's restful breath.

"Father in heaven, thank You for this." He closed his eyes and relived the lingering dream. Then he heard the door open.

He watched her head for the crib. Had she glanced his way before he opened his eyes?

She leaned over and touched their daughter. "Baby girl, what are you doing in here all alone?"

"She's not alone," Chase said softly. "She's with her dad."

Mel shot straight up and gasped. She stared at Chase for a moment before lifting her hands over her mouth.

"I didn't mean to startle you. It's all right, sweetheart." He pushed up in the bed.

She ran to him and fell into his embrace. And wept. And laughed. And prayed.

"I knew you'd come back to me," she whimpered.

He pressed his face against her neck and breathed in the faint scent of lilacs. The last time he'd held her, the sweet fragrance had left her and something like death had replaced it. But God didn't let her die. "How did you know?"

"You had to wake up." Her voice grew louder and she pushed off him. "So I could beat some sense into you." She slugged his arm.

"Ouch, Mel, that hurt." He rubbed his arm.

She fell onto him again and wept. Again. And then the door flew open. And people started talking. And the baby cried. Mel eased off the bed and wiped her face. But her eyes stayed with his. And he knew she loved him as much as he loved her.

Robert rushed in and boxed his hands around Chase's cheeks. "I told them not to expect a miracle. But here it is!" He laughed and rubbed Chase's head. "How do you feel, son?"

"What are you doing here?"

"I got your message and latched onto the exoself without being detected. And then I used the programs designed for the underground to get a ride into the city. It was simple, really. I made it in before the roadblocks went up. I wormed into WR data—again through Melody's programs—and filed a report indicating I was taking a tour of the new laboratory in the EU. No one knows otherwise. Once I got here, I saw I was too late. You were dying. But as your people say, God has restored you!"

"I still feel like death warmed over."

"We'll put the exoself back and you'll regain your

strength."

"Why didn't you put it back already?"

Amos stepped close, and Chase grasped his outstretched hand.

"That exoself of yours has done some"—Amos looked at Robert—"amazing things. The Feds are so spooked they've stopped trying to come into the city. But they're still out there. They have us surrounded."

"We need a strategy meeting," Chase said. "We'll figure this out."

Mel cleared her throat, and Chase looked up to find her watching him, the baby in her arms.

"Robert, can I unplug from the IV now?"

"Oh, yes, yes. How about some food?" He carefully slid the catheter out of Chase's arm.

"Sounds great. Can Mel and I have a few minutes? Then I need to see Switch. Somebody go find him for me."

Mom came near and kissed Chase's forehead. "We'll take care of everything. Switchblade will be so glad to see you. But he might beat you up. Maybe you should get your superpowers back first." She went to Mel and hugged her.

Chase rubbed his arm. "Yeah, I don't want to get beat up." He smiled at Mel.

She returned the smile. "We'll see you all in a few minutes," she said as the others left the room. Then she carried the baby to the bed and laid her next to Chase. "I've spent so many hours staring at you, willing you to wake up. Praying over you. I'm sorry I wasn't here."

"Mom told me where you were. You must be crazy, Mel. And look at that getup you're wearing. A man-sized dragon sweatshirt? Who gave you that? And this cap." He pulled off the ball cap she wore backward over her braided hair. "I saw you drop the gun on the dresser when you came in." He leaned close and kissed her. "And I know you're a bad shot."

She wrapped her arms around his neck and met his lips with a relentless kiss. Then she gazed into his eyes. "You gave up your last trip to Eight Mile for me. I carried on for you. I love you."

"I love you, Melody." He kissed her again.

The baby made one of those squeaky noises, and Mel leaned back and opened up the blanket. "Look at her, Chase."

The baby wiggled, opened and closed her tiny hands. "I'm looking. At *her*," Chase said.

Mel pursed her lips and lifted her brows. "Yeah, OK, I was wrong. But I'm so glad she's ours. You need to get to know her. She's so sweet."

"She doesn't have a name." Chase caressed the baby's soft curls.

"I was waiting for you to name her. So, you got any ideas?"

"You've waited a month. Can I have a day or two?"

"Sure." She gave him another kiss. "She has my mother's skin tone, and that's definitely my father's chin. But she has your eyes. She weighed only four pounds when she was born. But her breathing and everything else was perfect. When you get the exoself back, will you be able to tell…?"

"If she's transhuman? Does it matter?"

Mel cupped his face with her hands. "No." Her tears fell again, but she laughed. "Welcome back, Chase. I am so glad you're here with us."

56

Time seemed unimportant while Chase held his baby for the first time. The tiny girl mesmerized him. Mel said it didn't matter if the baby had anything transhuman in her. And it didn't. But once he got the exoself back, Chase would know. He needed to know. For his daughter's sake.

He lifted her to his shoulder and rubbed his cheek against hers. Then he coughed out a breath. Nothing about *this* girl smelled like lilacs.

"Um, Mel, what do we use for diapers in the underground?"

Mel had gone into the bathroom to clean up and get out of her "street clothes," as she called them. She spoke through the open door. "Oh no. I'm coming."

She stepped to the edge of the bed. Her hair hung loose now, and she wore a pink top and white jeans. Chase laid the baby on the bed and pulled his wife close for a kiss. "Now, there's the woman I love. But the street punk was kind of cute."

She laughed, and the sound of it filled him. Almost like heaven.

"We have a good supply of cloth diapers. Once you're up and feeling like yourself again, I'll give you a lesson." She took the baby to the crib. "And by the way, the street punk is a better shot now. Got some pointers on the mission field."

"That's comforting. I think."

"Did you eat the food your mom brought?"

Chase set his feet on the floor and stood. But he dropped back to the bed. After a moment he stood again and headed for the bathroom. "Yeah, and I'm feeling a little stronger."

"Are you all right? Let me help you."

"Take care of the baby. I'm fine." His drawstring pajama bottoms and white T-shirt seemed fresh. Mel had been caring for *him*, as well as a newborn. *And* the people on Eight Mile. And a number of other things, no doubt.

"Is Amos still running the show? Or did you step back in as leader?"

"Don't worry—I haven't taken on too much. He's still in charge. If it stays that way, I won't complain. If he needs me to take over some things, that's OK too."

Chase showered and returned to the bed to find jeans and a button-down shirt laid out for him. He dressed while Mel rinsed out the dirty diaper.

"Tell me about Switchblade," he said. "Mom told me he's waiting in the lobby down the hall. What's he been like since I did the forbidden?"

"He was hurt. And scared, though he wouldn't admit it. And mad. Not just at you but at Dani. He says he's done with her." Mel came out of the bathroom.

"Then you know what she did."

"She confessed. I forgave her, but it was hard. We were becoming close friends. She betrayed me and I felt like it was her fault I was losing you."

"And Switch feels that way too."

She nodded. "Even more so. They were getting really tight. You know? And she went against him."

"I'll talk to him."

The baby began to cry again.

Mel picked her up. "I've got to feed…what's-her-name."

Chase smiled and kissed his wife. "I want to stay while you feed her."

"I know, but we've got a lot to do now that you're back. And Switch is sitting out there, waiting for you to surface. Go ahead—as long as you feel strong enough. I'll catch up with you. But don't go up to eighty-nine without me. OK?"

"I won't." He kissed her again and kissed the baby's head before leaving the room.

Switchblade sat alone on a sofa, his elbows on his knees. His head in his hands.

Chase stepped close. "Hey, brother. You waiting for me?"

Switchblade met his eyes. "Robot. I heard you was back from the dead. How you feeling?"

"Little scared right now. I'm not strong enough to take you on, and I heard you might want to beat me up."

Switchblade rose and folded his arms. "I was considering it. But I'll settle for a handshake."

"Not me." Chase embraced his friend.

Switchblade drew his arms around Chase and pounded a fist into his back. "You never shoulda done it, robot. But when I look at that little squirming baby…at Melody all healed…I know you did what you had to do."

Chase dropped his arms and stepped back. "I'm glad you see it that way. It was God's will. No matter what anyone else thinks, I know it was."

"I ain't arguing. Just wish you woulda let me be the one to help you."

Chase shook his head and smiled. "*You* wouldn't have and you know it. God made a way. He used Dani. And you need to let it go."

Switchblade walked toward the lifts. "She didn't have no right. *She* should've told me, even if you wouldn't."

"Do you love her?"

He licked his lips and raised his brows. "What's love without trust? She could've gotten us all killed by helping you do this thing. She didn't know the exoself was up there on its own. She was just—"

"She was just following God. Forgive her." Chase grabbed hold of Switch's shoulder. "I need to go to the command center. Not sure I can get there on my own."

"I'm with you." Switch stepped into the lift.

Chase followed. "I'm pretty sure I haven't been told everything. What's really going on out there in the city? And why the heck have you been taking my wife to Eight Mile Road?"

Switchblade's hands went to his hips. "*Me* take *her*? That woman's been dragging me to Eight Mile every time I turn around."

"Relax," Chase said with a smile. "Thank you for watching out for her."

"All right, then. You're welcome. Girl's good with those folks—what's left of 'em. Lot more believers in the hood now."

"What about the ones still holding out to get you?"

"Dead. Some of the dragons tried to run. WR got 'em in the woods outside of town."

"How do you know that?"

"People on Eight Mile told us they ran. And Amos and that crazy old doctor have been reading the data just like you used to do. Only they use computers.

Report said nine rogues was killed. The numbers match."

"The underground is running well without me. But I'm sorry about the people who got caught. Don't know if I could've done anything."

"I'm not so sure about that. Sparky's doing fine with the details. But he ain't got no heart, Charlie. He ain't you."

"What do you mean?"

"I mean the exoself don't know what to do to save lives. You're the one who made it happen. You manipulated the WR. Sparky just followed your orders."

"What you mean to say is I was the one who fed lies into the system. But no more. I'm through lying."

Switch stepped out of the lift. "What happened to you while you was out? And how are we supposed to get out of this mess we're in if you don't feed bull to the Feds?"

57

Activity in the command center overflowed into the hall, and several people met Chase with a handshake or hug. Finley and then Brax nearly knocked him off his feet.

"Easy now," Switchblade said. "He ain't got his strength back yet."

Finley wrapped her arms around his neck and kissed his cheek. "I'm glad you decided to wake up. We need you."

Brax pulled Chase in among the computers. "Can you get the exoself back in you now?"

"I plan on it. Didn't think there was any rush, since I heard you can come and go as you please. But I haven't heard everything. Have I?"

Ridge joined them. He patted Chase's back but offered no smile or reassurance. "Come over here, brother. You need to see this."

They stopped in front of the holographic display. Ridge lit it up, and the west end of town rose from the black surface. The familiar road to Ann Arbor stretched to the edge of the display. Too many bodies to count covered the highway and other roads. Parking lots. Grassy areas. Abandoned vehicles lined the roadways. Cyber-guards lay in heaps. Drones had crashed on top of WR self-drives and larger transports. Four uniformed gunmen patrolled the area.

Chase circled the display. "The WR is taking a beating. Who's doing this?"

Then the display showed two men with assault rifles rushing the patrols and firing. The four tried to run. But they fell to the ground.

"I don't understand. Why didn't the Feds return fire?"

Amos was beside him now. "They didn't defend themselves because their laser weapons have ceased to function. Not enough old-fashioned firepower to make a difference, but the WR keeps sending troops close to the city to monitor the situation. And the dissenters keep taking them out."

"Where'd the dissenters get that much ammunition?"

"Most of the fallen didn't die that way. Federal troops—all of them implanted with neuro-prosthesis devices—started moving in two weeks ago. And—"

"And Sparky blew up their brains."

"Yes. You're looking at a cyber war zone. And the exoself is winning."

Chase found Switchblade's eyes. "I can't believe you've been taking my wife out of this building. It stops now."

Switchblade pulled him to a window. "Look outside, Charlie."

Chase glanced out the glass, then at Switchblade, and back to the window again. A few dozen people walked the streets. No gunfire. No Federal activity.

"Somebody explain this," Chase said.

Switchblade pulled him back to the holograph. "We're close to the center of the city. Feds can't get within ten miles of here. Eight Mile Road is no different. Whoever don't got an NP gets taken out by the dissenters." He pointed at the display. "But somethin's gotta give, Charlie. Only a matter of time before they figure out how to outsmart the exoself."

Chase sank into a chair. He'd have to allow the exoself inside him again. But what he'd feared had happened—it had become a killing machine. Would Sparky even let him take back control? "Mel didn't mention any of this."

Amos sat beside him. "Of course she didn't. She was too overjoyed at having you back. But she's worried, son. Like the rest of us."

"What am I supposed to do?"

"Get us into that room on eighty-nine," Amos said.

Mel came in. Chase rose from the chair, and she grasped his hands.

"You saw what's happening out there," she said.

"Yes. And you are not leaving this building again. I don't care how safe you think it is."

She nodded. "Whatever you say. Robert's waiting by the lifts. You need to try to get us in on eighty-nine."

"Mel, what are you talking about? And where's the baby?"

"She's fine—the grandmothers are fussing over her. Come with me." She headed out the door and toward the lifts.

Robert folded his arms. "We're hoping this will work, son. Come into the lift."

The door dissolved. Robert stepped in, followed by Mel and Chase.

Chase motioned to Switchblade and Amos, who'd accompanied him from the command center. "Come with us."

They both stepped in.

"Eighty-nine," Mel said. But the door didn't appear. "I can't go up, Chase. Neither can Robert, although his voice was programmed to access that floor just like mine was."

"I told Sparky to trust the people I trust."

Robert shook his head. "After you separated? It's not a puppy, Chase. You can't give it voice commands once you've pulled it out of you. It has to be programmed."

"That's not true, Robert. I've talked to it before when it was out of me. What's going on?"

"The exoself has joined itself to the supercomputer," Robert said. "While it allows us to view WR intel, programming is not permissible. But it gained enough from your imprint to know the Feds must be kept away, and the church must be protected. And it doesn't want interference."

"But it knows you—both of you." Chase sucked in a breath. "Eighty-nine."

The door appeared and the lift shot upward.

Mel clung to Chase's arm. "I should've told you, baby. I was just so happy to have you back. And I thought..."

"What, sweetheart? Don't be afraid."

"It seems saving my life was what started the war."

Chase held her close. "No. The Feds started this war. And the dissenters are fighting it. It was bound to happen. The exoself just gave it a nudge."

The door dissolved. Chase stepped out and stood in front of the door barring him from the exoself. "If the lift wouldn't bring you up, why didn't you take the stairs?"

"Tried it, Charlie," Switch said.

Mel held Chase's hand. "The door from the stairwell is electronically sealed. It wouldn't open for me. Or for the various power tools Switch brought up with him. Even if we'd gotten in, I doubt *this* door would have allowed entrance." She stepped closer. "Open."

The door remained shut.

"Open," Chase said.

And the door swung wide.

58

Chase eased into the presence of the exoself. And then he shut the door behind him. Just like when he'd locked himself in the safe room with Mel, the people on the other side started banging on the door. Only this time, Mel was one of them.

He circled the phantom display hovering right where he'd left it. But it'd grown taller and wider. It stretched closer to the array of screens and displays, which were all lit up and flashing code.

"Hi, old friend. I'm here. We need to go back to the way we used to be. Working together. I know you've changed the access code. But I'm sure I know what it is. Thirty-two, seven."

The exoself surged with light. Lines of code fell and numbers rose. But it meant nothing to Chase. He eased to the gurney and held the electrodes close to his head. They flew from his hands and clung to his temples. He stepped as close to the exoself as the wires attached to him would allow.

"We've had enough experience to do this on our own." He stretched out his hand to touch the display, and he pulled down seven lines of code. Every processor in his body sparked. The shock reeled him backward. His neck stiffened. His eyes wouldn't blink.

"I don't know how to lift the number. I don't even know where to find it."

The number filled his sight. Or maybe just his

mind. It floated upward as the exoself diminished in size and brightness. Chase stumbled to the gurney to lie down. He faced the screens flashing at his right side. And he let the data pour in through his eyes.

"Sparky, don't drop our shield while you're moving back in. You're protecting us. But I need to take control now." Chase arched his back and let out a groan. Then he fell against the gurney and spoke a command as the exoself disappeared.

"Open."

The door gave entrance. Mel and the others rushed to him.

"I can't believe you locked us out," Mel said.

"I didn't know what to expect and I had to protect you. Run a check on my systems. The sensors and processors. And your code."

She hurried to the displays and ran her fingers over multiple screens. Robert joined her. Amos and Switchblade stood next to Chase.

"Everything's in order," she said.

Chase yanked off the electrodes. "Robert, how many other people have this thing inside them? Kerstin and who else?"

Mel faced him. "The exoself is tracking Kerstin?"

"Yes. And *she's* tracking the exoself. And there are others." Chase met his doctor's eyes. "I can feel them but I can't count them. How many, Robert?"

"Six hundred," the doctor said quietly.

"An army. You couldn't have built them all by yourself." Chase stepped off the gurney and flexed the muscles in his arms. "But you had a hand in programming them. Right?"

"Yes, and I know how to shut them down. There are two ways. You can decode them, much like the exoself has done with every laser weapon and drone in the WR. Or you can shoot them. They all have NPs, but not like the ones the exoself so easily disables. More like the device inside you, son. Any wound will quickly heal—so quickly that they'll be hard to kill."

Robert touched the spot behind his left ear. "This is the place of their NP implantation. If you can put a bullet in the NP, you can destroy the exoself. And the person. But you can't shoot six hundred soldiers from the safety of this building. I suggest you start decoding them."

Chase lifted his eyes to the ceiling. "Amos said this is a cyber war. He's right. The exoself is preparing to take on an army of its own kind."

"The exoself doesn't know right from wrong," Robert said. "It has nothing to lose. *You* must fight. You were revived for this. Your God is with you. And the soldiers are coming."

Amos threw his hands up. "And you knew about it? Why didn't you tell us sooner?"

"When I left the Helgen, the transhumans had not been awakened. I should have been kept informed, but I knew nothing of the plans until I came into this room. It seems the Feds have labeled me a rogue. The exoself has latched on and it's sharing the information. It's right there on the screen." Robert pointed to the display.

Switchblade stared at the readouts. "Melody, you understand this nonsense?"

She nodded. "Robert's right."

Switch shook his head. "One exoself against six hundred? Charlie, this don't look doable."

Chase ran his own systems check. All there. "A transhuman army isn't the first Goliath to come against

God. The battle is the Lord's."

Switchblade nodded. Mel smiled. Amos shouted, "Amen."

Robert raised his hands to his cheeks. "Yes. Amen."

"Thank you, Robert," Chase said. "Please continue to help us. You have a calling too."

"I'm not sure the calling is mine, son. But I'm at your disposal."

Chase understood every coded readout. The exoself seemed to surge inside him. Not with defiance, but with complete submission.

"We have two days," he said. "We need to round up everybody left in the city."

"And bring them inside the Cos?" Switchblade asked. "What if they won't come?"

"The dissenters won't stop fighting. But the people on Eight Mile and anybody else left out there needs to come in with us. Go tell them. Bring as many as you can."

"All right—I'm on it. I'll round up a crew."

Chase grabbed his arm. "Before you go, talk to Dani."

He let out a huff. "We got more important things to do right now."

"No, we don't. Talk to her."

Switch headed for the open door. "This ain't no way to win a war, robot. But I'll go find her."

Chase reached for Mel. "I need you. We're in this together."

Her eyes seemed to smile. "What's next?"

"Next, we go see our baby."

"To see if she's..."

"I need to know if she's susceptible to

programming."

Fear clouded her trusting gaze. "But you can protect her."

The doctor joined them. "If I had the right equipment, I could've already told you with a blood test. If the theories are right, her DNA will have a marker."

Mel drew her brows tight. "Nobody's taking blood out of my baby."

"I understand how you feel, dear. Chase will be able to tell."

Amos nudged the doctor. "Come with me to the command center." He said to Chase, "You two join us as soon as you can."

Chase nodded. "Analyze the data on transits moving in from the west. I'll send you the reports."

Amos headed for the lift. Robert followed.

Chase and Mel went down to their room to find Mom holding the baby. Mama Sameea was rinsing out another diaper.

Mel took her daughter and held her close. "Things have changed," she told the ladies. "We need to bring everyone left in Detroit inside the Cos."

"Chase, what's going on?" Mom asked. "Have you got the—"

"The exoself is back where it belongs, and I'm fine. Now both of you go recruit some others to help you prepare. We're about to have a lot of company."

"OK, son. Come on, Sameea."

They left the room. Chase held his arms open. "Let me have her."

Mel lifted the baby to her shoulder.

"Trust me, Melody."

She handed the baby over and crossed her arms.

Chase carried his little girl to the sofa. He cupped the baby's tiny face in his hand and gazed into her blue eyes.

"Well?" Mel sat beside him.

He inhaled and faced his wife. "Her DNA has the marker."

Mel seemed to wilt. "She's transhuman."

"Her brain is bio-organically designed to accept data from outside sources without any processors."

"Then it will take someone with an exoself to program her."

"Yes. I'm doing it right now."

Mel jumped off the sofa. "Chase, I don't want her to be—"

"It's all right. I'm programming her to never under any circumstance accept code from anyone other than me."

"You can do that?"

"I just did. She's safe now. A baby like any other."

"Nanobots?"

"Yes, and they're active. It just means she won't have any health issues. Nobody else has to know."

"Oh, Chase. This is—"

"This is our life, Mel. You and me and..." He smiled.

"You have a name?"

"God has answered."

Mel tilted her head.

"That's what it means. Her name is Eliana."

"Eliana. I love it. And her. And you." Mel kissed him.

"And I love you. Both of you." Silent, desperate prayer welled up inside Chase. "Now let's go down and get this battle started."

59

Mel stayed behind to nurse Eliana. Chase took the lift to the command center. Data flooded the exoself concerning the WR's plans to take over Detroit, wipe out the dissenters, and capture the rogue transhuman. And his Christian followers. Laughable. They seemed to think Chase had secured leadership of a cult.

The exoself reported another squadron of patrols and agents with NPs had attempted to rush the roadblocks. Sparky systematically took them out. No input from Chase. The killing machine still killed. For the sake of his people, Chase allowed it. But soon those coming in would be transhuman. The exoself's method of elimination wouldn't stop them. Six hundred soldiers. People who got turned into something they might not have wanted to be. Or maybe they volunteered. Either way, they were…

He stopped at the door of the command center. "They're like me."

Dani approached, and Chase dismissed the troubling thought. She wrapped her arms around his neck and he embraced her.

"Thank you," he told her. "I know it was a hard decision."

"I did as I was led. But I'm so relieved you woke up." She let him go. "Switchblade just…Well, he forgave me. I know you talked to him. Thanks."

"Did he tell you what's going on?"

"That we're taking on a transhuman army? I guess after all we've been through, there's no sense in panic now."

He smiled and tugged on the long red braid hanging over her shoulder. "Just another day in the Underground Church. I guess I'd better get in there." He pushed the door open.

"I'll be in the clinic. Praying." Dani headed for the lift.

Chase entered the busy room.

Amos rose from his chair. "I guess you already know the transits from the Helgen have arrived in Chicago."

Chase took the seat at Mel's station. "They'll spend the night at the SynVue Estate and undergo systems analysis. Tomorrow they'll head this direction in old buses. The Feds know I could shut down their high-tech transits."

"So, why didn't you do that today?"

"And slow them down? Let's get on with this."

Robert pulled a chair to the station. "Are you feeling all right, son?"

"I'll feel better when my wife and daughter are safe. Robert, how many of these second-edition transhumans wanted it? And how many had it done to them? Like me."

"The best of the military were chosen. Only about a third came willingly. The rest were forced. A few tried to run and were eliminated."

Chase slumped into the chair. "And now there's no way to know which ones complied and which ones didn't."

The doctor's gaze dropped. "Even they don't

know. They're all the same now."

Switchblade walked into the room. "People from Eight Mile are coming. Most folks left in the city are coming. But like you said—the dissenters will fight to the end."

"They won't stand a chance," Chase said.

"Sparky can't shut down the weapons like he's been doing for the past two weeks?" Switch asked.

"They're recoding the transhumans and their lasers every few hours. The exoself won't be able to keep up."

Amos shook his head. "So your plan to decode them is out? What'll we do now?"

"I need to take out the programmer. Then maybe we can spare some of the transhumans. And most of the dissenters." Chase met Robert's troubled eyes. "Do you remember what I told you in my message before the transfusion?"

"Unplug the WR."

"Who's the programmer? What branch of the government is in control now? The input has changed. I can't tell where it's coming from. Who's behind this?"

"I've been studying the data too. It's clear the scientists at the Helgen have lost control. As have the Feds. There is no programmer." The doctor rested his elbows on his knees and rubbed his wrinkled face. "The WR has been unplugged. By the system. We're up against a faceless beast of cyber engineering and we've lost control. I fear it's hopeless, son. The best you can do is get as many as you can into the safe rooms under this building."

Even as Robert spoke, some of the trails into WR intel went dark. But hope flooded Chase's spirit. "No. My people are not going underground. Not anymore."

60

By late evening the following day, buses filled with transhumans had lined up in Ann Arbor. Men and women augmented by the WR unloaded into the warehouse district where Bloodless still ushered rogue citizens to their deaths. Chase could access the data as usual. Names of the dead included Dr. June, Hillary, Jeff, Ep, and what remained of the dissenters at the recently discovered campground. Chase had no time to mourn. But he'd remember them.

Sitting next to Mel in the command center, Chase followed a data trail listing the dead from a deeply encrypted file handled by one programmer. Kerstin. She still held her post at the warehouse. And until an hour ago, her exoself and Chase's seemed to fight their own battle. Chase didn't try to hide his location. But Kerstin had gone dark. What was she up to?

By her recent input into Federal systems, Chase knew who, or what, now directed the cyber coup. Not the Western Republic, but SynVue. Computers taking over the country were property of the same organization Chase had once dedicated his life to.

"I never knew who was really in charge anyway," he said.

"Baby, what are you talking about?" Mel rested her fingers on the computer's keypad.

"The entertainment phenomenon we used to work

for is taking over the country. Maybe the world."

"Not news. They've been running things for years. Tell me how long we've got until the transhumans start taking out the dissenters."

"I'd say about twelve hours. Data is sketchy. They're trying to throw me off."

She dropped her hands to her lap. "Then it could be sooner."

"I can still hack satellites. We'll know when they move this direction."

She slid her chair closer and rubbed his back. "But you can't fool the system the way you could before." She grinned. "Now that the inept humans, as you once called them, have taken a back seat to the computers."

"I was tired of lying anyway. But this...whatever it is...can see right through me." He grasped her hand and kissed it. "Doesn't matter. The battle—"

"The battle is the Lord's." She kissed him softly. "I'll go check on our daughter."

"Time to feed her?"

"No. I just want to see how she's doing up there with Mama."

"Let me go. You stay here and monitor the intel."

"All right. Bring her back with you. I miss her."

Chase rose and headed toward the door. "Be back in a few."

He found Eliana sleeping in her bed.

"Your mother will come soon, and I will go help in the kitchen," Sameea told him.

"Go ahead. I'm taking the baby to the command center for a while."

"She will be safer here." Sameea crossed her arms.

"She'll be safer with her father. We just want to see her for a few minutes."

Sameea relaxed her arms and nodded. "You are a good man. I will send your mother for her in half an hour." She left the room.

Chase grabbed a blanket and wrapped it around his daughter. Before he got to the lift, Mel sent a message through the exoself.

Chase, we have stragglers trying to get in at the lobby door, but you have the building on lockdown. Can you let them in?

Do you see them on the monitors? How many?

Three, I think. There are some shadows. Maybe four.

I'll go down and get a visual before I open the door.

Have you got Eliana? Bring her to me first.

Yeah, OK. I'm coming.

He stepped into the lift. "Twenty." The lift shot down. But it didn't stop. In only a moment the door dissolved to reveal the first floor.

Mel, something's wrong. The lift refused my prompt and took me to the lobby.

No response.

Chase eased into the hallway, the baby still at his shoulder. He stayed close to the wall as he entered the lobby.

Darkness filled the place. The flashing messages that'd once welcomed visitors to the Cos had ceased. Chase didn't instruct the building's security system to unlock the big glass door.

But it opened.

And as if she belonged, his old nightmare walked in.

"Lights on," she said as she entered the lobby.

Chase clutched the baby tighter. He swallowed. "What's wrong, Kerstin? Can't you see in the dark?"

"Of course I can. But they can't."

Three men followed her as she glided into the Cos. Not transhuman soldiers, or they'd have night vision. No NPs, or the exoself wouldn't have allowed them to get this far.

"I've come with some of your backward Christians." She laughed. "But look who *you've* brought. Tell me it isn't yours. That would be so unfair."

"Unfair?"

She stood ten feet from him. "The plan—before you went rogue—was for you and me to produce the first transhuman child. But you've done it without me. Haven't you? Let me see him."

The exoself surged, and Kerstin stumbled.

She righted herself. "Stop it! You can't beat me. These men are implanted with hydro-explosive devices. You and your son come with me and live. Your followers can go to—"

"The baby's a girl. And yes, she's mine."

"Let me see her."

Chase hesitated.

"I want to see her!"

He cupped the baby's head with his hand, lowered her in his arms, and spread the blanket open.

Kerstin laughed again. "I guess I don't need to ask who the mother is. You hooked up with that assistant of yours."

"She's my wife. And you are not getting near her or anyone else in this building."

Kerstin paused. She slung her long black hair over her shoulder. "Agreed. Come with me and I won't destroy them. Fight me, and I'll lock these wired-up idiots in here with you and your half-breed kid and blow you all to bits." Her lips curled upward and her green eyes filled with fire. Her exoself assaulted Chase's.

He fought back. He nodded to the men behind her. They showed no fear. Chase could almost feel their prayers. He reached deep into his processors, but Kerstin didn't falter. She'd become what Chase called the soldiers—a second-edition transhuman.

"All right," he said. "But not until your human bombs are outside the city. And the baby stays here."

"Don't be silly, darling. She has the marker. I can feel it. I can't program her—not yet. But I will. And I'll be her mother. Just the way it was supposed to be." She stepped forward. "Give her to me. Now!"

Chase pulled the baby to his chest.

The single shot of a pistol echoed through the lobby.

Kerstin's head jerked back. She dropped. Blood seeped from behind her left ear.

The baby cried. Chase shifted his sight from Kerstin's dead body to the point of execution. Twenty feet to his right. From the alcove leading to the stairs.

Mel.

Chase rushed to her and drew her into his embrace, the baby between them.

Mel stowed the gun behind her waist and lifted Eliana from Chase's arms. She threw a glance at Kerstin. "I had to…"

He kissed her forehead. "You did the right thing."

The three men at the lobby door seemed relieved, but they didn't move.

"What can you tell me about the devices?" Chase asked. "Are they imbedded?"

"Yes," one of them answered. "She already detonated others to get past the roadblock."

"Why didn't I see it? How could she get this far?" Chase latched onto her fleeing exoself and chased it into the multiplying SynVue program. "She used the real-time view. Everything we've seen on sat-feeds has been false."

Mel grasped his hand. "If she was feeding us past images, then what's really going on out there?"

"I've cornered her exoself and set the program back to current feed." He looked out the door. "She led the army here. They're on foot. A mile out."

61

"Chase, what do you mean you've got her exoself cornered? It's still functioning?" Mel hugged the crying baby.

"Yes. Her exoself is the key to us getting into SynVue. I followed it in and I'm latching on."

Switchblade ran into the lobby from the direction of the lifts. "I saw your message on Mel's screen." He stopped when he saw the body. "Is she...?"

"My pistol-packing wife put a bullet in her NP."

Switch grinned as he eyed Mel. "All that target practice paid off, huh?"

She headed for the lifts. "No time for compliments. The soldiers are almost here."

Chase eyed the exit. "Switch, get Mel and the baby to the floors above eighty-nine. I can stop them from getting past there."

"You think I'm leavin' you down here? And who are these jokers?" He motioned to the three men.

"Human bombs. I..."

Mel spoke from behind him. "I don't think you can help them. Come on, Chase. We stay together."

He faced her. "Please, Mel. For the baby's sake. I've already sent instructions for Amos to move everyone up. But I'm meeting this army head-on."

Switch crossed his arms. "You know I'm going with you."

Chase exhaled. "One day your loyalty will get you killed." He reached for Mel. "You need to go up. I love you."

She wrapped her arm around his neck and kissed him. "I love you. Please be careful."

Chase kissed his daughter's forehead. "I'll see you soon. I promise."

She hurried for the lifts. Switchblade stepped toward the three men.

"Back away," one of them said.

Switchblade stopped. "Charlie?"

"Imbedded explosives."

"Can you deprogram them?"

"No."

"Can you detonate us?" the youngest of the men asked.

"Through Kerstin's exoself. Yes."

"Then do it," another said. "We'll meet the soldiers and slow them down. It'll give your...our people more time."

"There has to be another—"

"You can't leave us here. If you try to cut us open to remove the devices, they'll blow. When the soldiers come, they'll detonate us. It's the only option. You're out of time."

Chase prayed. Then he let them go.

And he and Switchblade followed them into the street.

62

Midnight. Clear sky. No moon. Not a sound on the streets of Detroit. The three believers about to sacrifice themselves disappeared into the old Highland Park area. The soldiers were coming up Davison Avenue.

Chase and Switchblade held back.

One of the men cried out, "Now!"

And Chase set off the explosion.

The sky lit orange. Chase sensed the retreat of an exoself into SynVue's massive cyber being. Then another. Twelve of them. The transhumans could be killed after all. But Chase would try to save some.

"It's done," he said. "God rest their souls."

"Amen," Switch said. "What now?"

"I sent out Sparky's imprint. They'll come after me. I'm deep into the system and I can access their programs."

"Like I said, robot...what now?"

"You got a gun?" Chase asked.

"Yeah. You?"

"Mel slipped me her pistol."

Switchblade snorted. "Two guns. Six hundred transhumans we gotta shoot behind the left ear."

"Five hundred eighty-eight. The blast was powerful enough to take out a few."

"Thank the Lord for that, but—"

"I hear boots on pavement. Only a few. Probably

scouts. I have visual," Chase said. "Dear God, help us."

"What is it?"

"They're armored. Bullets won't penetrate their helmets."

"Should we run?"

"Won't matter. I've got to decode them." Chase used Kerstin's exoself to push into the main system. He smiled. "I've got this group. Ten of them. I shut down their strength sensors."

"Weapons?"

Chase closed his eyes. "I took out the lasers of the whole army." Fighting the programs of other transhumans—better transhumans—threatened to short-circuit him. But the Spirit remained constant. He bent to rest his hands on his knees. His lab-grown heart seemed to skip a beat.

"Charlie, heads up."

The first ten approached, attempted to fire. Then tossed their useless lasers to the ground and surrounded Chase and Switchblade.

Chase grabbed hold of a well-armored transhuman. And threw him fifty feet. Another moved in, and Chase wrestled him into a stranglehold and ripped off his helmet.

He was just a man. As much as Chase was just a man.

But he growled. "What have you done? I can't—"

"I'm threading my way into your programs. To set you free. I don't want to kill you."

"I'm programmed to kill *you*," the man screamed.

Others pulled Chase off their comrade. The rest attacked Switch. Chase twisted loose. He grabbed an armored man around the torso. Threw him against three others, who had Switchblade pinned. Two went down. One pivoted, jumped on Chase. They fell backward.

A gray helmet banged against Chase's forehead. The partially disabled transhuman possessed enough strength to hold Chase to the ground. But only for a second.

Chase pushed him off as Switchblade's big arm reached around the guy's neck. The helmet came off and the bullet went in.

The unmasked transhuman fell dead.

"Behind you," Chase yelled.

Switch swung around, threw his attacker into an old light pole. The blow knocked the man out.

Six down. Four ready for more.

Chase grabbed the light pole and yanked it loose.

"That's right, boys," Switch yelled. "The original transhuman's got this. Y'all just go on back where you came from."

One of the four dropped his own helmet. He cornered Switch with a knife.

Switchblade pulled out his namesake blade. "All right. Come on."

Chase roared and swung the pole. One man fell. Then two. Then three. Like bowling pins. He reached for Mel's gun and fired.

A swift move by the last of the ten made a shield of Switchblade, and the bullet grazed his shoulder.

"Watch it, robot!" He elbowed the soldier in the gut and broke free.

Chase fired again. The transhuman reeled back, the bullet in his chest. Blood circled an inch around the point of impact. But no more. The man heaved, coughed. And kept coming.

Nanobots.

Switchblade plowed into the man. Pinned him against a building. "Now!"

Chase aimed and fired.

The shot ripped through the transhuman's NP. The man fell.

Switchblade sank a bullet behind the left ear of the others sprawled on the ground.

Ten down.

More footsteps.

"Do you hear that?" Chase asked.

"Don't hear nothin' but my heart trying to crawl out of my chest."

"Not soldiers' boots. Just..."

Approaching steps. From the direction of the Cos. Chase squinted. Another army headed in from the far end of the street.

"It's our people."

63

They marched forward. Maybe a hundred. Ridge led the brigade. Brax. Leo. Terrell. Even a few women. Not Mel, thank God. But Dani joined the front line, a gun in one hand, a medical bag in the other. She rushed to Switchblade.

Chase studied the crowd. Dissenters. Eight Mile refugees. Believers who'd come all the way from Quebec and locals who'd only recently joined the underground. Chase could rebuke them. Send them back to the top of the Cosimo, where he'd told them to go. But the words wouldn't come. Only gratitude.

"Thank you," he said. "All of you. Several hundred more transhumans are coming. We've taken out a few and I've disabled their weapons. I can shut down their strength sensors. If I can reprogram them, I can make them stop fighting. But for now, it will be a fight. You know how to kill them. But…"

"But we'll try to save some," Ridge said.

Chase eyed his brother-in-law and nodded.

Ridge stepped closer. "My sister is on eighty-nine in the lab. She's trying the same thing—to decode them."

Chase blinked at the lighted superscraper. He opened his mind to the massive computer Mel had once used to get inside his brain.

Are you there, sweetheart? I thought I felt you a few

minutes ago.

I'm here. I didn't want to distract you.

Our little army arrived. Keep trying to decode the transhumans. They're closing in.

Pray, Chase. The battle is the Lord's.

Prayer already streamed through him in an unending appeal.

Switchblade's hands were on Dani's shoulders. "You gotta go back," he told her.

"Too late for that," Chase said. "We've got three minutes."

Dani locked elbows with Switch. "I came to treat the wounded and I'm not going anywhere until we go back together."

Chase faced his defenders. "Spread out."

They formed a line crossing the road and extending in front of the buildings. The rhythm of boots on pavement grew loud.

Mel. Now. Work with me.

I've got it, Chase. Weave into SynVue. Follow my lead.

Chase sent the exoself into a collision with Mel's threaded code. He clenched his jaw and held his breath.

The transhumans came into sight. Rows of them. One line behind another. They had to know their weapons were useless. But they were strong. Stronger than Chase.

Until that moment.

He hacked SynVue's programs and disabled the transhumans' sensors. Not just strength, but night vision, hearing, speed, and communication. SynVue's hold on them let go.

Some stopped. Others kept coming, pulling out knives and pistols.

About two-thirds of the army retreated. Of those remaining, some began wrestling weapons away from their comrades.

"They're turning on each other," Chase shouted. He backed against a wall, fighting the cyber battle as his own would-be soldiers met the flesh-and-blood enemy. Helmets hit the broken pavement. Bullets found the NPs.

Soldiers fell. Others rushed in. Gunfire filled the night. The army from the Cos thinned. But so did the number of transhumans.

Shadows appeared overhead. Then lights. Chase eased into the street.

Mel, we have drones. Dozens of them. I thought they were grounded.

I used Kerstin's exoself to reprogram them. They're headed west to take out SynVue's base in Ann Arbor.

Chase's head reeled back as a strong arm circled his neck. A blade went into his gut. His ears roared. He gripped his stomach as the transhuman soldier ran past him.

Chase, baby, what's wrong? Your programs are resetting. Stay with me.

He dropped to his knees and coughed. Blood coated his tongue. He held to Mel's last words. To the exoself. He clung to the Spirit.

Switch and Dani knelt beside him. Dani grabbed a coded plexi-patch from her bag, lifted Chase's shirt, and secured the high-tech bandage.

Switchblade pulled Chase to his feet. "You got enough nanobots left in you to take care of this, robot. I know you do."

Chase forced his eyes open.

Chase, answer me.

I'm here, Mel.

A shot rang close and Chase hit the pavement. Switchblade fell on top of him. Dani screamed. Chase groaned, flexed, and pushed the big man off.

Switchblade fell back, his eyes shut.

More bullets.

Chase stood and lifted Switch, carried him to an alcove behind a crumbling wall, and laid him down.

Dani knelt beside him. "Tell me."

"Bullet hit a rib and lodged close to his left lung. Must have hit his head when he fell, but I don't think he'll be out too long."

"We can't move him or the bullet will shift. We'll have to carry him back on a gurney."

"We'll get him back, and Mason will take care of him. Stay here." Chase left them and slinked along the side of the building.

Some of the transhumans seemed to have given up. Others wrestled with opponents. Ordinary humans were taking them down. A few more shots, then the gunfire ceased. In the distance, the blast of the drones' lasers met the cries of the retreating army.

Chase bent low and headed toward a group of enemy soldiers—a dozen of them—leaning against a wall.

"I'm sorry for what they did to you," he said. "We won't harm you. But we'll defend ourselves against the ones still fighting."

"What have you done?" one of them asked. "I feel like...myself. Like the transhuman is gone."

"It'll never be completely gone. But your mind is free. If you're willing, help us end this. Then we'll take you back to our base."

The men rushed into the street. Others nearby

followed their example. Less than fifty transhumans still fought for the cause of SynVue. Those released from the system's grasp seemed to know how to stop their comrades. A few more shots. More fallen transhumans.

But some would be saved.

As the fighting wore down, the exoself latched onto every stronghold SynVue had established. Communication systems around the world crumbled. The newly birthed cyber beast threatening to end mankind's dominion on earth ceased to function. Chase shut the thing down.

And the giant fell.

The last transhuman holding to the hope of a SynVue singularity took a bullet in the NP. From the gun of one of his own.

Mel, sweetheart, it's over. I'll be home soon.

Praise God. I love you, Chase.

He didn't tell her how many had been lost—he didn't know for sure. But some of their people were among the dead.

"Switchblade." Chase ran across the bloodied street.

Dani leaned over the big guy and caressed his cheek.

"Robot, you got things under control?" Switch asked.

"Did you think I couldn't handle it without you?" Chase knelt and touched Switchblade's arm. "Don't try to move. We'll find something to make a gurney and carry you back. You'll be fine."

"We lose anybody?"

Chase stood. "Dani, let's go see if we can..."

"Yeah. I'm coming." She bent to kiss Switchblade.

"Don't move. You understand?"

"I got it, girl. Go on."

They faced the street and stepped between the fallen. Chase knelt next to Leo.

"He's gone."

"God bless him," Dani said. "Chase, what about you? Are you OK?"

"The bleeding stopped and the wound closed up. Just took a few minutes."

Ridge came running, with Brax right behind him.

"Thank God," Chase said.

"About half of the ones who came with us are dead," Ridge told him. "We've got some wounded. These transhuman soldiers seem to have some medical know-how."

"They can help us get our people back to the Cos," Chase told him.

Brax shook his head. "We're taking the SynVue robots with us?"

Chase rested his hand on the young man's shoulder. "They need to hear what I have to say. Come daylight, we're having a meeting. With the world."

64

Mel met him in the street in front of the Cos. She embraced him, kissed him until a man cleared his throat.

Chase looked up. The transhuman soldier carried an injured believer in his arms, even though his superior strength was gone.

"Follow the others," Chase told him. "We have a clinic."

The man nodded and headed into the lobby. But he turned back. "Thank you." He faced the double doors and walked in.

Two more transhumans carried Switchblade between them on a sheet of plywood.

Mel let go of Chase. "Mason's waiting." She bent to kiss Switch on the cheek and then grasped Dani's outstretched hand. "We'll see you after the surgery."

Fourteen wounded from bullets and blades. Mason and Dani would be busy for a while. Twenty-two believers dead. Twenty-nine dissenters. All the tough guys from Eight Mile Road survived.

And forty-four transhuman soldiers came willingly into the welcoming shelter of the Underground Church. Others might have survived the drones. But their leader—the cyber beast that had taken over the government—was as gone as a non-living thing could be. Maybe one day someone would wake it up.

But not today.

Chase and Mel spent an hour in the command center. "I'm going to check on Switch," Chase said. "Hopefully, before sunrise he'll be able to take a ride to the rooftop."

Mel lifted her brows.

"Go tell everyone to meet on the roof at seven o'clock."

"Chase, what on earth?"

"Just do it." He kissed her and ran toward the lifts.

Transhumans in the clinic seemed to have retained their cyber knowledge. They worked with Mason to remove bullets and patch the wounded. Switch was already in recovery, but not awake.

Dani joined Chase there. "He'll be out for a while," she said.

"When he wakes up, can you get him in a wheelchair?"

"Sure, but why?"

"I need him on the roof with me at sunrise. Take him to the top floor and have some men help him up there."

"Chase Sterling, you are a strange man. But OK."

He smiled and touched her cheek. "See you up there."

65

For the next two hours, Chase and Mel reached into what was left of communication programs. The EU and other government entities held their power when the WR fell. The lives of most of the world's citizens would not change. Believers in other countries would still face persecution. Possibly extermination. But not by the device called Bloodless. Chase eradicated the program, sealed the records, and disabled the machines when he shut down SynVue.

He studied communication between rogue groups. "The Dissenters of the Republic have taken over what used to be Washington, DC, with plans to establish a new government. One that will strive for freedom. But the WR is prey to invasion. No telling what will become of this land."

He wormed his way into every satellite feed and graphic station he could access, and he and Mel installed a transhuman connection.

Her fingers slid across the keypad as code lined up on her screen. "The cameras are set up, and the sound system. But I don't see how we can tap into so many systems with an illegal feed."

"By using the building," he told her. "Those triangles on the roof are transmitters. Sort of like old-fashioned antennas."

"How long have you known this?"

"I'm not sure." He remembered his last dream. Or whatever it was. Was that when he found out? "For a while."

"Tell me all your secrets. What do you plan to say when you address the world?"

He gazed into his wife's beautiful brown eyes. How he loved her. "You know."

She smiled and kissed him. "Yes. But you're not dressed for this grand event. Where's your designer suit?"

"I have no idea. Today I'm not the one who matters."

They rode the lift to the top floor at five minutes till seven and took the stairs upward. An audience of about three thousand waited on the stone rooftop. Mel retrieved the baby from her mother, who stood at the front of the crowd with Ridge and Brax. Dani, Mason, Finley, Robert. And Mom.

Mel carried Eliana onto a stage erected by transhuman soldiers. Chase followed. Amos stood to the side of the platform.

Switchblade waited there too, in a wheelchair. He pushed himself close to the edge of the stage, where he stood and crossed his arms. Always the faithful bodyguard.

"Listen up," he said in a booming voice. "This man's got something to tell you."

As the first rays of sunlight swept over the rooftop, Chase met Mel's reassuring gaze. He grasped an old microphone from its stand. Cameras surrounded the stage. The lighted triangles now towered fifty feet above the Cosimo. The satellite feed carried this moment around the world.

Then Chase Sterling, uncensored, a Christian

transhuman in a world ruled by evil, spoke.

What Chase Said

"Believers. Transhumans. Dissenters. Hiders and refugees. Enemies seeking to shut down this transmission. My name is Chase Sterling. Hear me. We've been silent for...

"Well, I've never been silent. I had a lot to say back when I changed lives. When I welcomed the worship of fans. But that life ended. I became a new man. Not by what the government did to me, but by what Christ did for me. I became the citizen of a holy nation.

"But they were a quiet people. A remnant who'd forgotten their mission. Who'd perhaps forgotten their King would soon return and set things right. They failed to give warning.

"But I'm here to issue a caveat. So take heed.

"We will not hide. Love is too strong and judgment too certain for us to remain nothing but a whisper of weakness. By the blood of Christ, my people and I will go out with hope. With the promise of redemption. And we will take what comes.

"Believers around the world, hear me. Meet this mission with the strength of the Lord. Enemies, hear me. Turn to Christ and live. It's your only hope. We will escape the fury of this world. But you will meet your end by the hand of our God.

"Now hear these words. Not my own—they come from the God of the universe. Maker of heaven and earth. Spoken by Him who paid your redemption. He said, 'I came to seek and save the lost.'

"And from His word, a testimony I claim as my own: 'Here is a trustworthy saying that deserves full acceptance: Christ Jesus came into the world to save sinners—of whom I am the worst.'

"Citizens of the nations, hear me. We are unrighteous. Lost. Our destiny is death. Our Redeemer is life. Our time is short. Follow Christ and live.

"As for me, I am His possession. Redeemed. As life is His, so it is mine. Not by my accomplishment. I'm powerless. I couldn't change my own life and I can't change anyone else's. I never could. Only Jesus.

"And that's all I have to say. But my people will speak. Loud and long and clear. Until we are gone from this world."

You Can Help!

At Pelican Book Group it is our mission to entertain readers with fiction that uplifts the Gospel. It is our privilege to spend time with you awhile as you read our stories.

We believe you can help us to bring Christ into the lives of people across the globe. And you don't have to open your wallet or even leave your house!

Here are 3 simple things you can do to help us bring illuminating fiction™ to people everywhere.

1) If you enjoyed this book, write a positive review. Post it at online retailers and websites where readers gather. And share your review with us at reviews@pelicanbookgroup.com (this does give us permission to reprint your review in whole or in part.)

2) If you enjoyed this book, recommend it to a friend in person, at a book club or on social media.

3) If you have suggestions on how we can improve or expand our selection, let us know. We value your opinion. Use the contact form on our web site or e-mail us at

customer@pelicanbookgroup.com

God Can Help!

Are you in need? The Almighty can do great things for you. Holy is His Name! He has mercy in every generation. He can lift up the lowly and accomplish all things. Reach out today.

Do not fear: I am with you; do not be anxious: I am your God. I will strengthen you, I will help you, I will uphold you with my victorious right hand.

~Isaiah 41:10 (NAB)

We pray daily, and we especially pray for everyone connected to Pelican Book Group—that includes you! If you have a specific need, we welcome the opportunity to pray for you. Share your needs or praise reports at http://pelink.us/pray4us

Free Book Offer

We're looking for booklovers like you to partner with us! Join our team of influencers today and receive at least one free eBook per month. Maybe more!

For more information
Visit http://pelicanbookgroup.com/booklovers